Praise for *More Happy Than Not*

"A beautiful debut novel [that] manages a delicate knitting of class politics through an ambitious narrative about sexual identity and connection that considers the heavy weight and constructive value of traumatic memory . . . Aaron's Bronx universe [is captured] with a precision that feels at once dreamy and casually reportorial . . . Mandatory reading."

—*The New York Times Book Review*

"[An] important addition to speculative fiction for young adults . . . Silvera's tale combines the best features of science fiction with social justice in this engaging read, as Aaron finds a place where he belongs." —*Los Angeles Times*

"Heartfelt . . . The futuristic twist, with its poignant repercussions, drives home a memorable, thoroughly contemporary theme . . . Lose your memories, lose your pain, lose yourself."

—*Chicago Tribune*

"This is definitely at the top of my YA list. There's a realness to its main character, Aaron Soto, and his struggle to be who he really is. It confronts race and sexuality in a way I haven't seen in the genre before." —*Latina Magazine*

"For its explorations of sexuality, poverty, and race in the Bronx along with its subversion of the traditional hero's journey, *More Happy Than Not* is one of this summer's most anticipated YA debuts. An absorbing, thought-provoking, and timely read for people of all ages." —*NEXT Magazine*

"A gut-wrenching story of race and sexuality." —*The Guardian*

"Smart . . . Sensitive 

Housekeeping

"A bold, inventive, raw look at male sexuality in an irresistible sci-fi package." —*The Globe and Mail*

"Aaron is one of the most interesting, authentic teen narrators I've met, and his story is told with incredible courage and unflinching honesty. Silvera managed to leave me smiling after totally breaking my heart. Unforgettable."
—Becky Albertalli, National Book Award nominee and author of *Simon vs. The Homo Sapiens Agenda*

"Adam Silvera explores the inner workings of a painful world and he delivers this with heartfelt honesty and a courageous, confident hand. Combine these with a one-of-a-kind voice and a genius idea, and what you have is a mesmerizing, unforgettable tour de force." —John Corey Whaley, National Book Award finalist and author of *Where Things Come Back* and *Noggin*

"Adam Silvera is a voice missing in YA fiction. The honesty of his words and his ability to tell a story make you realize that we've been waiting for him. I'm blown away."
—Holly Goldberg Sloan, author of *Counting by 7s* and *I'll Be There*

"An important new voice in YA literature . . . Adam Silvera has created a passionate, searing narrative with characters who feel unique and totally familiar . . . *More Happy Than Not* is an unforgettable read." —Alex London, author of *Proxy* and *Guardian*

"A debut as deft as it is sharp, as honest as it is assured, and, above all, extremely moving . . . [It] left me spellbound—and reminded me why I love to read." —Adele Griffin, author of *The Unfinished Life of Addison Stone*

"Inventive and daring, Silvera's gritty debut kept me turning pages until 2 A.M. His writing crackles with challenging questions, searing and timely." —Aaron Hartzler, author of *Rapture Practice*

"Adam Silvera's *More Happy Than Not* is a fantastic magic trick I haven't stopped thinking about since I finished reading and suspect will stay with me for some time to come."

—Jasmine Warga, author of *My Heart* and *Other Black Holes*

"Adam Silvera harnesses a certain reckless energy and unleashes it through the voice of Aaron Soto . . . He sinks into your skin so you can't stop thinking about him even when you aren't reading. High on story, character, and some perfectly executed twists, I loved this book." —David Arnold, author of *Mosquitoland*

"Poignant . . . So engrossing that once you start it, you won't be able to put it down. Don't say we didn't warn you." —TeenVogue.com

"This is a beautifully written book that seems to get sadder with every page, but never feels hopeless." —Refinery29.com

"[Silvera] is a beautiful writer. Aaron's story is heart-wrenching, funny, inspirational, and eye-opening. This is a really special novel from an extremely gifted new writer." —Bustle

"This is a cry-on-the-subway book, so watch out." —MTV.com

"Silvera's debut is equal parts gut-punch and warm hug, not to mention sweet, funny, creative, and a really welcome entry to YA with regard to having characters coming from a lower socioeconomic background." —B&N.com

"A compassionate read that you'll want to pass on to everyone you know." —*Metro US*

"Easily one of the most heart-wrenching [stories] you'll read this year." —PasteMagazine.com

"No matter who you are, *More Happy Than Not* is almost impossible not to enjoy." —*Bucks County Courier Times*

"Heartbreaking, funny and hopeful." —*The Spencer Daily Reporter*

"A dramatic and heart-wrenching story of first loves, first heartbreaks, grief and the quest for happiness."

—Shelf Awareness, Starred Review

"Vividly written and intricately plotted . . . Silvera pulls no punches." —*Publishers Weekly*, Starred Review

"[A] well executed story of a teen experiencing firsts—first love, first sex, first loss—and struggling with his identity and sexuality . . . Ingenious."—*Booklist*, Starred Review

"A multifaceted look at some of the more unsettling aspects of human relationships. A brilliantly conceived page-turner."

—*Kirkus Reviews*, Starred Review

"A gripping read—Silvera skillfully weaves together many divergent young adult themes within an engrossing, intense narrative." —*School Library Journal*, Starred Review

"Silvera draws wonderfully complex characters and deftly portrays the relationships among them." —*VOYA*

"The novel takes an unexpected, complex turn that Silvera ably constructs . . . Refreshing."

—*The Bulletin of the Center for Children's Books*

MORE HAPPY THAN NOT

ALSO BY ADAM SILVERA

History Is All You Left Me

They Both Die at the End

What If It's Us (co-authored by Becky Albertalli)

Infinity Son

MORE HAPPY THAN NOT

☺ ☺ ☺ ☹

ADAM SILVERA

Copyright © 2015 by Adam Silvera
Introduction Copyright © 2020 by Angie Thomas

This is a work of fiction. Names, characters, places, and incidents either are the product of the author's imagination or are used fictitiously, and any resemblance to actual persons, living or dead, businesses, companies, events or locales is entirely coincidental.

All rights reserved.

Published in the United States by Soho Teen an imprint of
Soho Press, Inc.
227 W 17th Street
New York, NY 10011

Library of Congress Cataloging-in-Publication Data

Silvera, Adam, 1990–
More happy than not / Adam Silvera.

ISBN 978-1-64129-194-1
eISBN 978-1-64129-276-4

[1. Memory—Fiction. 2. Dating (Social customs)—Fiction. 3. Gays—Fiction. 4. Coming out (Sexual orientation)—Fiction. 5. Single-parent families—Fiction. 6. Bronx (New York, N.Y.)—Fiction. 7. New York (N.Y.)—Fiction. 8. Youths' writings.] I. Title.
PZ7.1.S54Mor 2015 [Fic]—dc23 2014044586

Interior design by Janine Agro, Soho Press, Inc.

Printed in the United States of America

10 9 8 7 6 5 4

For those who've discovered happiness can be hard.

Shout-out to Luis and Corey, of course, my favorites who sucker punched me in the best ways.

MORE HAPPY THAN NOT

INTRODUCTION

Without question, *More Happy Than Not* changed me.

From the very first line, the story of Aaron Soto reeled me in. I vividly remember picking up a copy while at a local bookstore and flipping to the first pages—I always read the first lines of books as opposed to the jacket flap. The first line led to me reading the entire first page, then the second and third. I was hooked. I was also struck, because while reading those first few pages, it hit me:

These were characters I knew.

Aaron, Genevieve, Brendan, Baby Freddy, and even Me-Crazy were all people I knew from my own neighborhood. No, I wasn't from the Bronx—I was a world away in Mississippi, where subways and bodegas don't exist—but these characters were still familiar. Reading about their experiences and their lives felt like seeing my own world but through a different lens: a unique, fascinating lens, unlike any other thing I'd seen in young adult literature.

Suddenly, by crafting a world that resembled his own, Adam Silvera had given me permission to do the same. Here was a book about young people of color who were allowed to be the stars and not just the sidekicks. Aaron was allowed to be complex and complicated and never confined to a stereotype.

I must admit, at times the novel gutted me, as it should. I won't spoil the ending, but I will say I was a mess for days afterwards. I couldn't shake Aaron and his story and found myself wanting to check on him as if he were an actual person. (In fact, in my first conversation with Adam, I asked how things were going for Aaron.) But with that gut-wrenching ending, Adam reminded me of something else—it's okay to have not-so-happy endings or rather, it's okay if things are less happy than not. Young people especially need to know that it's okay if they don't get their "fairy tale ending." After all, for them this is truly just the beginning. *More Happy Than Not* reflects that, and as a result of seeing it in this novel, I decided to do the same with my own novels.

I hope *More Happy Than Not* reels you in and guts you. I hope it reminds you that it's okay not to be okay. Even more than that, I hope you never forget it.

Thank you, Adam.

Thank you, *More Happy Than Not.*

Love,
Angie Thomas, author of *The Hate U Give*

HERE TODAY,
GONE TOMORROW!

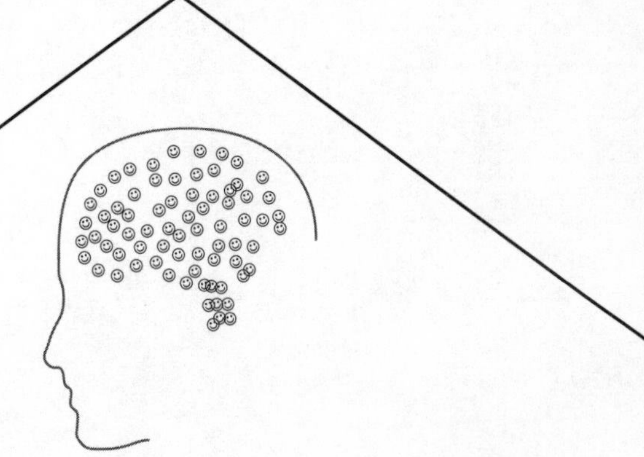

Suffering from unwanted memories? Call the Leteo Institute at 1-800-I-FORGET to learn more about our cutting-edge memory-relief procedure!

PART ONE: HAPPINESS

1
SUCKER-PUNCHING MEMORIES

It turns out the Leteo procedure isn't bullshit.

The first time I saw a poster on the subway promoting the institute that could make you forget things, I thought it was a marketing campaign for some new science fiction movie. And when I saw the headline "Here Today, Gone Tomorrow!" on the cover of a newspaper, I mistook it as something boring, like the cure for some new flu—I didn't think they were talking about memories. It rained that weekend, so I hung out with my friends at the Laundromat, chilling in front of the security guard's old TV. Every single news station was interviewing different representatives of the Leteo Institute to find out more about the "revolutionary science of memory alteration and suppression."

I called bullshit at the end of each one.

Except now we know the procedure is 100 percent real and 0 percent bullshit because one of our own has gone through it.

That's what Brendan, my sort of best friend, tells me at least. I know him as much for his honesty as I know Baby Freddy's mother for her dedication to confirming the gossip that comes her way. (Rumor has it she's learning basic French because her neighbor down the hall may be having an affair with the married superintendent, and the language barrier is a bit of a block. But, yeah, that's gossip too.)

"So Leteo is legit?" I sit down by the sandbox no one plays in because of ringworm.

Brendan paces back and forth, dribbling our friend Deon's basketball between his legs. "That's why Kyle and his family bounced," he says. "Fresh start."

I don't even have to ask what he forgot. Kyle's identical twin brother, Kenneth, was gunned down last December for sleeping with this guy Jordan's younger sister. Kyle was the one who actually slept with her, though. I know grief just fine, but I can't imagine living day by day with that—knowing the brother I shared a face and secret language with was ripped out of my life when the bullets were meant for me.

"Well, good luck to him, right?"

"Yeah, sure," Brendan says.

The usual suspects are outside today. Skinny-Dave and Fat-Dave—who are unrelated, just both named Dave—come out of our local bodega, Good Food's Store, where I've been working part-time for the past couple of months. They're throwing back quarter juices and potato chips. Baby Freddy glides on by with his new steel orange bike, and I remember when we used to give him shit years ago for still needing training wheels—but the joke is on me since my father never got a chance to teach me to ride at all. Me-Crazy is sitting on the ground, having a conversation with the wall; and everyone else, the adults mainly, are preparing for this weekend's community event of the year.

Family Day.

This will be the first time we're celebrating Family Day without Kenneth and Kyle, or Brendan's parents, or my dad. It's not like Dad and I were gonna have father–son wheelbarrow races or father–son basketball games; besides, Dad always paired up with my brother, Eric. But father–son anything would've been better than this. I can't imagine it's any easier for Brendan, even though his parents are both alive. It might be worse, since they're just out of reach in boxy jail cells for separate crimes: his mother for armed robbery, his father for assaulting a police officer after he was caught dealing meth. Now he lives with his grandfather who is thugging it out at eighty-eight.

"Everyone's going to expect smiles from us," I say.

"Everyone can go suck it," Brendan replies. He pockets his hands, and I bet there's weed in there; dealing pot has been his way of growing up faster, even though it's pretty much what landed his dad in prison eight months ago. He checks his watch, struggling to read what the hands are saying. "I have to go meet someone." He doesn't even wait for me to respond before he walks off.

He's a guy of few words, which is why he's only my sort of best friend. A real best friend would use a lot of words to make you feel somewhat good about your life when you're thinking about ending it. Like I tried to. Instead, he distanced himself from me because he felt as if he had a duty to hang with the other black kids—which I thought and still think is bullshit.

I miss the time when we took full advantage of summer nights, ignoring curfew so we could lie down on the black mat of the jungle gym and talk about girls and futures too big for us—which always seemed like it might be okay, as long we were stuck here with each other. Now we come outside because of routine, not brotherhood.

It's just one more thing I have to pretend I'm okay with.

HOME IS A ONE-BEDROOM apartment for the four of us. I mean, three of us. Three.

I share the living room with Eric, who should be home any minute now from his shift at the used video game store on Third Avenue. He'll power on one of his two gaming consoles, chat with his online friends through a headset, and play until his team bows out around 4 A.M. I bet Mom will try and get him to apply to some colleges. I don't plan on sticking around for the argument.

There are stacks of unread comics on my side of the room. I bought a lot of them for cheap, like between seventy-five cents and two dollars at my favorite comic shop, without any real intention to read them from start to finish. I just like having a collection to show off whenever one of my more well-off friends comes over. I subscribed to one series, The Dark Alternates, when everyone got into it at school last year, but so far I've only gotten around to flipping through them to see if the artists have done anything interesting.

Whenever I really get into a book, I draw my favorite scenes inside them: in *World War Z*, I drew the Battle of Yonkers where zombies dominated; in *The Legend of Sleepy Hollow*, I drew the moment we meet the Headless Horseman because that was when I suddenly cared about an otherwise so-so ghost story; and, in *Scorpius Hawthorne and the Convict of Abbadon*—the third book in my favorite fantasy series about a demonic boy wizard—I drew the monstrous Abbadon being split into two from Scorpius's Sever Charm.

I haven't been drawing very much lately.

The shower always takes a few minutes to heat up so I turn it on and go check on my mom. I knock on her bedroom door, and she doesn't answer. The TV is on, though. When your only living parent isn't responding, you can't help but think of that time when your father was found dead in the bathtub—and the possibility that beyond your home's only bedroom door life as an orphan awaits you. So I go inside.

She's just waking up from her second nap of the day to an episode of *Law & Order*. "You okay, Mom?"

"I'm fine, my son." She rarely calls me Aaron or "my baby" anymore, and while I was never a fan of the latter, especially whenever my friends were around, at least it showed that there was life inside of her. Now she's just wiped.

Beside her is a half-eaten slice of pizza she asked me to get her from Yolanda's Pizzeria, the empty cup of coffee I brought her back from Joey's, and a couple of Leteo pamphlets she picked up on her own. She's always believed in the procedure, but that means nothing to me since she also believes in Santeria. She puts on her glasses, which conveniently hide the sunken lines around her eyes from her crazy work hours. She's a social worker at Washington Hospital five days a week, and spends four evenings handling meat at the supermarket for extra cash to keep this tiny roof over our heads.

"You didn't like the pizza? I can get you something else."

Mom ignores this. She gets out of bed, tugging at the collar of her sister's hand-me-down shirt she recently lost enough weight to fit into because of her "Poverty Diet," and hugs me harder than she has since Dad died. "I wish there was something else we could've done."

"Uh . . ." I hug her back, never knowing what to say when she cries about what Dad did and what I tried to do. I just look at the Leteo pamphlets again. There *is* something else we could've done for him—we just never would've been able to afford it. "I should probably shower before the water gets cold again. Sorry."

She lets me go. "It's okay, my son."

I pretend everything is okay as I rush to the bathroom where steam has fogged up the mirror. I quickly undress. But I stop before stepping in because the tub—finally clean after lots of bleach—remains the spot where he took his life. His memories sucker punch my brother and me at every turn: the pen marks on the wall where he measured our height; the king-sized bed where he would flip us while watching the news; the stove where he cooked empanadas for our birthdays. We can't exactly just escape these things by moving into a different, bigger apartment. No, we're stuck here in this place where we have to shake mouse shit out of our shoes and inspect our glasses of soda before drinking in case roaches dived in while our backs were turned.

Our hot water doesn't run hot for very long so I jump in before I miss my chance.

I rest my head against the wall, the water sliding through my hair and down my back, and I think about all the memories I would want Leteo to bury. They all have to do with living in a post-Dad world. I flip over my wrist and stare at my scar. I can't believe I was once that guy who carved a smile into his wrist because he couldn't find happiness, that guy who thought he would find it in death. No matter what drove my dad to kill himself—his tough upbringing in a home with eight older brothers, or his job at the infamous post office up the block, or any one of a million reasons—I have to push ahead with the people who don't take the easy way out, who love me enough to stay alive even when life sucks.

I trace the smiling scar, left to right and right to left, happy to have it as a reminder not to be such a dumbass again.

2

A TRADE DATE

(NOT A DATE WHERE YOU TRADE YOUR DATE)

Last April, Genevieve asked me out while we were hanging out at Fort Wille Park. My friends all thought this was an epic case of gender role-reversal, but my friends can also sometimes be close-minded idiots. It's important for me to remember this—the asking-out part—because it means Genevieve saw something in me, the life of someone she wanted to lose herself in, and not someone whose life she wanted to see thrown away.

Trying to commit you-know-what two months ago was not only selfish, but also embarrassing. When you survive, you're treated like a child whose hand has to be held when crossing the street. Even worse, everyone suspects you were either begging for attention or just too stupid to get the job done properly.

I walk the ten blocks downtown to the apartment where Genevieve lives with her dad. Her dad doesn't really pay her a whole lot of attention, but at least he's alive to ignore her. I buzz the intercom and am desperately wishing I could've ridden a bike here. My armpits stink and my back is sweaty, and the shower I just took is now completely pointless.

"Aaron!" Genevieve calls, sticking her head out from her

window on the second floor, sun rays glowing against her face. "I'll be down in a sec, I gotta wash up first." She shows me her hands, wet with yellow and black paint, and winks before ducking back in. I'd like to think she was drawing a cartoonish happy face, but her hyper-imagination is more likely to draw something magical, like a yellow-bellied hippogriff with pearl-black eyes lost in a mirrored forest with nothing but a golden star to guide it home. Or something.

She comes down a couple minutes later, still in the ratty white shirt she wears to paint. She smiles before hugging me, and it's not one of those half smiles I've grown used to. There's nothing worse than seeing her sad and defeated. Her body is tense, and when she finally relaxes, the pale green tote bag I got her for her birthday last year slips down her shoulder. She's drawn a lot on the tote; sometimes there are tiny cities, other times it's an imagining of a song lyric she loved.

"Hey," I say.

"Hi," she says back, tiptoeing to kiss me. Her green eyes are watery. They remind me of a rain forest painting she gave up on a few months ago.

"What's wrong? My armpits stink, right?"

"Totally, but that's not it. Painting is stressing me out like whoa. You're rescuing me just in time." She punches me in the shoulder, the aggressive way she chooses to flirt.

"What were you painting?"

"A Japanese swallow angelfish walking out of the ocean."

"Huh. I was expecting something cooler. More magical with hippogriffs."

"I don't like being predictable, dumb-idiot." She's been calling me that since our first kiss a couple days after we started dating. I'm pretty sure it's because I might've accidentally bumped heads with her twice like the biggest amateur in the history of inexperienced kissers. "You in the mood to go see a movie?"

"How about a Trade Date instead?"

A Trade Date is not a date where you trade your date for someone else. A Trade Date—Genevieve made it up—is when I choose a spot to go to that will interest her, and she does the same for me. And it's called a Trade Date, obviously, because we're trading favorite pastimes with each other, and *not* each other.

"I could settle on that, I suppose."

We play Rock, Paper, Scissors. Loser has to choose first and my scissors cut the hell out of her paper. I could've just volunteered to go first because I already know where I want to take her, but I'm not 100 percent sure yet of the words I want to say, and I could use the extra time to make sure I get them right. She brings me to my favorite comic bookstore on 144th St.

"I guess you're done being unpredictable," I say.

COMIC BOOK ASYLUM
We've Got Issues

THE FRONT DOOR IS painted to resemble an old phone booth, like the kind Clark Kent dashes into when he needs to change into Superman. While his monogamous relationship with that particular phone booth outside the *Daily Planet* never made much sense to me, I'm as close to super as I've felt in a while. I haven't been here in months.

Comic Book Asylum is geek heaven. The cashier in the Captain America shirt is restocking seven-dollar pens shaped like Thor's hammer. Pricey busts of Wolverine and the Hulk and Iron Man gloriously line a shelf modeled after the fireplace in Wayne Manor. I'm surprised some forty-year-old virgin isn't having a seizure over the Marvel and DC clashing going on here. There's even a closet full of classic capes you can either buy or rent for an in-store photo shoot. But my favorite spot is the clearance cart with the dollar comics, since, well, they're carrying dollar comics and that's a hard price to beat.

They even have action figures Eric and I would've played with when we were younger, like a combo pack of Spider-Man and Doctor Octopus. Or a set of the Fantastic Four, though we would've probably lost the Invisible Woman—Get it?—since my favorite was the Human Torch and his was Mister Fantastic. I even had a soft spot for the bad guys, like Green Goblin and Magneto, because Eric always preferred the heroes and that made it more fun.

Genevieve continues to choose this place on Trade Dates because she knows it makes me happiest, although the community pool where I took swimming lessons used to be a close second before I almost drowned. (Long story.) She wanders off and looks through their posters, and I cut straight for the clearance cart. I rifle through the comics for something badass that might inspire me to work on my own comic some more. I left off on a suspenseful panel of Sun Warden—my hero, whose origin story involves him swallowing an alien sun as a child to guard it. Right now he only has enough time to save one person from falling off a celestial tower into a dragon's mouth, and he's torn between his girlfriend and best friend. There's no doubt Superman would save Lois Lane, but I wonder if Batman would save Robin over his girlfriend of the week. (The Dark Knight gets around, man.)

Some guys are talking about the latest *Avengers* movie, so I quickly choose two comics and rush over to the counter so I won't have to Hulk out if they spoil anything. I never got to see the movie when it came out in December because nobody wanted to go. We were all in a funk over Kenneth.

"Hey, Stanley."

"Aaron! Long time no see."

"Yeah, I had a bit of an episode going on."

"Sounds mysterious. Leaping over tall buildings with a mask on, maybe?"

I take a second to answer. "Family stuff."

I hand him my gift card and he swipes it for the two-dollar charge. He swipes one more time before telling me, "Zero balance, dude."

"No, I have a few dollars left."

"I'm afraid you're poorer than Bruce Wayne with a frozen bank account," he says. He should be ashamed of himself—not because that's a rude thing to say to a customer, but because he's been recycling that same weak joke for months now. No shit I would be poorer than Bruce Wayne on his poorest day.

"Do you want me to put them on hold for you?"

"Uh, you know, it's cool. Yeah, I'll be fine."

Genevieve comes over. "Everything okay, babe?"

"Yeah, yeah. You ready to bounce?" My face warms up and I'm getting teary, not because I won't go home with these comics—I'm not eight years old—but because I'm just really fucking embarrassed in front of my girlfriend.

She doesn't even look at me when she reaches into her tote bag and pulls out a few bucks, which somehow makes me feel even worse. "How much is it?"

"Gen, it's fine, I don't need these."

She buys them anyway, hands me the bag, and starts talking to me about an idea for a painting, one where starving vultures chase shadows of the dead down this road, unaware the corpses are above their heads. I think it's a cool enough idea. And as much as I want to thank her for the comics, her changing the subject so I didn't have to feel shitty about myself was probably a better move.

☺ ☺ ☺ ☺

"REMEMBER THAT TIME KYLE got the Leteo procedure?"

Remember That Time is a dumb game we play where we "remember" things that have happened very recently or are going down now. I'm getting the game running to distract her while we walk through Fort Wille Park on 147th Street, close to the post office where my dad worked, near a gas station where Brendan and I used to buy candy cigarettes whenever we felt stressed. (We occasionally joke about how dumb and childish that was.)

"How can anyone know for sure if no one's seen him?" Genevieve is holding my hand as she hops onto a bench, walking along the back with the worst balance ever. I'm positive she's going to crack her head open one of these days and I'll be begging Leteo to make me forget witnessing it. "A lie could've snuck its way into Freddy's mom's rumor mill. Also: saying he *forgot* Kenneth is a little extreme since Leteo *suppresses* memories. They don't erase them." She's never believed in the procedure either, and she once believed in the power of horoscopes and tarot cards.

"I think it counts as forgetting if you never remember it again."

"Good counter."

Genevieve finally loses her balance and I catch her, but not in that heroic way where I could carry her away into the sunset, or even in a funny way where she lands perfectly horizontal on top of me and we kiss. It's more like her body twists and I catch her under her arms but her legs drop and skid back, and now her face is facing my dick, and it's awkward because she's never seen it. I help her up and we're both apologizing; me for no reason, and her for almost falling nose-first into my crotch.

Well, there's always next time.

"So . . ." She pulls her dark hair away from her face.

"What would your battle plan be if zombies came at us right now?"

This time I change the subject so she doesn't have to feel

embarrassed. I hold her hand and lead her through the park. She shares her half-assed strategies about climbing apple trees and waiting them out. Spoken like a true dumb-idiot.

Genevieve's mother used to bring her here as a child, when it was more kid friendly with seesaws and monkey bars. She stopped coming here as much after her mother died in a plane crash a couple years ago on her way to visit family in the Dominican Republic. Whenever we have Trade Dates, I usually take her to other places, like the flea market or the skating rink on half-off Wednesdays, but today we're going to remember that time she asked me out.

We get to the sprayground—one of those fountains where water sprays up from the ground in timed bursts. All ten hoses are now clogged with filthy leaves, cigarettes, and other trash.

"It's been a while," Genevieve says.

"I thought it'd be cool if I asked you out here," I say.

"I don't remember us ever breaking up."

"Is that really necessary?" I ask.

"You can't ask me out if we're already dating. That's like killing a dead person."

"Good point. Break up with me."

"I need a reason."

"Fine. Um, you're a bitch and your paintings suck."

"Broken up."

"Awesome," I say with the biggest smile. "I'm sorry for calling you a bitch and telling you your paintings suck just now and for trying to you-know-what myself. I'm sorry you had to live through that and I'm sorry I was such a dumb-idiot to think I didn't have any reason to be happy because it's pretty damn clear you're my happiness."

Genevieve crosses her arms. There are still spots of paint on her elbow she missed when washing up. "I *was* your happiness until I broke up with you. Ask me out again."

"Is that really necessary?"

She punches me.

"Okay. Genevieve, will you be my girlfriend?"

Genevieve shrugs. "Why not? I need something to do this summer."

We find shade under a tree, kicking off our shoes as we lie down with our feet in the grass. She tells me for the millionth time I never had anything to apologize for, that she didn't hate me for grieving and suffering. And I get that, but I needed this fresh start for us, even if we were just joking around. Not everyone can afford to go to Leteo to have life undone and I wouldn't if I could. If I did, I wouldn't be able to re-create big life moments like today without the memories to remember.

"So . . ." Genevieve is tracing my palm lines like she's about to tell me my future, and she kind of is. "My father is going upstate with his girlfriend on Wednesday for an art show."

"Good for him, I guess."

"He's going to be gone until Friday."

"Good for you."

Only then do I see where this is going. A sexy lightbulb moment flashes, and when it does, I get up and jump so high I think I might've left an Aaron-shaped hole in the clouds. But when I come back down, I remember something very crucial: Fuck, I have no idea how to have sex.

3
MANNING UP

I am so screwed later on.

Okay, poor choice of words, but yeah, I'm going to give it my best, and once Genevieve sees how seriously I'm trying she'll probably laugh so hard she'll cry and I'll cry too but not because I'm laughing with her. I was hoping I could watch an unhealthy amount of porn to memorize techniques, but it's almost impossible in a one-bedroom apartment. I can't even wait for Eric to fall asleep because he stays up all night gaming. I've considered maybe watching porn in the morning while he's knocked out, but even naked bodies can't wake me up.

I know I'm lucky just to have a cell phone, even though it has the shittiest Internet connection ever, but with a laptop I could sneak into the bathroom for "research." Instead, we have a big-ass computer in the living room, and Eric is busy online right now building a free website for his video game clan, The Alpha God Kings. Fuck.

I'm doodling on the back of the report card I got yesterday. Students had to return to school to clean out our lockers and sign up for summer school if needed. My grades dropped in the last couple of months because of, well, you-know-what, but I passed everything (even chemistry, which can go in a corner and melt in hydrochloric acid forever). My guidance counselor tried getting me to talk to her about how I should use this summer to get back in a better headspace for senior year. I totally agree, but right now I'm more concerned about tonight than I am about high school.

The apartment feels extra small, my head even smaller, so I go outside to breathe for a second or minute or hour, but no longer than that because I am having sex tonight whether I know how to or not. I spot Brendan heading into a staircase, call his name, and he holds the door open. He got his first blow job at thirteen from this girl Charlene, and he would go on and on about it whenever we played video games. I hated him for achieving something I hadn't, but he's actually the kind of person whose ways I should tap into.

"Yo. You got a second?"

"Uh." We both look down at his hand and he's carrying weed in a Ziploc bag. Long gone are the days when he was a solitaire whiz. "I actually gotta go handle this."

I make my way past him before he can close the door. The staircase smells like fresh piss and I see the puddle on the floor; it was probably Skinny-Dave who is very territorial. "You blazing or dealing?"

Brendan checks his watch. "Dealing. Customer is coming in a minute."

"I'll be fast. I need to know how to have sex."

"Let's hope it's not fast for your sake."

"Thanks, asshole. Help me not fuck this up."

He shakes his pungent weed in my face. "I gotta make some bank, A."

"And I gotta make my girlfriend happy, B." I pull out the two condoms I bought from work yesterday and shake them in his face. "Look, just give me some tips or tell me girls don't really care about their first times or something. I'm freaking out right now that I'm not—I swear to God I will pay Me-Crazy to destroy you if you repeat this—that I'm not going to be good enough."

Brendan rubs his eyes. "Fuck all that. I boned a bunch of girls just so I could get off and get better."

"But I would never treat Genevieve like that." I wouldn't use any girl like that. Maybe Brendan isn't the right person to ask after all.

"That's why you're a virgin. Go ask Nolan for advice."

"Nolan, who's fathered two kids at seventeen? No thanks."

"Aaron, don't be some little boy who everyone will think is a punk or fag if you bitch out."

"I'm not trying to bitch out!"

Brendan's phone rings. "It's my customer. You gotta bounce."

I don't move. I expect my sort of best friend to step his game up during this big day for me. "I need you to do better than that."

"What, did your father not give you a sex talk before he kicked it?"

Really crude way of labeling my dad's suicide, I know. "No, he would always joke that we had HBO. I overheard him telling Eric some stuff one time, though."

"There you go. Ask your brother." I'm about to protest when he stops me. "Look, unless you're about to buy this weed off me, you need to go." Brendan fake-smiles with a hand out for money. I turn away. "That's what I thought," he says. "Man up tonight."

THERE'S A LIST OF things I would rather do than have the sex talk with my brother, but dying a virgin isn't on it.

Eric is playing the latest Halo game—I've lost count to which one this is—and his match is finally coming to a close. I have no idea what to say. We sometimes play racing games together, less so these days. We definitely never talk to each other about monumental life things, not even Dad's death. His match ends and I stop acting like I'm reading *Scorpius Hawthorne and the Crypt of Lies* and sit up from my bed.

"Do you remember Dad's sex talk?"

Eric doesn't turn, but I'm sure the words are sinking in. He speaks into his headset, telling his "soldiers" he needs two minutes, and then mutes the microphone. "Yeah. Those talks are always really scarring."

We aren't looking at each other. He's staring at the postgame stats, probably analyzing how his team could've done better, and I'm shifting from the worn yellowed stains in the corners of the room to outside the window where life isn't awkward. "What did he say to you?"

"Why do you care?"

"I want to know what he would've told me."

Eric taps buttons that have zero effect on the menu screen. "He said he didn't think about feelings when he was our age. Grandpa encouraged him to just have fun when he was ready, and to always make sure to wear a condom so he didn't have to grow up too soon like some of his friends did. And he would've said you're making him proud if you actually feel ready."

Eric echoing Dad's words is not the same.

I miss my dad.

Eric switches his microphone back on and turns away like he regrets ever talking to me. I shouldn't have forced him to remember Dad when he was distracted; the grieving need their peace whenever they can get it. He resumes playing, instructing his team like the alpha he is. Like Dad was whenever he played basketball and baseball and football, and anything else he did.

I pull a shirt out of my dresser that smells like concentrated dish soap. That's what happens when you share your clothes with a brother who rubs everything against cologne samples. Before I leave, I tell him, "I'm spending the night at Genevieve's. Tell Mom I'm at Brendan's playing some new game or something."

These words knock him out of his zone. He looks at me for a second before remembering he's totally disinterested in my life, and goes back to playing.

I'M TORN WALKING TO Genevieve's.

I'm overthinking everything. Why am I not running? If I really want this, I should be running, or at least jogging, in the interest of saving some energy. But if I don't want to do this, I should be dragging my feet and flipping around to go home before I reach her door. Maybe I'm playing it cool by just walking there, not too eager, not thinking too highly of this completely monumental rite of passage to manhood. Here I am, a lanky kid with a chipped tooth and first chest hairs, and somebody wants to do this with me. And not just anyone. It's Genevieve: my artist girlfriend who laughs at all my unfunny jokes and doesn't abandon me during anything-but-fun times.

I step into this corner store, Sherman's Deli, and pick up a little something for her since it feels like a dick move to take a girl's virginity without some kind of present. Skinny-Dave says flowers are the perfect deflowering gift, so if that's what he thinks, it's gotta be the wrong move.

As I approach Genevieve's door and knock, I look down at my crotch and say, "You better do what you were made to do. So help me God, I will ruin you if you don't. I will absolutely massacre you. Okay, Aaron, stop talking to your dick. And yourself."

Genevieve opens the door in a sleeveless yellow shirt and bedroom eyes. "Good conversation with your dick?"

"Not nearly as deep as I would've liked it to be." I lean forward and kiss her. "I'm a little early so if you need a few more minutes with your other boyfriend I can wait out here."

"Get in here before we break up again."

"You wouldn't dare."

She starts closing the door.

"Wait, wait." I reach into my pocket and pull out a pack of Skittles.

"You're the best."

I shrug. "It seemed weird to come empty-handed."

Genevieve grabs my hand and drags me inside. The apartment smells of the huckleberry candles her mother gave her and also of hot paint, probably Genevieve mixing up a shade she couldn't find inside of a Home Depot.

After my dad passed, I spent a lot of time on that living room couch crying into Genevieve's lap. She promised things would eventually be okay. Her promise actually carried weight since she lost a parent too—versus my friends, who consoled me with pats on the back and awkward glances.

Genevieve is the reason things got better.

Colorful paintings line the hallway walls. There are canvases of alive gardens, circuses where clowns watch ordinary people do tricks, glowing cities below a deep black sea, clay towers melting underneath a harsh sun, and so much more. Her father doesn't say much about her art, but her mother always bragged about how Genevieve painted rainbows in their proper order before she was old enough to spell her own name.

Creepy china dolls crowd a mail-littered table with a dish for keys. A brochure with Genevieve's name catches my eye. "What's this?" I ask, looking at the cabin on the cover.

"Nothing."

"Nothing is nothing, Gen." I open the booklet. "An art resort in New Orleans?"

"Yeah. It's a three-week stay out in the woods working on art with zero distractions. I thought it could be a good space for me to maybe finally finish something but . . ." Genevieve gives me this sad smile and I hate myself.

"But you couldn't trust your dumb-idiot boyfriend to be alone." I hand her the brochure. "I'm done holding you back. If you don't go, make sure it's because you want to have sex all summer."

Genevieve flings the brochure back on the table. "I should probably make sure it's worth staying for first, right?" She winks and walks deeper down the hall, vanishing into the living room.

This apartment was so confusing my first time here that I walked in on her father comparing blueprints for a new mall he's assisting with. Yeah, he has an office in his apartment, and meanwhile I share a living room with my brother and am limited to masturbating in my bathroom. Life sucks that way.

The scent of huckleberry grows stronger as I step inside her bedroom. I see the two candles sitting on top of her bureau, the only source of light in a room dark with unfinished paintings and two sixteen-year-olds about to grow up. Her bed is made with deep blue covers. Genevieve looks like she's sitting in the middle of the ocean. I drop my bag and push the door closed behind me.

This is it.

"We don't have to do this if you don't want to," Genevieve says. Seems very role-reversal based on all the bad TV I've watched, but sweet of her to offer. Or not offer.

The last time we tried having sex I got sick from movie popcorn. It was some romantic comedy thing—we were on a double date with our classmates Collin and Nicole (who are expecting a kid now, crazy)—but I'm ready to do this. I'm not backing out.

"Are you sure you want to?"

"Get over here, Aaron Soto."

I imagine myself tearing my shirt off and charging toward her for awesome sex, but I'm more likely to get tangled in my shirt, tripping over my feet, and making this everything but awesome. So I just walk over, managing not to trip, and sit down beside her, nice and simple. "So. You, uh, come around here often?"

"Yes, I come around my house often, dumb-idiot."

She hugs my neck and squeezes. I choke for a second, collapse backward on her, and play dead. Genevieve smacks my chest, and between giggles says, "No one suffocates . . . that quickly! You suck . . . at dying! You are the . . . *worst* dead guy ever!"

Confidence floods through me in this little moment where I poorly played dead and she called me out on it, and it's a joke that will remain between us because it happened in our personal space where we were about to do a very personal thing and I know I want this with her without a doubt. I break free from her not-quite-tight grip, slide up on her, and kiss her lips and neck, and everything else I instinctively feel is right. She pulls my shirt off and it sails over my shoulder.

"Remember that time you were half naked in my bed?" Genevieve asks, looking up at me.

I take off her shirt and leave her in a bra.

She unzips my jeans and I kick them off with much awkward difficulty while she laughs. If I thought there was any chance Genevieve would've laughed seeing me in my boxers, I would've faked a reason to get out of this. But I can't recall a time where I felt more exposed and comfortable in my life. I care for her so hard, whether Dad would've advised that for my first time or not, and my happiness and her happiness will be one of my greatest hits.

4
MANHUNT ON FAMILY DAY

It's Family Day. While everyone's setting up outside, I'm manning the counter at Good Food's because the owner, Mohad, had to pick up his older brother from the airport. The work doesn't bother me, especially after the night I had. I handled the morning shipment without bitching. I even upsold all the honeybuns that are expiring tomorrow so we wouldn't have any waste. Throughout the morning, my friends popped in so I would spill all the details. It's probably bad form to tell your boys all about your deeds the day after it happens, but there's just no way you can't *not* talk about it.

Brendan grilled me for very personal details about Genevieve—who isn't due to show up until later—but eventually backed off after a line was forming behind him. Skinny-Dave wanted to know how many times we did it (twice!) and how long I lasted (not long but I lied). Baby Freddy wanted to compare first-time tales, except his sounds like bullshit, and to this day, Tiffany denies ever doing anything with him. Lastly, Nolan asked me if I actually went through with it. This, when he came in to buy baby wipes for his two girls; he always uses condoms, but he must be wearing them really wrong. That's more than can be said for Collin, who didn't bother using a condom with Nicole.

On our block, there are guys and girls in their late twenties who we've grown up calling "the Big Kids." We've watched them kick each other's asses, date, and hook up with each other's exes. Some have even gone to college and stayed away. Others, like Devon Ortiz, are still around. Devon comes in to buy panty hose for his mother and congratulates me. This concerns me because it means word is getting around quickly, but also makes me feel kind of proud, like I'm finally one of the Big Kids myself.

By the time Mohad gets back, Brendan has also returned, crowding the counter with Nolan and Skinny-Dave. "When do you get off? We want to get a game of manhunt going."

"Mohad asked me to stay until one," I answer.

From across the store, Mohad shouts in his thick Arabic accent, "Soto! You're good to go now if you and your smelly friends clear out of here."

They all cheer. We bounce.

The energy out here is different from when I started work at 8:00. Nearby, my brother is shuffling cards with his gaming friends: there's Ronny, who always talks shit online but hasn't ever won a fight in real life; Stevie, who met his girlfriend, Tricia, on a dating website for video game fanatics (except he hasn't actually *met her*-met her yet); and Chinese Simon, who is actually Japanese but didn't speak up until a year too late.

My mom is handing out hot dogs to Fat-Dave and his younger healthy-sized brother. She made them on her neighbor Carrie's grill and I hope they're not waterlogged like they were on my twelfth birthday. Brendan and I spat them out behind her back and went to Joey's to split a meatball sub.

Skinny-Dave's mother, Kaci, pushes a shopping cart of blue shirts toward us. The shirts are all paid for months in advance, but I know Mom couldn't afford them for us this year so we'll look like oddballs in any pictures taken for our community center. Kaci hands Fat-Dave his extra-large shirt, which is great since there are now mustard stains on the white shirt he's wearing. Kaci hands her own son his shirt before approaching Brendan and me. "You two are both mediums, right?"

"Yeah, but I don't think my mom ordered one for me," I say.

"I didn't order one either," Brendan says.

Kaci hands us shirts. "Your family has taken care of you, boys. Have fun today and let any of us know if you need anything."

We thank her and slip our shirts over the ones we're already wearing. The shirts are sort of lame. You'll rarely see them worn after tonight except maybe when you're doing laundry or when sleeping over at a friend's house. But I do kind of, sort of, definitely like the sense of unity they bring. They really make this four-building complex feel less like a shitty place where we happen to live and more like a home.

My mom calls me over. She hasn't looked happy in so long, but she looks especially *not* happy with me right now. Whatever she's talking to Baby Freddy's mother about—a conversation I can't make out because she rarely uses Spanish at home—she cuts herself off and snaps, "I'm very proud of myself for not storming into your place of work after I learned you weren't at Brendan's last night."

Not really sure why Baby Freddy's mother is hanging around since gossip is pointless when everyone already knows what's going on.

"Who told you?"

"Your brother."

I was hoping it was just word of mouth. "Judas."

"You are under our watch, Aaron, and you don't have the same freedom your father and I once allowed you, not anymore. If you're going anywhere, *I* know about it and *I* have to speak with the adult who's going to be there."

"Okay, yeah. Fine. Can I go?"

"Were you safe?"

"Yes, Mom." Fucking kill me. The smell of burnt hot dogs catches her attention and I head back to my friends. Brendan, Skinny-Dave, and Baby Freddy all give me the yo-you-just-got-in-trouble-like-some-little-kid look. "Fucking Eric snitched on where I spent my night." I flip him off even though his back is turned to me. "Let's just get a game going, okay?"

HOW TO PLAY MANHUNT: One person is designated as the hunter and everyone else has two minutes to hide somewhere inside our block. Once the hunter catches you, you're on his team and you have to help him capture other players until everyone's caught or the hour is up.

It's sort of like tag, except way more intense.

Baby Freddy asks for any volunteers to be the hunter. He's automatically out because the last time he was hunter, his mother called him upstairs for his 9:00 curfew and left us all hiding for an hour before we realized he was home. Both Daves hate hunting. Deon bites the bullet and counts down.

Brendan and I try keeping up with Me-Crazy as he storms into the garage where we're sure we'll see Skinny-Dave any minute. He always hides underneath cars (which almost ended badly . . . twice). Me-Crazy is our resident manhunt fanatic, and we're pretty sure he will become a threat to society the next time he's really bored. But for now, he's a bit of a pioneer when it comes to the best hiding spots. He was the first to discover the third-floor hallway window of Building 135 opens up to the connecting rooftop—where we throw all our deflating handballs and empty Top Pop bottles and Arizona cans from ground level. He's also the only player to this day to ever hop a ride on top of a moving Nissan to get away from six hunters. No joke, but his name is *also* Dave. He nicknamed himself Me-Crazy after all these not-so-sane stunts, and because of that one time he clipped the wings of a wounded bird for a laugh. We're lucky he likes us.

Me-Crazy's Timberland boots don't slow him down, but his footsteps are so loud I'm surprised they never give him away. "Stop following Me-Crazy," Me-Crazy says. "Yah going to get Me-Crazy caught."

"Not if we all hide together," I gasp. Brendan is lagging behind.

Me-Crazy halts, and it's not so he can point out his next hiding space. He rolls his eyes back until all we see is white. He punches his own face and jogs in place.

Oh shit: Crazy Train Mode. When he's like this, he lifts people up onto his shoulders and bangs them against walls and cars and whatever the fuck else is around.

"We'll stop following you, goddamn it," I tell him.

We jet around him while he stands still, not turning back; he knows we know better.

"Fucking psycho," Brendan says as we reach the far end of the garage and run into Building 155. We sneak into the unoccupied maintenance office and catch our breath. It smells like dirty mop water and toilet plungers. Brendan spits inside this sink that's filled to the brim with yellowed water. "You have to tell me about Genevieve's tits now."

"No way."

We hear footsteps and crouch, keeping our backs against a broken-down table.

"Punk," Brendan whispers, peeking over the table for Deon or custodians. "Props to you, A. I thought for sure you were going to pull some fag shit and not go through with it."

"You wish," I whisper back. "It was pretty fucking incredible."

"I bet. No homo, but I would watch that sex tape to see your girl in action. Not you."

"I'm really uncomfortable right now," I joke.

"FUCK."

I turn to see what's got Brendan wilding out. Deon is coming toward us. We both hop up and separate so he'll have to choose. I don't like my odds. Deon is fit from years of being on the football team and once he grapples me, I'm done. (Yeah, you gotta basically bear-hug someone for three beats of "Manhunt one, two, three. Manhunt one, two, three . . ." to capture them.) Deon fakes coming for me and grabs Brendan, setting me up for escape.

I bolt, my heart pumping hard. I skip stairs, slamming open the door. I'm running out of breath but I can't get caught now, not unless I want to spend the rest of the game figuring out where the fuck Me-Crazy is. We'd all have a better chance finding Bigfoot playing with the Holy Grail. I head to the little alleyway where I can hide inside a Dumpster—hell no, scratch that—hide behind a Dumpster. But the gate is locked.

Upside: I'm skinny enough to squeeze my way through if I can pry the gate open.

Downside: I'm too skinny and lacking the muscle needed to pull this off.

Someone behind me whistles. I almost jet down the block toward Dead Man's Corner, named so because it's easy to get cornered if you're up against two hunters. But it's not Deon or Brendan. Some stranger-guy with light brown skin and thick eyebrows is standing at the curb. He's with a short girl with dyed red hair who looks frustrated or sad or both.

"You okay?" he asks me.

"Yeah, playing manhunt," I manage. "And it's going to be game over in a sec." I keep pulling and pulling, trying to squeeze in but am just going to get stuck. "Fuck you, gate!" Eyebrows

Guy says something to the girl, turns his back on her, and walks over to me. She looks fucking murderous and finally walks away while he nudges me to the side. He pulls open the gate. "Get in there."

"Awesome, thanks." I slide in and take cover behind some cinder blocks since the Dumpster chokes me with its stench of hot garbage. I hear footsteps stampeding our way and I lie flat on the ground, the concrete warming my face and smelling like baked tar.

I hear Eyebrows ask, "You looking for some tall kid?" I can only assume Deon and Brendan nod because he then says, "He went that way." The footsteps continue on toward Dead Man's Corner. "Coast is clear, Stretch."

I get up and approach him, wrapping my fingers around the chinks of the fence dividing us. "Thanks, yo."

"Happy to help," he says with a smile that probably bags him a lot of girls. "I'm Thomas, by the way."

"Aaron," I say, extending my hand to shake his, but we're still on opposite sides of the gate. He laughs a little. "So what was going on with that girl?"

"I was breaking up with her."

"Yikes. Why?"

"She's not really right for me anymore."

"Why's that?"

"Nothing you would care about."

I'm half nervous Brendan and Deon will sneak up from behind me, but I'm also half curious to know why this stranger-guy named Thomas broke up with his girlfriend. "So our one-year anniversary is today," he says breaking the silence. "I went to the mall to buy Sara's favorite perfume. I didn't remember what it was called, and I know I knew it before. I didn't think it was a big deal, I knew what it smelled like and I could figure it out from there." He pulls out a couple movie tickets from his wallet. “Then I saw these ticket stubs. I couldn’t remember if I saw these movies with Sara or my cousins.”

“Okay . . .” I wonder when this story will take a crazy twist, like he slept with her sister or something.

“If I can’t remember, I’m wasting her time. Dragging it out will just lead her on and stop me from finding someone new,” he says.

“Makes sense,” I respond. “I mean, if Romeo and Juliet didn’t think the other could offer ultimate happiness, the both of them would’ve survived.”

He laughs. “So basically make sure I find someone worth downing poison for?”

“Exactly,” I say. “Do you live around here?”

“Yup.” Thomas points to the Joey Rosa Projects.

“Do you want to play?”

“Isn’t manhunt for thirteen-year-olds?”

“Nah. We go hard, like tackle each other and shit.”

“How late you guys going to playing for?”

“Different games throughout the day, I don’t know.”

“I have to head home. Maybe I’ll find you later. It seems like you need someone to watch your back.”

“I’m sure I’ll be fine from here on out.”

“How sure?”

“Bet-my-life sure.”

Thomas points behind me, and there goes Deon and Brendan. They’re winding down, but they’re close. Thomas pries open the gate and I sneak back to his side.

“I should probably run.”

“You should probably run.”

“See you later, Thomas.”

“See you later, Stretch.”

☺ ☺ ☺ ☺

TEN MINUTES LATER, AFTER making the stupid move of hiding inside the tunnel slide like an amateur, Deon catches me. Now I'm searching for others in staircases and the garage, when I feel magnetized back to the gate where I just was. No one is there. Not Baby Freddy or Nolan or that kid Thomas. I move on.

☺ ☺ ☺ ☺

NOT LONG AFTER 4:30, Genevieve joins the Family Day festivities. The guys all cheer and whistle as she approaches. I half expect her to play-choke me like she did before we had sex last night, except for real. But as we hug she whispers, "I told my friends too." Then she punches me. When my friends begin asking probing questions about how good I was, she and I ditch them for an unoccupied bench.

"How you doing?" I ask.

"Pretty happy, I guess."

I stare at her bare neck until my eyes fall a bit. Normally I'm better at not staring at her cleavage whenever she wears these baggy-cut shirts, but my post-sex hormones are at a high. I'm weak to it all. She raises my chin until our eyes reconnect. "I've created a monster, haven't I?"

"I swear I like you as a person too."

She's not smiling, though. "I'm going to miss you, Aaron," she says.

She grabs my hand. I'm so fucking confused.

Then I see it in her face. It feels like someone has knocked the air out of me. She's breaking up with me. She only wanted me for sex. Maybe the sex was bad. I was bad at sex because we rushed this. Maybe we should've never had sex, ever. It would be a hard life but an even harder life is one without Genevieve who never gives me shit whenever I run out of things to say at the end of a long day.

"What did I do?" I ask.

She places a hand on my cheek, a pity palm. "I enrolled to the art camp, dumb-idiot. I was a really late admission obviously, but I called and someone dropped out. But I don't leave until after my birthday, so this doesn't ruin whatever big plans you have."

Yeah, I am indeed the biggest dumb-idiot this world has ever seen. But I'm also the luckiest dumb-idiot, because I have a girlfriend who gives so many flying fucks about her future. And she's definitely not leaving because the sex was so-so.

Probably not.

"I think I'll miss you too," I say back, and it sounds really cool, like when Han Solo told Princess Leia "I know" after she said she loved him.

The pity palm clenches into a fist and punches my shoulder. If I told her I didn't have any plans for her birthday yet, she'd probably punch me in the face. Whatever I decide on can't be too expensive because I have to give my mom some rent money before the month is up. "You probably want to spend your birthday at the park waiting for stars to come out, don't you?"

"That sounds pretty perfect, actually, yeah."

"Nah. Too boring. Let's go to NASA and try to fool around in a zero-gravity room."

"Sounds impossible and messy."

"I think it sounds outrageously fun."

"You're not winning this, Aaron." She gets up, smiling, and walks away.

I chase after her. "I'm sure they have stars at NASA somewhere . . ."

☺ ☺ ☺ ☺

THE GREAT ARGUMENT OF NASA vs. Park ended when Genevieve threw a "because I say so" my way. So, you know, it was never going to happen but it still sucks.

It's darker out now, maybe after 8:00. Colorful ribbons surround us from our water-balloon fight as fireflies flicker gold around the barbecue grill we're using to roast marshmallows. Genevieve has never had a roasted marshmallow before so I capture the moment on my phone's shitty camera. Her face sours, and she gives me a thumbs-down. "Too burnt," she mumbles, spitting it out.

"Real ladylike," Nolan says.

Genevieve flips him off. "How about this?"

All the other guys burst into a chorus of "Oooooooooh!"

I eat the rest of the marshmallow for her and we sit back. My brother is still playing cards with his friends underneath a streetlamp; my mother is trying to socialize over the pounding salsa; some dads are playing horse with beer cans, a trash bin as their basketball net . . . and that Thomas kid is here, lost and looking around.

I unwrap my arm from around Genevieve's shoulders and run to catch Thomas. "Yo!"

"Stretch, thank God!" Thomas gives me a fist bump. "I couldn't find you. What's going on out here, someone's birthday?"

I point to the shirt, which I guess he didn't register earlier. "Family Day. It's an annual celebration for us Leonardo Housing residents. You guys have something like this over at Joey Rosa?"

"Nope. Is it okay that I'm here? I can leave if it's just a community party." He looks around with this face that screams, *I know I don't belong.*

"You're chill. Come meet my friends."

We make our way back to the crew. "Yo, this is Thomas." Genevieve looks back and forth between us. "And this is my girlfriend, Genevieve."

"Hey," Thomas says. "Happy Family Day, everyone."

They all give halfhearted waves and head nods.

"How do you know each other?" Baby Freddy asks.

"Bumped into him earlier. He just broke up with his girlfriend and I thought some games could cheer him up."

"Wait." Deon sits up. "Didn't I see you outside the gate this afternoon?" He nudges Brendan with his elbow. "This is the dude that sent us to Dead Man's Corner?"

"That what you call it?" Thomas places a hand over his heart and raises the other. "Guilty, by the way. I gave Stretch here a much-needed assist."

"Where you from?" Fat-Dave asks.

"Down the block. Joey Rosa's."

They all glance at one another. Sure, we've had some BS with Joey Rosa kids over the years, always getting into fights whenever they invite themselves over to our block, but I can tell Thomas isn't like them.

Skinny-Dave doesn't care about the rivalry. "You know Troy? He still with Veronica?"

"I know him, but I don't like him," Thomas answers. "My neighbor Andre was pissed at Troy for some reason and I overheard him asking Veronica what she saw in him and she had no idea what he was talking about."

"YES!" Skinny-Dave jumps. "I knew that fucker was lying. I should go call her."

Thomas scratches his head. "I hate to break it to you, but she's seeing Andre now." We all laugh at Skinny-Dave who falls back into his seat.

"How'd the rest of the manhunt game go?" he asks me. "You win?"

"I got caught ten minutes later," I say. I sit back down with Genevieve and hold her hand. She pulls away—and then I see why: she's holding out her palm as a landing place for a firefly. It's easy to forget it's there when it's not glowing, until all of a sudden it comes back and surprises you; it reminds me of grief.

"Did you know fireflies glow for mating purposes?" Thomas says.

"Nope," I say. "I mean, I believe you, I just didn't know that."

"Imagine if we could glow to attract a mate instead of spraying on cologne that chokes everyone in a fifty-foot radius," he says, which is weird since I don't think his cologne smells all that bad.

"Aaron and Genevieve know enough about mating," Nolan throws out.

Genevieve flips Nolan off, again. "Did you all know fireflies also glow to lure prey? It's basically the equivalent of a girl who gets you to follow her into an alley with her great ass, and then eats you."

"What a crazy fun fact." I wrap my arm around her shoulders in the hopes she'll never eat my head off in an alley because I never realized girlfriends existed in the same predatory universe as hungry fireflies.

☺ ☺ ☺ ☺

ME-CRAZY BULLIES BABY FREDDY into going to Good Food's to buy another handball since he knocked the other onto the roof earlier during the baseball match. They go back and forth for a while until Thomas reaches into his pocket, pulls out a dollar, and hands it to Me-Crazy. It's a thank-you to everyone for letting him crash Family Day. Me-Crazy nods, doesn't thank him, and hands it to Baby Freddy—who sucks his teeth, victorious enough that he didn't have to buy another ball with his own money, but still enough of a loser that he has to go get it. When he returns from Good Food's, he bounces the handball over to Me-Crazy.

"Now what?"

"Suicide," Me-Crazy says in a low growl, which sounds fucking crazy even without the growl, but he's not actually suggesting we all somehow use this handball to kill ourselves because that would be a) insensitive to me—not that he cares, I guess—and b) impossible.

Genevieve looks up at me as if we're all some cult run by Me-Crazy.

"It's a game," I tell her.

How to Play Suicide: It's every man for himself. Someone throws a handball against the wall, it bounces back, and if that ball touches the ground, someone else throws it. But if someone catches it, the original thrower has to race to the wall and shout "Suicide!" before anyone has a chance to bean them.

" . . . and the game goes on until you're the last one standing," Brendan explains to Genevieve.

"Sounds barbaric," she says.

"You can opt out of a beaning," Baby Freddy says.

He's right. There's a rule we reserve for girls and younger kids, where instead of hitting them with the ball you try and throw the ball against the wall before they reach it and eliminate them that way.

"Or you can not play at all," I offer. I don't want to see what happens when she's running to the wall when Me-Crazy is armed.

"I can handle it," she says.

"You ever play this?" I ask Thomas.

"Been a few years."

We walk over to the wall under my window. There's a white residue fogging up one panel because of our shitty air conditioner or something. You can see a couple of my sketchbooks sitting on top of a pile of comics next to my dad's trophies.

Me-Crazy throws the ball first. It's possible no one caught it on purpose in case you hit him too hard and he flips out. Nolan throws the ball next and Brendan and Baby Freddy bump into each other trying to catch it while both making contact with the ball. Nolan is safe whereas Brendan and Baby Freddy book it to the wall. I quickly snatch up the ball and bean Baby Freddy.

He's out.

Brendan shouts "Suicide!" before someone else can sweep up the ball and hit him too. But shouting "Suicide!" on Family Day is a poor move. Everyone, especially my mom and brother, are instantly hyperalert as to whether or not I've you-know-what'd myself. It takes a moment for them to realize we're playing a game they've begged us to rename over and over through the years.

The game goes on. Fat-Dave manages to eliminate Nolan, Deon, and Skinny-Dave because, overweight or not, he has a pitcher's aim. He throws the ball and Genevieve catches it.

"Don't miss," I beg her.

Genevieve throws the ball, and, well, it's good to know if we ever get into a big fight where she's threatening to throw a knife at me I won't have to move a single muscle.

"Suicide!" Fat-Dave shouts.

It's so tense right now you'd think there are mines planted on the ground.

Genevieve doesn't run for the wall (like she should).

No one makes a move for the ball (like they should).

Finally, Brendan goes for it.

"Don't do it," I tell him. I should've grabbed the damn ball myself.

Genevieve runs and is a couple feet from the wall when the ball hits her in the shoulder. She spins around, rolls her eyes, and folds her arms. "Is that what you've all been so afraid of?"

"I went easy on you," Brendan says as she takes a seat with the other losers. Brendan throws the ball and it rebounds right into Thomas's hands. Thomas chases him and hurls the ball, but hits Brendan after he shouts "Suicide!" and is penalized. The ball rolls toward Me-Crazy, which is just terrifying for the newbie, so I race for it myself, falling onto my shoulder in an attempt to grab it. I get up and Thomas hasn't run to the wall yet.

"You okay?"

"Throw it!" Me-Crazy shouts.

I throw the ball, but I fucking miss.

We both run for the wall, and Thomas shouts "Suicide!" and before I can call it myself, I've been beaned so hard I crash straight into the wall and sink to the ground.

"Aaron!"

Genevieve rushes over to me, but I'm fine, or should be in a few days, at least. She massages my temples and I turn to see Me-Crazy celebrating his hell of a hit. And Brendan is shaking his head, no doubt disappointed in my bad throw.

"You sure you're okay, babe?" We sit the rest of the game out, my head still pounding.

"I could down a bottle of Excedrin right now," I say, which are poor choice words for the guy with the suicide attempt on his life record. We watch the game while chatting about how she's going to miss having someone tall around to reach for high things when she flies to New Orleans on Tuesday afternoon. I'm about to tell her something that would be rated NC-17 if it were a movie, when Thomas beans the hell out of Fat-Dave so hard, Brendan claims *he* felt that one. And sure, they all sympathize for the dude with extra poundage as a shield, but when I get hit in the fucking head, the only one who makes a move for me is my girlfriend. That's gotta be contractual or something.

The game comes down to Thomas and Brendan and Me-Crazy. Between Thomas and Brendan, someone's balls gotta drop sometime in the next few rounds so Me-Crazy doesn't win out of fear. Brendan has a really bad throw (not that I'm going ahead and shooting *him* a disappointed look or anything) and it rolls toward my mom and our neighbors.

"I'll get it," I offer so I can test my motor skills after that hit to the head. To my relief, I don't walk like some toy with bad wiring. My mom has the handball by the time I get to her and I throw it back over to Brendan. "Rough game over there."

"I preferred the water-balloon fight," Mom says.

"Even when we were throwing bottles of water at Me-Crazy?"

"I don't think there's any more damage that can be done to that boy," Mom says a little too loudly, getting some laughs from some neighbors who I know without knowing, if that makes sense. But there's one woman I sort of, kind of, definitely recognize, something to do with her piercing green eyes and tousled mass of red-orange hair. That hair is like a candle's flame.

"Hello, kiddo," the redhead says in a light English accent that's got a tinge of South Bronx flavor to it.

"Evangeline!" I practically shout. She's my old babysitter and I had the biggest crush on her. It's weird seeing her casually drinking when I never saw her drinking as a kid, which, you know, made her a good babysitter. "I want to hug you or something but I'm really sweaty and, uh, dude-like right now."

She puts down her beer and hugs me anyway. She messes with my hair and looks me in the eyes. "So this is little Aaron Soto nine years later. You're so handsome. I'm sure you have plenty of gorgeous suitors fighting over you, yes?"

"Just the one girlfriend, actually," I proudly say. It's sort of awesome being able to tell my first crush that I'm basically off the market now. She shouldn't have turned me down when I asked her out after my Power Rangers marathon.

"One lovely girlfriend he snuck away to spend the night with yesterday," Mom grumbles. "Behind my back."

"How was London?" I ask Evangeline, ignoring Mom. If I remember right, she's only nine or ten years older than me. "You broke my heart to study abroad, right?" I cried and cried after she left, not that I'm going to own up to that right now.

"I was studying philosophy at King's College. Though if I could rewind time I would happily trade in courses about pre-Socratic ideologies in favor of playing race cars with you."

"That's all I wanted to hear." I smile. "So you're back. For good?"

"I am, I am. I need to figure out work now, but am simply relieved to be back in the states where I'll take our God-awful subway traffic over the London Underground any day of the week." She suddenly gives me the same sad look she used to have whenever she had to tell me my mom was stuck at work for another hour or two. "I'm sorry about your father. If you ever want to talk, kiddo, give me a holler, even if it's just to tattle on your brother for not sharing the Player One controller."

I pocket my hand so she won't see my scar. My mom lowers her head. Better to chat with Evangeline instead of Dr. Slattery, the awful therapist I spent a few weeks talking to. "For sure." I fake-smile because everyone wants happiness for me as much as I want it for myself. "Welcome back."

I head back to the game just in time to see Me-Crazy bean Brendan with the ball. Thomas must've been eliminated a minute or so before because he's already sitting down with Genevieve, probably chatting about fireflies again. I sit on the other side of Gen and Baby Freddy asks me, "Who's that redhead with your mother?"

"My old babysitter," I answer. "She's pretty gorgeous, right?" This catches Genevieve's attention. She stops talking with Thomas and turns around to scope out her competition. "I had the craziest crush for Evangeline as a kid. But I've moved on."

Brendan asks, "How didn't I know this, you punk bitch?"

"Because I haven't illustrated my autobiographical graphic novel yet, asshole."

☺ ☺ ☺ ☺

LATER I ESCAPE WITH Genevieve for some alone time before her father picks her up. She won't be around to meet tomorrow—her aunt is taking her shopping for her retreat—but we'll definitely be in touch and will see each other for her birthday on Monday. I walk her to the car. She punches me in the shoulder before joining her father, who grunts my way and guns the engine.

Thomas looks tired by the time I make it back to the courts. He's sitting by himself, watching the others drinking Arizona iced teas and laughing. "You good?" I ask him.

He nods. "More fun than I ever have on my block."

"You doing anything tomorrow?"

"I have work until five."

"Where do you work?"

"This gourmet Italian ice cream shop on Melrose."

"Sounds cold and terrible."

"It's very cold and very terrible."

"I'll meet you after work and you can actually play manhunt with us this time."

"Sounds like a plan, Stretch."

We fist-bump.

Once the courts are clear of adults who will be rocking hangovers tomorrow, we play basketball in trash bins rattling of beer cans and aluminum foil, and even a little handball before calling it a night ourselves.

5
A HAPPY FACE WITHOUT EYES

The next afternoon, I find myself on Melrose Avenue.

I'm picking Thomas up from his job, Ignazio's Ice Cream, and the air-conditioning is on full blast. I have zero interest in buying anything. If anyone else were behind the counter I'd probably be a pain in the ass and eat a sample and bounce, but Thomas doesn't look like he's in the mood for that nonsense. He's wearing the worst khaki apron in the history of the world, and his big eyebrows are knitted as he reviews some receipt at the register, punching in keys.

"Welcome to Ignazio's," Thomas greets me without looking up. "Would you like a cup or waffle bowl?"

"Just some eye contact," I say.

Thomas's head jerks up. He looks like he might stab me in the eye with a sample spoon, but just as quickly relaxes. "Stretch!"

"Thomas!" I don't have a nickname for him. "It's mad hot out. I take back what I said yesterday, it's not cold and terrible in here. You got it good here."

"Not for long."

"What do you mean?"

Thomas takes off his apron. He opens the door marked with a bronze MANAGER plate and says, "Hey, I quit." Then he drops the apron and joins me on the other side of the counter.

I don't know if I should clap or cheer or worry about his future.

He pushes me toward the door and shouts "WOOOOOOOO!" once we're outside.

I have to laugh. "What the hell just happened? Did you just quit? You quit, didn't you?" Considering how happy he looks, I take it I'm right. "Dude, I'm sensing a pattern here. You broke up with your girlfriend yesterday and now you've quit your job. You're twenty years too young for a midlife crisis."

"I always quit things I'm tired of dealing with," Thomas says. "Always will."

We make our way back toward Leonardo Housing, and he punches the air, but I'm not really sure what the hell he's fighting.

"I couldn't stand Sara's paranoia anymore," he says. "I couldn't stand people coming into the store for eight samples when they already knew what flavor they wanted. I couldn't stand pumping air into bike tires so I quit that too. If it's not doing something for me, I quit. There. I said it: I'm a quitter."

I don't know how to respond. This guy was a complete nobody to me yesterday. And now he's . . . what, I don't know, exactly. But he's more than a quitter. "Uh . . ."

"Have you ever quit anything, Stretch?"

"Skateboarding, yeah. I must've been ten or something. I went down this crazy steep hill, and saw my young life of playing with action figures flash before my eyes right before I crashed into a parked van."

"Why didn't you just hop off the skateboard?"

"Why are you questioning the irrationality of a ten-year-old?"

"Well played."

"But I get where you're coming from. I guess you can quit

whatever you want. You know, as long as you're not quitting something or someone that's a good fit for you."

"Exactly!" Thomas nods at me, like he's surprised that he's found someone who gets him. "Where's Genevieve today?"

"Hanging with her other boyfriend," I say.

"Aww. Is he nice?"

"He's a bit of a tool, but he's built like Thor so there's not a whole lot I can do. Nah, she's going on an art retreat in a couple of days and needs to go shopping for some craft tools and luggage. Tomorrow is her birthday and there's all this extra pressure to make it seriously awesome since we won't see each other for another three weeks afterwards."

Man, three weeks without Genevieve. Fuck that in the face.

"You should paint her nude, *Titanic*-style," Thomas suggests.

"I don't think I could get anything done with breasts in my face. I'll revisit that idea when I'm old and have seen enough of them."

Back at the block, we get a game of manhunt going. Nolan volunteers as hunter and everyone breaks up. Thomas launches into a sprint one way while Brendan goes the other; I follow Thomas, not wanting to be found early like yesterday. Good thing too, because Thomas makes the rookie mistake of running through the lobby of Building 135—right past a security guard. Before the guard can chase us, I lead him to the staircase with a broken lock, and head up, fast. We stop off on the third floor, open the hallway window, and climb out onto the rooftop—where there's an old generator and all the stuff we roofed.

From up here we can see the second court, the middle of three. There are dark brown picnic tables and the jungle gym where we used to play Don't Touch Green. We see Fat-Dave running from the third court. He's out of breath and gives up. Nolan tackles him and boom, man down.

Thomas isn't even paying attention.

"Nice treasures," he comments, crouching over to pick up a broken yo-yo. He tries spinning it, but the yo-yo detaches from the string and rolls into a headless Barbie. "So how long have you been dating Genevieve?"

"Over a year," I say. I pick up an old GameCube controller, spinning the wire over my head like a lasso before throwing it back down on the pebbles. "I'm lucky it's been that long. She didn't hate me when I gave her reason to."

"Did you cheat on her?" His tone becomes matter-of-fact. "When I started checking out other girls on the street, I knew I wasn't completely into Sara anymore."

"I didn't cheat. My dad died. Well, he committed suicide and that put me in a bad place." I don't talk about this a lot. Sometimes, because I don't want to; other times because my friends don't like dragging death and grief into things.

"Sorry to hear that." Thomas sits on the ground and stares at some empty bottles. Nothing fascinating there, but I'm guessing it's less awkward than looking me in the eye. "I don't get why you thought Genevieve would break up with you."

"There's more to it," I say. My eyes wander to the curved scar on my wrist.

"Tell me who you are," Thomas says.

"What?"

"Tell me who you are: stop hiding. I'm not going to sell your secrets, Stretch."

"Didn't you just sell out *your* friends yesterday to win over *my* friends?"

"They're not my friends," Thomas says.

I sit down across from him. Before I can change my mind, I hold my arm out so he can see the smiling scar, two words that don't fit together. From his angle it'll look more like a frown, but he shifts next to me, leans over, and wraps his hand around my arm. He pulls my wrist closer to his face, inspecting it.

"No homo," he says, looking up at me. "It's weird how it looks like a smile. A happy face without eyes."

"Yeah. That's what I always thought, too."

He nods.

"I kept blaming myself for not being a good enough son, and my mom swore he killed himself because he was unhappy, and it just got me thinking I might be happier dead, too . . ." I trace a nail over the scar, left to right, right to left. "So I did this as a cry for help, I guess, because I didn't like the bad place I was in."

Thomas traces the scar too and pokes my wrist twice. His fingers are dirty from the yo-yo and other crap on the roof. But now I see; he's added eyes with two dark fingerprints above the scar. "I'm glad you didn't do it, Stretch. Would've been a waste."

He wants me to continue existing. I want that too, now.

I pull my arm away and fold my hands on my lap. "Your turn: tell me who you are." His eyebrows meet in the middle, like he's considering the possibilities of who he might be. When he doesn't say anything, I ask, "Childish question, but what do you want to be when you grow up?"

"I think a film director," Thomas quickly answers. "Though you're probably catching on that I don't have a whole lot of direction in life."

"I wouldn't say that, but I wouldn't *not* say it either. Why a film director?"

"Been interested in it since I saw *Jurassic Park* and *Jaws* as a kid. I bow down before Spielberg, whose directing made dinosaurs and sharks even more terrifying."

"I've never seen *Jaws*."

Thomas's eyes widen like I just spoke in Elvish. "I would gouge out my eyes and give them to you if it meant you could see the magic that is *Jaws*. Spielberg does this awesome thing at the end where—actually, I won't spoil it for you. You'll have to come over and watch it sometime."

A window slams shut behind us.

We both freak out for a second and find Brendan and Baby Freddy standing there. I jump to my feet like someone just caught me with my pants down doing something with someone I really shouldn't be doing anything with. "Uh. Have you guys been caught yet?"

"Nah," Baby Freddy says. "What are you doing?"

"Catching our breath," I lie while Thomas simultaneously says, "Talking."

Brendan is looking at us funny, but then his eyes widen. I turn to see Nolan coming toward us while Fat-Dave is struggling to come through the window. We run back to the window on the other side. Thomas is beside me one second, down on the ground the next. I have a tenth of a second to decide to keep going or to help him out. I stop to see if he's okay.

Nolan grapples me. "Manhunt one, two, three. Manhunt one, two, three. Manhunt one, two, three."

I'm caught but don't really care. I crouch beside Thomas where he's massaging his knee. "You good?"

He nods, whistling in and out, and then it hits me that he could push me down and make a run for it and leave me chasing after him the rest of the game. Fuck that. I grapple him. "Manhunt one, two, three. Manhunt one, two, three. Manhunt one, two, three."

We all go back downstairs to search for Me-Crazy before the game ends. I pair with Thomas while Brendan and the others fan out in the garage. We run up to the balcony—Thomas limping behind a bit—and look for Me-Crazy in empty porches, behind barbecue grills, and under deflated pools.

"So I know a little about you and you know a little about me," he says, wincing as he tries to keep up. "Tell me Genevieve's story."

"I'll destroy you if you make a move on my girl."

"Don't worry about that, Stretch."

"Genevieve is . . . She is just the fucking greatest. She gets obsessive when she discovers new artists and is always sending me rambling emails about her favorites and why they should be more famous. She stays up late for daylight savings time so she can see the hours change on the clock. Oh, and she used to rely on her horoscope when she was younger and took it personally whenever it duped her." I look up at the sky and it's in that weird blue-and-pink phase without any stars. "She wants to go to the park to look at stars tomorrow, but I want to top that."

"Planetarium?"

"Ruled it out already. I'm scared she'll want to grab lunch or something like that and I can't afford it."

Thomas knocks over a shovel leaning against a wall in one of the porches and it clatters loudly. He quickly hops out and hides against the wall before the neighbors can come and curse him out. I crawl over to him and we wait it out a bit before running back down the stairs. "You have anything planned so far?" he asks, once we're safe.

"My mom's coworker gave me a two-for-one coupon for a pottery session. So in the morning we'll make something cool together, but I just need a good finish." Something tells me sex in a crappy motel room wouldn't count as a real gift unless you're a complete arrogant bastard in a high school prom movie. "Any ideas?"

"Show her stars like she wants," Thomas says. "I know where to get you some."

He tells me his plan and it's so fucking boss.

6
HER HAPPY BIRTHDAY

I like waking up from nightmares.

Sure, the nightmare itself is a mind fuck, but knowing I'm okay? That's what I like. The nightmare I've just woken up from started off as a dream.

In it, I was a kid, maybe eight or nine. I was at Jones Beach with Dad, just the two of us. We were throwing a football back and forth. I missed one catch and chased down the ball, but when I turned around Dad was gone. The sand around me exploded like land mines and riding on a wave of red water was my dad's corpse, and I woke up right after it splashed on me and took me under.

"Good morning," Mom says.

She's taking Dad's college basketball trophies off the window ledge, throwing them into a box stuffed with his old work shirts.

I jump out of bed. "What are you doing?"

"Turning our home back into a home." She bends over and picks up another box, packed with God knows what. "I'm done watching people lose their lives at the hospital only to come back to this graveyard."

That's why she's home; another patient lost to drug overdoses, abuse, who knows what today.

And I get what she means. I can see a drawing forming in my head now of what it would be like if we could set our home on fire: warped windows, concaved walls, flames eating everything we didn't want, and then all of us leaving our footprints in the ashes as memories melt and disperse around us. Except I would never draw myself surrounded by black smoke, because I'm not ready to watch it all burn away.

"Why do we have to do this now?"

Eric comes out of her bedroom, pulling himself away from the *Stars Wars* marathon he planned for himself on his day off. He actually helps Mom out with the boxes. This is the same guy who won't wash a single dish or fold his own shirts.

"My son, it's been four months already. What use do we have keeping empty cigarette cartons and unopened mail? It's too much. I don't like his ghost around me."

"But he was your husband," I say. "And our dad."

"My husband used to bring me ginger ale when I was sick. Your father played with you beautiful boys throughout your childhood. But we didn't lose that man—he took himself away from us." Mom chokes on her words and cries as she admits, "Part of me wishes I never knew him." I think back to the Leteo pamphlets on her bed.

"Maybe there's something more we should've been doing to keep him happy," I whisper. "You said so yourself a few days ago."

Eric scoffs. "That's zombie talk. He's gone, okay? Just shut it and leave her alone."

There's a hole inside me too, and questions in my head I can't just ignore. I miss the man my mom misses, who laughed when my friends and I were in his car pretending it was a spaceship being chased by alien invaders; who watched cartoons with me whenever I had a nightmare; who made me feel safe when he put me back in bed so he could leave for his night shift at the post office. I don't like thinking about the man he was right before we lost him.

Mom puts down a box. I think I've won, but instead she holds my hand and sobs some more while tracing the raised smile on my wrist. "We're scarred enough, okay?"

Eric moves some more boxes out into the hallway, where the next stop is the incinerator. I'm completely motionless. Soon all the boxes are gone.

☺ ☺ ☺ ☺

THOMAS MEETS ME IN front of his building, and we ride the elevator straight up to the rooftop. I ask him if the alarm above the doorway is going to go crazy, but he says it's been busted for the past couple of years, since some big New Year's party. He rarely uses this entrance anyway. He prefers the fire escape because of the view and exercise, but we're on limited time before I have to meet up with Genevieve. The sun is sinking behind the cityscape, and I can already feel the brutal heat dying down.

". . . so then Eric tells me I'm speaking in zombie talk because I don't think death is the end of a person," I say, catching him up on what went down earlier. I spot an orange cord trailing across the ground and follow it to the edge of the roof. "Well, when I say it like that I feel like I should be biting into a brain."

"Don't let that ruin your day, Walking Dead. And definitely don't let it ruin your girl's day." He picks up the cord and shakes it. "This connects down to my window and through my bedroom. It's all set up already, but text me if you have any issues."

I walk over to the small black-and-gray projector, facing toward an old chimney that's sealed off with cement. A smile spreads across my face.

☺ ☺ ☺ ☺

"I'M SO EXCITED," GENEVIEVE says. She picks out a pre-fired vase at Clay Land, a pottery studio on 164th Street that doubles as a tattoo parlor after 4:00—just in case someone wants to make a poor life decision after painting mugs for their parents. The pottery sessions cost thirty dollars with the two-for-one coupon, which sort of sucks for my wallet, but we're creating something that's lasting, like us. Especially considering her father mistook yesterday for her birthday.

We sit at this table in the corner. Genevieve doesn't wait for the instructor before she grabs a paintbrush and goes to work. Her hands race around like she's on a timer with only seconds left, and she traces yellow and pink lines around the vase from a starburst of red.

I paint a happy zombie on the mug I picked out. "I'm sorry we didn't do this sooner."

"No sad stuff on my birthday, Aaron." Genevieve's smile widens as she trails two fingers soaked in purple around the vase. "I love this more than a bath of Skittles."

She dropped That Word. Not at me, but about something we're doing together, and I freak out a bit in my head. And also not freaking out—she didn't say she loved *me*—but still freaking out enough that I almost knock over my mug. It might be the paint fumes, but I ask: "Do I make you happy?"

She stops rubbing the neck of the vase and looks up at me. Then she holds out her hand that's soaked in a blend of paints and when I reach for it, she punches me in the arm and leaves a colorful fist print. "You know you know the answer to that." She dips her finger in a can of yellow paint and traces a smile over my dark blue shirt. "Stop fishing for compliments, you tall dumb-idiot."

☺ ☺ ☺ ☺

GENEVIEVE PROBABLY THINKS I'M finally bringing her to my apartment, something I've always avoided since it's not very girlfriend friendly. It's always messy and smells like wet socks. We just keep walking past my building, into Thomas's, and we ride the elevator up to the roof.

The sun is now completely tucked away and the moon is doing its thing. There's a picnic blanket on the ground held down by the cinder blocks; this was Thomas's doing, and it's a surprise to both me and Gen. "So you're likely wondering what the hell we're doing here."

"I always suspected you were psychic," she says, still holding on to my hand like she's dangling from the edge. She looks up and finds some stars hanging out up there in the faraway sky, but I'm about to beat them.

We sit on the blanket and I press the proper buttons on the projector and CD player. "Okay, my plan to take you to the planetarium was a no go because of reasons you would punch me for getting worked up over. So I figured if I couldn't take you to some constellations, I would bring them to you." The projector whirs to life and a light beams onto the chimney. An ominous-sounding female voice says, "Welcome to the known universe." Thomas downloaded the star show from online and even got the audio onto the CD player for us.

Genevieve blinks a few times. There are tears forming in the corners of her eyes, and you shouldn't be happy when your girlfriend is crying, but it's okay when they're Aaron-did-something-right tears.

"From here on out you're in charge of my birthday," Genevieve whispers. "The picnic blanket, the pottery session, the stars, and now this woman who sounds like God."

"We both know God is a dude, but nice try."

She punches my arm. I pull her close to me and we lie down for our trip across the universe. It's pretty strange feeling sucked into the stars in front of us when there are actual stars above us. Artificial satellites orbit the planets and I act like I'm flicking them away, clicking my tongue each time. Genevieve punches me again and shushes me. I would've shut up anyway after seeing the planets fall into the distance so we can admire constellations, like the twins for Gemini (which she whoops at), the Pisces fish, the Aries ram, and the rest of the zodiac family. The constellations fall away. The captions tell us that we're a light-year away from Earth when boring radio signals zoom in . . . on and on until we end up in the Milky Way galaxy 100,000 light-years later. This feels like something straight out of a video game.

We travel 100,000,000 light-years from Earth—into other galaxies, where we see lots of greens and reds and blues and purples glowing against the black of space, like splattered drops of paint on a dark apron. I don't know how we're not space sick once we hit 5,000,000,000 light-years away from Earth. There's something shaped like a butterfly, and we discover it's the afterglow of the big bang, which is pretty damn beautiful.

Everything begins zooming away, space and time undoing its present to us, my present to Genevieve, and it throws us out of the cosmos. This trip changes everything for me. Or maybe doesn't change anything, only makes clear of what I can find here on Earth, my home. Space is pretty damn unreachable for most of us. I turn to Genevieve, to the girl I brought to the stars and back, who waits for me through times dark as space. I hold her hand and say, "I think I sort of, maybe kind of . . . I think I love you."

My heart is pounding. I'm so dumb. Genevieve is out of my league, out of this universe. I wait for a reaction, for her to laugh at me, but she smiles and blows all my doubts away—until her smile falters for a second. I could've missed it if I blinked or rolled my eyes back in relief.

"You don't have to say that," Genevieve says. I check her

hands to see if the ax she just slammed into my chest is as big as I think it is. "I don't know if that's what you think I want to hear."

"I'll be real. I didn't think kids our age could do this, you know, but you're more than my best friend and definitely more than some girl I like sleeping with. I'm not waiting for you to say it back—in fact, never say it. I'll be okay. I just had to tell you."

I kiss my girlfriend on her forehead, untangle our hands and legs, and get up. It's hard, seeing as there's this crushing weight in my chest that makes me feel like that time I tumbled under the waves at Orchard Beach. I follow the orange cord to the ledge and look down at the street: two guys are either shaking hands or swapping money for weed, a young mother is struggling to pop open a baby stroller and a couple of girls are laughing at her. This world is full of ugliness like drugs and hate and girlfriends who don't love you. I look over at my building a couple blocks down. I could really go for being home now.

Genevieve grips my shoulder and hugs me from behind. In her hand is a folded piece of paper. She shakes it until I take it from her.

"Look at it," she says, slightly muffled. This is a goodbye hug that comes with a goodbye letter with goodbye words. I unfold the wrinkled sheet and it's an illustration of a boy and a girl in the sky with a backdrop of many, many stars. The boy is tall and when I examine it more closely, the girl is punching him in the arm—it's a constellation of us.

Genevieve turns me to her and looks me in the eyes and I almost want to turn away. "I drew that after our first date and have carried it around a lot wondering when I could share this with you. All we did was walk around and it was easy, like we were hanging out for the hundredth time."

Then I realize our first clumsy kiss was the inspiration. "I laughed after we kissed and you didn't get offended or anything. You smiled and punched me in the arm."

"I should've punched you in the face. I guess I like hurting the boy I love."

I don't move. I told her to never say it but I'm damn glad she did. We're locked in some strange staring contest and our mouths are curving.

This is still an ugly world. But at least it's one where your girlfriend loves you back.

7
THAT TIME I'M ALONE

It hasn't even been twenty-four hours and I miss Genevieve. I would sell our firstborn child—a little guy I think we'll name something ironic, like Faust—just to have her back to punch me.

I didn't even change clothes when I woke up because the shirt had her fist print, not that I would ever tell my friends. I tried distracting myself with some Sun Warden sketches. Funny how *I* was so big a distraction to Genevieve that she had to fly to New Orleans just so she could get some work done.

I never do anything right.

These are bad thoughts for me to be thinking. That shitty therapist Dr. Slattery told me to speak to someone—friends, a stranger on the subway, anyone—whenever I find myself in an unhappy and lonely place: obvious advice and not worth the bank we spent on him. I go outside and search for Brendan since there's no one home for me to talk to. Not that I'd be chit-chatting with my mom and Eric anyway. I try calling Brendan; he doesn't pick up his phone.

Outside, Skinny-Dave is playing handball. He lets me join him, which is great because it keeps me busy enough to suffer through his small talk about "procrastination masturbation," where you save a porn link for later because you can't be bothered with the cleanup at that moment. But it's not long before he stops playing so he can check on his laundry, leaving me alone with a handball I "better not fucking lose" or he'll castrate me and my future sons. (Sorry, Faust.)

Twenty days.

I only have to survive twenty more days without her.

☺ ☺ ☺ ☺

"HELLO?"

"Hey, it's Aaron."

"I know, Stretch. What's up?"

"Nothing, which is a problem. I should be doing something instead of sitting here and only missing Genevieve. You free to hang out?"

"I'm sort of in the middle of something right now. You doing anything tomorrow morning?"

"Nope. Unless whatever you're about to suggest is stupid, in which case, yeah, I have plans to save the world or something."

"Well, if you're done saving the world before noon we could go see a movie."

"I guess the city can take care of itself for a couple hours. So what are you up to right now?"

"Nothing," he says.

He sounds kind of ashamed and dodgy, sort of like the way someone (not Skinny-Dave) gets really uncomfortable when you ask them if they watch porn or not, even if the answer is obvious. But I let it go and instead get him to talk to me about stupid things, like what superpower he would like to have—invincibility, which Skinny-Dave always confuses for invisibility.

It's better than handball, at least.

8
NO HOMO

Thomas looks tired as hell when I meet him on the corner of his block the next morning.

It's a little after 11:00. Not sure if he got any sleep or if he'll be able to stay awake for the entire movie.

"Are you cloning yourself?"

"What?" Thomas groggily asks.

"I'm trying to figure out what you're obsessively working on."

"I don't think anyone wants two clueless Thomases walking around." We take a shortcut through some shady projects to get to the theater as fast as possible. "I don't want to tell you or you'll think I'm some lost puppy."

"Nah, you're more like a work in progress. We all are," I say. I hold my hands up in surrender. "But I'll drop it."

"You're supposed to try and force me to spill the beans."

"Okay. Spill the beans."

"I don't want to talk about it."

So we don't.

Again.

Instead, he goes on about how he loves summertime mornings

because of the eight-dollar ticket charge for a movie, which usually doesn't even matter since he knows how to get in for free because he worked there for two weekends last summer before—you guessed it—quitting.

"But you want to be a director. Isn't working at the movies a good first step?"

"I thought it would be, but you don't get a vision for any projects working behind the concession stands. You're constantly burning yourself from popcorn oil, and your classmates bully you at the box office when you don't let them into R-rated movies. Ripping off tickets won't turn me into a director."

"That makes sense."

"I figure if I keep taking odd jobs I'll get some material for my own scripts. I just haven't figured out a story to tell yet."

When we get to the theater, Thomas pulls me by my elbow toward the parking lot. We pass a couple of emergency exits before continuing down an alleyway I know we have no business walking through. He pulls out a savings card for a drugstore and slides it down the crack of a door until there's a click. He turns and smiles when he opens the door.

I only feel slightly guilty, and it's such a rush that I'm not scared of getting caught. It's also a good trick to know for when Genevieve gets back, even if seeing a movie is the last thing I'll want to do after she's been gone for three weeks. The door leads us out by the bathrooms. We head for the concession stand, buy some popcorn—See? We're not total criminals—and go to the condiment bar where he drowns his popcorn in butter.

"I always come to this theater for midnight showings," Thomas says. "The energy always surprises me. No one on my block would ever dress up on a day that's not Halloween because they're not comfortable in their own skin. But for the midnight showing of *Scorpius Hawthorne*, so many people who I wish I'd made friends with were dressed up as demonic wizards and specters."

"I didn't know you read that series!"

"Hell yeah," Thomas says. "I brought my copy to the midnight showing and readers signed their names and underlined their favorite passages."

I wish I'd gone. "Did you dress up?"

"I was the only brown Scorpius Hawthorne," Thomas says. He tells me about other midnight showings too, where he had people sign the video game cases and comic book anthologies that inspired them all. These are all cool mementos. But I'm just happy to have another friend who's read and seen the Scorpius Hawthorne series.

We look at the movie posters to decide what we're going to see. Thomas wishes a new Spielberg movie was out but is ready to settle on a black-and-white film about a boy dancing on a bus. "No thanks," I say.

"What about that new movie, *The Final Chase*?" Thomas stands in front of a poster of a pretty blue-eyed girl sitting at the edge of a dock like it's a park bench, and a guy in a sweater vest reaching out for her. "I didn't realize this was out yet. You down?"

I'm pretty sure the commercial for this movie leans toward the romance side of things. "I don't think I can."

"It's PG-13. You are of age, aren't you?"

"Yeah, smart-ass. Looks like something Genevieve might like. There's nothing else you want to see?"

Thomas looks around and turns his back on movies promising explosions and gunfights. "I wouldn't mind seeing that French movie again. It starts in an hour, though."

It's obvious he doesn't want to see the French movie again because who in the hell would want to see a French movie twice? "Let's go see *The Final Chase.* I can always see it again when she gets back."

"You sure?"

"Yeah. If it sucks, she's on her own."

We go inside and there are plenty of seats available. "Preference?"

"The back row but don't ask why," I say.

"Why?"

"I have this pretty irrational fear of having my throat sliced inside a movie theater, so I figure that can't happen if no one sits behind me."

Thomas stops chewing on his popcorn. His eyes are grilling me on whether I'm being serious or not before he busts out laughing so hard he almost chokes. I sit down in the back row, and he collapses into the seat next to mine as his laugh winds down.

I flip him off. "Don't act like you've never been freaked out by something ridiculous."

"No, I definitely have. I used to bother my mother when I was a kid, maybe nine or ten, to let me watch horror movies, especially slasher flicks."

"Probably not the best thing to say to someone afraid of having his throat sliced."

"Shut up. So my mother finally gave in one evening and let me watch *Scream.* I was scared shitless and was up until five in the morning. Ma always encouraged me to count sheep when I couldn't sleep but it only made things worse. I was counting sheep that night and every time they hopped over the fence . . ." Dramatic pause. "The *Scream* guy would stab each of them and they would fall down, bloody and dead."

I laugh so loudly other people shush me, even though previews haven't started yet, and it's hard to stop. "You are so disturbed! How long did this go on for?"

"Never stopped." Thomas screeches and mimes someone getting stabbed. The previews come on and we shut up.

There's a rom-com, *Next Stop: Love,* which is about a train conductor crushing on this new attendant; a typical horror movie where creepy little girls appear after someone turns a corner; a miniseries called *Don't You Forget About Me* about a husband trying to convince his wife not to forget him with a Leteo procedure; and, finally, a comedy about four postgrad guys on a cruise ship that doesn't look funny at all.

"Those all looked terrible," I say.

Thomas leans over and says, "I will slice your throat if you talk during the movie."

☺ ☺ ☺ ☺

THIS MOVIE IS TOTAL bullshit.

It's supposed to be funny and the only thing I'm laughing at is how the studio managed to disguise an uncomfortably dark movie as a summer comedy.

It's about a guy named Chase who strikes up a conversation with some cute girl on the train about where she's going. She tells him, "Somewhere good." He digs deeper but she doesn't respond. She leaves her phone on the train, and Chase chases (sigh) after her to return it, but it's too late, so he goes through her phone and discovers a bucket list of things she wants to do before ending her life.

By this point, Thomas has fallen asleep. I should probably do the same thing, but I hope it gets better . . . and it never does. Near the end, Chase pieces together she's going to kill herself at the pier and when he finally gets there he's greeted by the blinding red-and-blue siren lights of police cars. He smashes the phone.

I want to smash something, too.

My recap to Thomas when he wakes up: "Bullshit, bullshit, bullshit."

He stretches and yawns. "Your throat looks fine, though," he says.

☺ ☺ ☺ ☺

I SORT OF, KIND of, definitely like summer in my neighborhood: girls chalking hopscotch; guys playing card games under whatever shade they can find; friends blasting their stereos; shooting shit on the stoops. And while my apartment is small, it's moments like these that make those walls feel bigger than they are.

I point to the red hospital across the street. "My mother works over there and manages to be twenty minutes late every morning." Down the block is the post office. "And my father used to be a security guard there." Maybe all that time alone with his thoughts was where he went wrong.

The fire hydrant on the corner has been wrenched open. The screaming kids remind me of all the times we filled up buckets and spilled water all over the playground, throwing ourselves down the wet slides since we couldn't afford to go to an actual water park.

"I don't know what my dad does," Thomas replies. "The last time I saw him was on my ninth birthday. I was watching him from my window go to his car to get my Buzz Lightyear, but instead he got in and drove away."

I don't know when we stopped walking or who stopped first, but we're both still.

"Asshole."

"Let's not go taking dark turns, okay?" Thomas eyes the sprinkler and mischievously raises his huge eyebrows before pulling off his shirt, his arms flexing. He's got some God of War–like abs coming in and all I have is serious rib cage. "Come on."

"I don't want to get my phone wet."

"Just fold it inside your shirt. No one's going to steal it."

"You do know we aren't in Queens, right?"

Thomas tucks his phone inside his shirt and leaves it against a mailbox. "Your loss, dude." He runs with an athlete's sprint and bounces back and forth through the sprinklers, the sun glinting off his belt buckle. Sure, some people are looking at him like he's insane, but he doesn't seem to care.

I don't know what possesses me, what chokes out all my insecurities and allows me to pull my shirt off, but it's freeing. Thomas gives me two thumbs-up. I don't feel like a scrawny kid right now.

I pull my phone out—but before I can roll it inside my shirt, it buzzes. Genevieve is calling. I freeze.

"Hey!" I answer.

"Hi. I somehow miss your dumb-idiot face already. Fly out here so we can build a house in the woods and start a family," she says.

"I miss you more but not as much as I hate camping."

"It wouldn't count as camping if we spent our lives here."

"Truth." I picture her smiling despite the distance and it makes me happy, no, happier. I want to beg her to come home, but I want her to stay focused on her art and not worry about me. "Have you started painting yet or is there some lame orientation?"

"The lame orientation was yesterday. We're taking a quick break before doing some still life on trees and . . ."

I nearly drop my phone when I see Thomas doing push-ups from inside the sprinklers, showing off for these girls across the street. I put the phone back to my ear when I hear Genevieve calling my name. "Sorry. Thomas is making a dick of himself." He doesn't care like I would've."

"You boys playing more Suicide?"

"Nah, it's just me and Thomas." I feel too exposed with my shirt off. "I think I'm heading home in a little bit, though. Pretty tired. You think you'll be free to call me tonight? I want to hear all about the five hundred paintings you'll finish today without me around to bother you."

"Yup. Call you tonight, babe." She hangs up before I can say bye or tell her I love her.

Now I feel like shit for getting distracted, but she'll call later. I'll explain how I really needed something fun to do, which is sort of her fault since she left me here, but if she hadn't left, it would've been my fault, so I guess I can't really go blaming her. Hopefully she'll send me a punch across the country and all will be okay. I tuck my phone inside my shirt and kick my sneakers off, leaving everything on the ground. I charge toward the sprinklers in jeans and socks and jump through the jets of water. I'm laughing when I land on the other side.

"Woo-hoo!" Thomas whistles. "About time."

I shiver from the cold. "Okay, uh, I miss my clothes."

"Be free for sixty seconds, Stretch." Thomas grabs on to my shoulders like he's prepping me for the last game of the season—what game that is, I don't know. "Forget about everything. Forget about your father. Even forget about your girlfriend. Pretend like you're the only one around." He lets go after coaching me and sits down on the ground. The water continues to wash over him.

I sit down across from him and get soaked. "I'm the only one," I quietly tell myself, shedding my worries as if they could sink down the sewage drains. I squeeze my eyes shut and count up, feeling lighter as each second passes, more myself. "Fifty-eight, fifty-nine . . ." I don't want to let go of the last second. "Sixty."

I open my eyes to a group of kids playing tag around us.

"It's going to be impossible to get out of these jeans," I say. I can barely hear myself with the water crashing into my ears and the splashing and the children. Thomas stands and offers to help me up.

I clasp his forearm.

He shouts, "No homo!"

We're both laughing as we go back to our abandoned belongings. Thomas dries his chest off with his shirt, soaking it up. "I don't know if it's because of that nap, but I feel great! I haven't had that much fun since . . . nothing comes to mind."

"Good to hear. I mean, sucks for you, but glad to know I'm not wasting your time." I start putting my shirt on but poke my head through the wrong hole and get lost. I wrestle with myself until I feel Thomas's hands steadying me.

"Stop! Stop!" Thomas is cracking up. There aren't enough No Homos to excuse us from the fact that he's dressing me right now. After some wrangling around, I'm sorted and find myself facing him. "I can't take you anywhere. You're making an ass of yourself."

I look across the street. The girls who were checking out Thomas are laughing at me. I would've probably been really pissed if I didn't have Genevieve. Then I see Brendan and Me-Crazy chilling not too far off, smoking the cigarettes Me-Crazy steals from his father. They're looking at me like they don't even recognize me. I nod my head to say hey, but they must be too high from smoking some of Brendan's weed earlier.

"You doing anything tonight?" Thomas asks. "Besides sleeping, which you can do at my house." He smiles. "Okay, that sounded wrong. No homo."

"What do you have in mind?"

"Since I feel like *The Final Chase* may or may not have slightly disappointed you—"

"It one hundred percent did," I interrupt.

"I thought we could watch *Jaws* on my rooftop."

"I'm down."

I've always felt the worst time to be treated like a kid is during the summer. Sure, most of the parents around here give us 10:00 P.M. curfews, but we normally stay out until midnight, sometimes even 1:00 or 2:00 A.M. This is not about rebelling or seeing how far we can push the adults before they come outside with a belt. (Fat-Dave has it bad like that.) It's just that we're exposed to more grown-up shit versus those in the safer boroughs and white-picket-fence neighborhoods. But when I call my mom to tell her I'm going to go stay over at Thomas's, she talks to me as if I'm five years old. She needs to meet Thomas to make sure he's not a drug dealer or some devil on my shoulder who might talk me off a roof.

We go wait for her by one of the brown picnic tables in the second court. This is the same spot where Brendan broke the news to me that he was going to spend the summer in North Carolina with his family when we were thirteen. I started drawing comics when he wasn't around and he came home to find himself drawn as a Pokémon trainer.

Mom comes downstairs in my eighth-grade gym shirt, and I wish she had left her keys at home so Thomas wouldn't see all her supermarket discount cards. "Hello."

"Hi. I'm Thomas," he says, offering a hand.

"Elsie," she says with a smile, shaking it. "Please tell me that's not sweat on you two."

"Sprinklers," I say.

"Thank God. What are your plans tonight, boys?"

"The movie we just saw bombed, so I thought I could show Stretch here *Jaws*," Thomas says.

Mom looks at me. "You didn't call and tell me you were going to the movies."

"I got back in one piece."

Her eyes fall on my scar and then back at me.

"He knows," I say.

Thomas cuts in, "If it helps, Ms. Elsie, I can give you my address, my phone number, and my mother's phone number. But I feel like Aaron hasn't lived until he's seen *Jaws.* You're more than welcome to join us if you haven't seen it yourself."

This gets my mom smiling again. "I saw it in the theaters when I was a young girl. Thank you."

Thomas almost looks jealous that she was alive when the movie came out. Maybe he thinks Back Then was a better time to be born. I personally think Much Later would've been a better time instead of Right Now.

"I'll be at the supermarket late tonight anyway, so you can go," Mom tells me.

I'm smiling like a dumb-idiot. I haven't gotten this excited about a sleepover since Fat-Dave's mother took us all to buy the newest Throne Wars game at midnight, and everyone stayed up all night playing at his house.

"Thomas, please make sure he's asleep before two, remind him to use the bathroom first, and don't let him spend more than a dollar on candy."

I would make a you-know-what joke for how embarrassing she's being, but it would prolong the agony. Mom hugs him, and then me. She thanks him for letting me sleep over, takes down all of his information—address, his number, his mother's number—and we start walking away.

"Your mother's cool," he says.

"Yeah, when she's not treating me like a little kid. I should probably go grab some clothes to sleep in."

"Don't worry about it, I have stuff."

We're only going a couple blocks down, but as someone who will likely never have enough money to go see the pyramids in Egypt or boat down a canal in Venice, this day away from home already feels like I'm headed to another country.

THE ORANGE CORD FOLLOWS us to the rooftop and snakes across the pebbled ground, where all evidence of my night with Genevieve is gone. Thomas props the projector up, but it's still light out so we can't watch the movie yet. I lie down with my arms spread out like I'm going to try and make a snow angel.

"What are you doing?" Thomas asks.

"Drying off." I shut my eyes, but can still see spears of orange and feel the sun cooking my face. I can't tell how much of my drenched shirt is water and how much is sweat. Summer sucks that way, but winter can go die twice because I always refuse to leave the house—even whenever Genevieve wants to go out and build snowmen and take silly couple photos.

"No homo, but you should take your shirt off," Thomas says.

I look up and his shirt is already off and he's draping it over the ledge to dry. I sit up, take my shirt off too, throw it at him, and sprawl out. The baked pebbles burn, but it's not any worse than the sand at Jones Beach. Speaking of which, two shirtless guys on a rooftop isn't all that different from two shirtless guys at the beach, so we really shouldn't have to No Homo this.

Thomas plops down next to me. "I used to watch movies with Sara up here. Well, we would start watching something and then start messing around."

"You had sex with your ex up here?"

He laughs. "Nah, never sex. Just other stuff."

"Was she your first?" I ask.

"Yeah. You?"

"Yeah, Sara was my first too," I say. Thomas smacks my shoulder so hard it leaves his handprint. I punch him above his heart but his chest is firmer than mine. "Your breasts are hard."

"They're called pecs, and I paid a lot of money for them."

For some reason I feel uncomfortable talking about his body, probably because it's better than mine. "Do you miss Sara? Be real."

"No and yes," he answers. "I had to break things off with her because we really weren't right for each other anymore. I just miss having someone to call and go out and have fun with. But it never *had* to be Sara."

"I get that."

We drop it and talk about random things as the sun falls out of sight behind the city's buildings: video games and favorite comics; how much we hate school and the hot teachers and girls who make it easier; his birthday coming up—on the same day Genevieve gets back—and how he's never smoked before, not even a cigarette. He looks disappointed when I admit to blazing up with Brendan and the others a few times. To keep it light, I admit something incredibly shameful: "I don't know how to ride a bike."

"How is that even possible?" he asks.

"No one ever taught me. My mom doesn't know how to either, and my dad was going to but never got around to it."

"I'll have to teach you then. It's a basic life skill, like swimming and masturbating."

☺ ☺ ☺ ☺

THE SKY IS DARK now.

The quality of *Jaws* is really poor since a) the movie is old, and b) we're watching it on a brick wall. But I wouldn't trade in this experience for a perfectly clear DVD on a big-screen TV.

It's getting chilly, but I can't pull myself away to get my shirt because I'm too concerned about the girl running into the ocean like she doesn't know she's in a shark movie. "How many times have you seen this?"

"Lost count," he says. "More than *War Horse*, less than *Jurassic Park*."

After some serious "Oh shit!" moments where the shark eats more people and the survivors' boat blows the hell up, we put our shirts back on, pack up the projector, and carefully go down the fire escape—even though the roof door is open.

"Ma should be sleeping by now so we need to be quiet," Thomas says, opening the window and climbing through.

His room smells like clean laundry and pencil shavings. The walls are green and decorated with posters of movies and pictures of his favorite directors. I step over the balled-up socks on the floor and see the toy basketball hoop fixed to the door where he must play when he's bored. Drawn all over the door are deadlocked games of tic-tac-toe, quotes from Steven Spielberg movies, doodles of dinosaurs, a spot-on drawing of E.T., and lots of randomness I can't make out.

His bed isn't made but it looks comfortable, unlike mine. My bed is basically one level better than a cot. He even has his own desk, whereas the only surface I can sketch on is a textbook on my lap. There's an open notebook on the desk where it looks like he crossed out some music notes he was composing in favor of a screenplay he hasn't gotten very far with.

Thomas opens his closet door—something else I don't have—and starts throwing some shirts on his bed. "Come find something to sleep in, Stretch."

I check out the shirts. Most are too baggy, too tight, too childish, too geriatric, and, I shit you not, too extraterrestrial. It turns out the last shirt was a gift from his aunt's visit to Roswell, New Mexico. I settle on a white T-shirt and quickly change into it. In the corner of the room behind his laundry basket is a board with a pie chart and several notes thumbtacked to it. It reads: *LIFE CHART*.

"What's this? Old school project?"

"That's what I've been working on the past couple of days," Thomas says, changing into his Snoopy pajamas and a tank top. "I decided I would direct myself on the course of life I want to take. You know, like Maslow's hierarchy of needs, except not something that will make me so obsessed to figure out every last detail."

I have no idea who this Maslow guy is, but Thomas's chart seems plenty obsessive. Thomas carries the board across the room and props it against his dresser. We sit down in front of it. The categories in this pie chart are divided by school/work, health, self-actualization, and relationships.

"I think I'm doing okay with health. I eat right and work out. I'm struggling a bit with financial security because I can't seem to find a job I love. The money in my savings account can't even buy me a movie ticket."

At least he *has* a savings account, something that might suggest he once had enough money worth putting away. If I get birthday or Christmas money, I usually slip almost all of it inside Mom's purse since she knows where we need it most. It sucks paying for a home you don't love living in, but it beats the alternative. See? Silver linings.

"I'm finding my biggest struggles are with love and purpose," Thomas continues. This chart is the work of a madman who wants his happy ending; I should imitate his insanity. "It might've been a blow to my self-esteem after breaking up with Sara. But chilling with you kept me from falling into a black hole about it, I think."

"You're welcome," I say. My phone vibrates inside my pocket and I see it's Genevieve. I screen it. I'll hit her up before bed.

"I'm serious. You gave me something. Whatever it is, I can't get it from my missing father, overworked mother, or ex-girlfriend. So maybe you have to help me figure out my true potential."

I study his room for a moment. This place belongs to someone who lives as many lives as possible. There are unfinished sheets of music, movie scripts. (Later I learn that there's even an abandoned musical in his closet about a robot that time-travels back to the Mesozoic era to study dinosaurs while singing about surviving without technology.) There are boxes of Legos stacked in the corner, a colorful tower from when he wanted to be an architect and set designer.

It's like when you're a kid, and you want to be an astronaut before accepting it might be impossible—even though everyone says nothing's impossible, and they go so far to pinpoint moments from history to make you feel stupid. But you move on anyway. You know your capabilities and circumstances, so you start thinking that maybe being a boxer would be cool even though you're too skinny. No problem, you can bulk up. But that all changes when you want to write for the newspaper and dream of having your own column, so you start doing that. And one day when you're writing someone advice on how to be more organized, you think about piloting a ship into space again.

This is how Thomas lives his life, one misfired dream after the other. That journey may stretch for a lifetime, but even if he doesn't discover that spark until he's an old man, Thomas will die with wrinkles he earned and a smile on his face.

"If you help me stay happy so I don't end up like my dad, you got a deal," I say.

"Deal."

9
BEYOND DEAD ENDS

The only thing that sucked about last night was that I never got a chance to call Genevieve back. It's the first thing I think of when I wake up.

Thomas's desk chair creaks—the one where he sat last night to show off his "mad origami skills." (Except when he tried to make a seashell it just looked like crumpled paper.) I sit up and rub my eyes. I can tell it's early because of the slant of the sunlight through the windows. I can't believe he's already awake, hunched over, writing something while quietly tapping his foot; it's like he's taking a final exam and doesn't want me copying off of his test.

"Yo. What are you doing?"

"Journaling."

"You journal a lot?"

"Pretty much every morning since seventh grade," Thomas says. "I'm almost done. How'd you sleep? Are my sheets still dry?"

"Fuck you." My back does hurt a bit, but not so much that I can't get used to it.

"I left a new toothbrush and towel out for you in the bathroom if you want to wash up before breakfast." His eyes are still on the page.

"You're cooking breakfast?"

"Yeah right. I only know how to make toast and Pop-Tarts. We'll figure something out." Thomas smiles and returns to journaling.

I have to wait a second before I throw off the covers because of that thing that happens to guys when they first wake up. But he isn't even looking at me. I hurry out of his room and can only assume his mother's gone off to work already by the way he's freely letting me walk around the place. I find the bathroom and take a piss while looking around the shelves piled with clean and fluffy towels. At home, we share the same batch, raggedy and torn, washed at best twice a month. When I'm done brushing, I go back to Thomas's room, and he's already gone.

I follow the sound of clattering utensils into the kitchen, stopping once to check out all the photos on the wall. There's Thomas as a kid playing baseball—the same crazy eyebrows. The kitchen is twice the size of mine. There are red pots and pans hanging from the wall and they look so spotless. There's a mini TV on top of the fridge, and Thomas has the news playing like a grown man, but he's not listening because he's on the phone.

". . . I can mail those back to you," he says, pouring Corn Bran into two bowls, handing me one. "No, Sara, I think it's too soon to meet up . . . Look, I . . ." He looks at the phone before setting it on the counter. "She hung up."

"Everything okay?"

"She wants every letter and card she wrote to me. I don't know . . . She's hoping I'll reread them or something so I'll miss her." He sits down across from me, and shrugs. "Anyway, enough with that. Sorry to report this was the only cereal we had left. I ate all the Lucky Charms the other night, but we have cookies and marshmallows. And a leftover chocolate bunny from Easter we can use. I hope that's cool."

The last time I sat down for a meal in a kitchen was at my grandparents' house, and they're both dead now. Still, I jump out of my seat and crumble Chips Ahoy into my cereal, and Thomas gives me the biggest smile.

☺ ☺ ☺ ☺

AFTER BREAKFAST, WE HEAD out, walking nowhere in particular—in fact, walking away from my block. "So who are your friends around here?" I ask him.

"You," Thomas says. "And I think Baby Freddy and Skinny-Dave like me just fine."

"I meant on your block."

"I know you did. It's embarrassing. My only friend here is Mr. Isaacs on the first floor. He's big on cats and obsessed with factories." He shrugs. "I had to outgrow my friends after they played me."

I'm a little nervous asking, but I have to. "What'd they do?"

"After what my father did on my birthday, I stopped wanting to celebrate it, but last year my friend Victor kept calling. He was going to throw a party, a night of board games and drinking. I was about to go to Victor's house, but then he called and canceled last minute to go to some concert with our friends. I thought it was part of some bigger surprise. My phone never rang after that. I was too depressed to drink alone so I just sort of sat in my room and did nothing. They didn't even bring me back a T-shirt."

Without knowing Victor, I know he's an asshole. "You don't need dickheads like that in your life anyway. They slow you down."

Thomas stops walking, turns me toward him, and says, "This is what I like about you, Stretch. You care about what happens to you. Everyone else seems resigned to grow up and become nobodies who are stuck here. They don't dream. They don't think about the future."

I have to look away because all this talk of the future shakes me. I massage my scar. "You're wrong," I say. Maybe I should turn around and go home so I don't waste his time. "I thought death was a happy-ending exit strategy. I appreciate everything you're saying, but—"

"But nothing." Thomas grabs my wrist. "We all make mistakes. Every wrong job I take is a mistake, but it's also a step in the right direction. If nothing else, it's a step away from the wrong one. You would never do that to yourself again, right?" He's looking at me, forcing me to meet his eyes.

"Never."

Thomas lets go and keeps walking. "And that alone makes you different."

We continue down the block in silence until a young woman with a picket sign walks past us in the other direction.

LETEO IS HERE TODAY BUT NEEDS TO BE GONE TOMORROW

I chase after her, and Thomas follows. "Excuse me, excuse me. Sorry. What's with the sign?"

"A girl has gone brain dead because of Leteo," the woman answers. Her voice is grave, and her eyes look vacant. "She's the fourth this week. We're rallying to shut this place down." The woman sounds proud, self-important. She's probably also one of those crazy PETA people who throw fake blood at elderly women in fur coats.

"We?"

The woman doesn't answer. Thomas and I exchange a glance. We follow her. The closer we get to 168th Street, the louder we hear a crowd hidden by buildings. There are cop cars blocking the street, their sirens failing to warn other people away. We round the corner, and the street is as crowded as a holiday parade, except instead of character balloons in the air, there are picket signs being raised.

10

AN UNFORGETTABLE RALLY

I've seen pictures of the Bronx district Leteo Institute before, but the unhappy rioters add an edge when seeing it up close. You'd think the institute would look more futuristic, like the Apple Store in Manhattan, but honestly, the Museum of Natural History looks more cutting-edge than Leteo does. The building is four floors high with bricks the color of ashes.

Leteo is getting the bad rap of a good morgue with their body count. It's still strange to me how hospitals never incite this sort of reaction when they're guiltier of more cases of malpractice. Maybe it's because Leteo is supposed to only exist in old science fiction shows and this advancement scares people.

A bald guy fills us in on the recent botched surgery. Apparently some schizophrenic girl in her early twenties was having a procedure done to wipe her mind clean of imaginary characters that have shadowed her since childhood. Instead, she never woke up at all, near death but not close enough. Representatives of the institute haven't come forth with any additional information about the girl's coma.

A curly-haired woman and an older man are trying to squeeze through the crowd, unsuccessfully. They both have signs:

NO MIRACLES FOR CRIMINALS

GRIEF IS NATURAL. GUILT IS DESERVED.

It doesn't match the brain-dead bit.

"You did a criminal a favor!" the older man shouts over the crowd, as if someone from Leteo is listening to his complaints in person. "What, you going to save some terrorists next?"

"Excuse me, sir," Thomas says. "What's with the signs?"

It's the woman who answers us. "We're here to speak out against the car accident, of course."

"We don't know what you're talking about," I say.

She nudges the man. "Harold, tell these boys about the wreck. You tell it better than I do."

"You kids should get off your phones and watch the news," Harold says. I turn to Thomas, who smirks. "A few months ago some yahoo crashed his car and killed his four-year-old son and wife. For some bizarre reason, the hellions at Leteo agreed to wipe the memory of his wife's and son's existences after he tried to kill himself in jail."

"Why would he want to forget his family?" I ask.

"Guilt," Harold says. "Leteo says he's able to function better with prison tasks under the belief he killed strangers. Maggie and I believe that is nonsense. That guilt is *his* to feel."

"It's worse than a hit-and-run, truly," Maggie says. "They view us all as clients, not patients. Big difference." She turns her back on us and pumps her sign up as high as she can, screaming, "No miracles for criminals! No miracles for criminals!"

Police charge through the crowd in an effort to reach the entrance. Thomas drags me back so we don't get caught up in any of it. I turn one last time, bumping shoulders with a couple people, and I see a child on a man's shoulders waving a sign that reads NO TO TABULA RASA. The kid definitely has no idea what it means, but if anyone snaps a photo it's bound to go viral.

On the other side of the crowd, there are Leteo supporters. Maybe only a fourth of the protesters, but they're here. They're probably friends or relatives of forgetters who appreciate how Leteo repairs lives. I half expect Kyle's parents to be there, though I can't possibly imagine what sort of sign they would have. Maybe GOOD JOB ON MAKING MY SON FORGET HIS TWIN. HE ALWAYS WANTED TO BE AN ONLY CHILD. No, if they were around here, they'd more likely be inside Leteo to forget Kenneth too; I would if I had to live with someone who had his face and his laugh.

Thomas finally lets go of me when we get to the corner, but we stop and watch as a chant begins: "Never forget! Never forget!"

"I USED TO THINK the procedure was the shadiest scam in all of Scamville," I tell Thomas as we walk home, keeping my voice low as we passed a crowded bus stop—as if the entire country doesn't know about Leteo. New York hosts three institutes, one here in the Bronx, another in Long Island, and a third in Manhattan. I wonder if there are riots going down in front of the ones in Arizona or Texas, California or Florida. "I know someone who went through it. I don't know him anymore. I mean, I know him, but he's different now, you know."

"Wait, what?"

"Kyle, this kid I grew up with. His twin brother was killed and it was sort of his fault, so he forgot Kenneth ever existed so he could live. I hope he's doing okay and not having any weird delayed reactions," I say.

"You don't see him anymore?"

"Nope. His family moved away before they got it done. I'm not even sure where they went. Baby Freddy's mom somehow found out about the procedure and our entire block knew by the end of the day. It would've been impossible keeping everyone he's ever met from asking about his twin, so leaving made sense."

Kyle and Kenneth, the Lake twins. We don't remember them nearly enough. In every generation on my block, a group of friends loses someone. One of the Big Kids, Benton, drunk-rode his bike into traffic a couple years ago. I don't know the details beyond that, but I guess it could be said that Kenneth took one for the team. The least we could do is fucking remember him, especially when Kyle can't.

My heart is racing just thinking about it, the way it pounds when I'm the last one standing in a game of manhunt. "Would you ever do it? The procedure?"

"I have nothing to forget, and I wouldn't if I did," Thomas says. "Everyone plays a purpose, even fathers who lie to you or leave you behind. Time takes care of all that pain so if someone derails you, it'll be okay eventually. You?"

"When you put it that way, I have nothing I'd want erased either," I say. "Well, maybe clowns. I could go without circus memories."

"Doctors should work on erasing clowns. Period."

11
TRADE HANGOUT

I've been picking up extra shifts at Good Food's because Mom's not feeling well. She's missed work two days in a row already, and it's really going to set us back. Mohad even trusted me to close up last night, and all my friends naturally wanted to lock themselves in and have a party with every beer and cigarette and snack available to us. The last thing this family needs is me getting thrown in jail and sued.

It's my first day off since witnessing the Leteo rally with Thomas, the last time I saw him. I'm meeting him in a bit, but until then I'm chilling with Brendan and Baby Freddy on a staircase. On one of the steps, Brendan is rolling up some weed on top of graph paper and overdue bills.

"I thought your clients do all that themselves."

"These aren't for my clients," Brendan says, licking the tip of his freshly rolled-and-folded blunt. "I'm branching out. I'll work some corners and colleges and if I roll it myself they won't realize I'm skimming them twenty percent of what they're paying for."

"My boss is looking for another dishwasher," Baby Freddy says. "If you want to stop dealing."

"Washing dishes is for spics like you and Skinny-Dave. I'm good."

"Whatever. Can I get a freebie?"

"You can have half off." Brendan's smart. I've seen Baby Freddy trying to smoke and it would be a waste of the weed he's saving from shorting others.

"Kenneth liked to smoke," I say.

Brendan looks up. "Fucking shame Kenneth's brother fucked the wrong guy's sister. A guy with a gun."

Baby Freddy ignores him. "He loved acting like he was Kyle even though Kyle hated that."

"Maybe that's the real reason Kyle forgot about Kenneth," Brendan says, lighting up the blunt he just rolled and inhaling deeply. "Great, now you got me smoking someone else's shit." He tosses all his blunts into a Ziploc bag and sprinkles the remaining weed in. "Let's go get a game going. I feel like running."

"I'm about to link up with Thomas, actually. I'm down when I get back, though."

"Okay then," Brendan says.

We all leave the staircase and a security guard sees us with Brendan's Ziploc bag. He calls us delinquents but carries on. Baby Freddy tells me he'll see me later. Brendan keeps it moving.

I definitely should've left the memories of Kenneth and Kyle dead and buried.

☺ ☺ ☺ ☺

"WHAT SHOULD WE DO?"

"I have this thing I do with Genevieve—"

"If you're thinking what I think you're thinking, that's off the list," Thomas says, patting my back.

"Hilarious. No, this isn't going to sound great either, but we have Trade Dates."

"Is that where you hang out with another couple and swap girlfriends or something?"

"No. God, why doesn't anyone get this?" I hate repeating myself almost more than anything in the entire universe, but I tell him what a Trade Date is in the hopes we can do something fun like it, but in a No Homo way. "I was thinking we could go maybe do a Reverse Trade Date—without calling it a Reverse Trade Date or a date at all—where you take me somewhere personal for you and I'll do the same."

"Sounds cool. We'll skip the rooftop since you've already been there. Let me think about it. You go first."

We go to Comic Book Asylum. I tried applying for a job before, but they told me I have to wait until I'm done with school because of some bullshit, like labor laws or something, I don't remember. I can't think of a cooler atmosphere to work. "This is the best fucking place ever," I say as we arrive. "I mean, look at this fucking door. Isn't this the best fucking door you've ever seen?"

"It is the best fucking door I've ever seen," Thomas says. "You curse a lot."

"Yeah. My mom used to get really pissed whenever the bus driver told her I was cursing on the school bus with Brendan, but once a year she would host late night spelling bees for me and my brother only using curses. I think it was her way of letting us get it out of our systems."

Thomas laughs. "Your mom is f-u-c-k-i-n-g awesome."

He goes straight over to the cape closet and tries on both Superman and Batman capes, quoting lines from each movie. ("KRYPTON HAD ITS CHANCE!" and "SWEAR TO ME!") He follows me over to the bargain cart, picks up a comic, and says, "I hate how superheroes can be twenty for thirty years so comic book artists never have to create new characters. It's lazy." Some hard-core comic geeks turn around and glare at him. I'm a little concerned for his life.

"I don't know. At least those cash cows finish their comics. My comic—"

"You have a comic?"

"Not one for sale."

"Where is it?"

"Not here."

"Can I read it?"

"It's not done."

"So what?"

"It's not good."

"So what? Stretch, I let you use my rooftop for your girl's birthday. You owe me."

"I thought I was going to help you figure out who you are."

"Just let me read your comic."

"Fine. Soon."

I think about the page where I left off in the comic, with Sun Warden torn between saving his girlfriend or best friend from becoming dragon food. If someone asked me to choose between saving Genevieve or Thomas, I would rather dive head-first into the mouth of the dragon. I'm about to tell him how I haven't drawn a whole lot since my dad's death, but I look up and see Collin from school—and he sees me too.

I feel a little shitty. I wasn't 100 percent supportive or sympathetic toward him when he told me he got Nicole pregnant. But, well, sex is basic math: condom equals less chance of having a baby, and no condom usually equals baby. And I shouldn't have to feel like a dick because he didn't think to properly wrap his up. Even though I'm a firm believer that everyone in the universe will one day cut the bullshit—as in politely nod at one another instead of wasting their short lives with pointless conversations—I feel obligated to say something.

I walk up to Collin. He smells of a cheap drugstore-brand cologne.

"Hey. How's your summer been? We miss you around the courtyard, dude." It's a bit of a lie since he always thought manhunt was child's play. He's not wrong, but he never fully beasted at it like we do. He preferred sports, mainly basketball.

Collin's eyes are red. Not stoned, but very similar to how I look whenever I'm beyond exhausted and frustrated or bottling in an insane amount of anger. I can't blame him since I hear he's working two jobs to pay for a baby he likely didn't want and definitely isn't ready for. The last thing I should've done is reminded him how much fun he's missing out on. He's holding Issue #6 of *The Dark Alternates,* that series I never got into—I get my magic fix from Scorpius Hawthorne.

He doesn't say anything so I ask, "How you liking that series?"

"Please leave me alone," Collin says without looking at me. "Seriously. Back off." Before I can apologize, he flings the comic onto the floor and run-walks out.

I turn around. Thomas is wearing the Superman cape again. "Did you see that?"

"Nope. Don't tell me I missed someone shooting webs out of their hands."

"No, and Spider-Man fires webs from his wrists, not his hands," I correct. (It's a very crucial distinction.) "I used to go to school with this asshole and he just blew me off."

"What's his story?"

"He had sex without a condom and is now expecting a kid. The end."

"He's probably stressed." Thomas browses for a little bit longer, knocks on the fireplace. "Pretty cool place you picked."

"Thanks. I'm ready to bounce whenever you pick a place."

"I decided. I hope you're game for a run," he says while walking toward the door.

"Thomas?"

"Yeah?"

"Can the store maybe have its cape back?"

☺ ☺ ☺ ☺

WE'RE AT HIS HIGH school's track field.

The gate is wide open and apparently it's available to the public all summer. There are six people running the track right now; two are listening to music, and the others are forced to hear the 2 and 5 trains as they speed past. Because it's a high school field, it doubles for other sports, like soccer and football. There's a nice breeze here, and it's exactly the kind of place to come to when life is suffocating.

"Are you on the track team?"

"I tried out but wasn't fast enough," Thomas says. "But I bet I'm faster than you."

"Yeah right. I've seen you run during manhunt."

"There's a difference between racing and being chased."

"Not for me. I'm always ahead."

"Loser has to buy winner ice cream."

We make up our own start and finish lines and crouch like we're pros. "I'm thinking pistachio," I say. "FYI."

Three.

Two.

One.

GO!

Thomas takes the lead, putting all his speed into these first few seconds, whereas I know to be fast but to also pace myself. After about ten seconds, he's already winding down. He may be a month or two away from a six-pack, but I've been running relay races with Brendan since the better part of my childhood. My feet pound against the pressurized rubber, and the sneakers are way too tight on me, but I run, run, run until I pass him and I don't stop until I leap over the discarded water bottle we marked as the finish line. Thomas doesn't even finish; he just collapses onto the grass.

I jump up and down until my rib cage hurts. "I dusted you!"

"You cheated," Thomas pants, catching his breath. "You have a height advantage. Longer legs."

"Wow. That's going into the Bullshit Hall of Fame." I fall face-first next to him, and the grass stains the knees of my jeans. "Maybe don't choose a place next time where you'll get your ass handed to you. Why here anyway?"

"I'm used to quitting things—"

"Really?" I punch him in the shoulder.

He punches me back. "Yeah, really. But this place rejected me from becoming someone and that was a first."

"Way to make me feel guilty for proving how slow you are."

"Not at all. It's not like my heart is in running or anything like that, but at least I learned that you can't always choose who you're going to be. Sometimes you're fast enough to run track. Sometimes you're not." He tucks his hands behind his head, still catching his breath. "Anyway, it's a pretty chill place to just remember and think, you know?"

I do now.

We don't go and get ice cream. We wait for our rib cages to stop killing us, counting overhead trains go by, and then we race up and down the bleachers before flopping onto the grass again.

☺ ☺ ☺ ☺

WHEN I GET BACK to the block, my friends are sitting on a brown picnic table, their bikes surrounding them. When we were younger we would play Shark here. The game starts with one person (the shark) trying to drag you off the table (the raft) by your ankles. Once you're off, you become a shark too. Sometimes when there were too many sharks, some players would hop on their bikes and just circle the survivors in a menacing way.

"Hey. You guys game for manhunt?" I'm pretty drained from running around before, but if I can find a decent hiding spot it won't matter.

"I think we're going to ride bikes instead," Nolan says.

"We played manhunt already," Deon says.

"And smoked too," Skinny-Dave says, laughing.

"I'll go upstairs and get my rollerblades," I say, and I turn to run upstairs when Nolan stops me.

"Bikes only, dude."

I look over at Brendan. I don't know why I expected him to defend me but that was stupid. He's obviously still pissed I brought up Kenneth and Kyle. He obviously told the guys. "It's cool. I'll go home and read *Scorpius Hawthorne* or . . ."

They don't wait for me to finish. They mount their bikes and pedal away from me.

12
FIGHTS AND FIREWORKS

Yes, it took Brendan three whole days to get over his little bitch-fit. If he had waited one more day, it would've been his longest grudge since we were fourteen—when he got mad at me for not choosing him as my partner for a gaming tournament on Third Avenue. Basically, Brendan thinks that if you're not with him, you're against him. It's ridiculous, but whatever. I'm just glad he grew up just in time so I could rush out of Yolanda's Pizzeria with him and the other guys.

Me-Crazy is fighting some twentysomething in the middle of the street.

I was nine when I got into my first fight with someone who wasn't my brother. I didn't know how to make a fist so Brendan had to help me. Every time the kid, Larry, would hit me, I would run back to Brendan to ball my fists for me until I couldn't take it any longer.

Yeah, I lost my first fight over a plastic whistle to a kid named Larry.

But learning how to make a fist helped me later in a fight against Nolan. We were all wrestling and he slammed me too hard against the mat. I got pissed and clocked his jaw. I lost again, but I got a couple good swings in before Brendan broke it up.

No one is breaking up Me-Crazy's fight, and, well, Dumb Son of a Bitch asked for it. That's what I'm calling him because you would have to be a dumb son of a bitch to pick a fight with Me-Crazy. It's true: Me-Crazy bumped into the guy at the pizzeria and didn't apologize. But Dumb Son of a Bitch shouldn't have called him a "homeless waste of life" just because Me-Crazy has bad acne, yellow teeth, and smells like he hasn't showered in over a week. To be fair, there's no way Dumb Son of a Bitch could've known the word "homeless" is Me-Crazy's only soft spot since he and his family have been evicted twice. But let this be a lesson to all never to fuck with someone who looks like they may not have a future outside prison.

So, Me-Crazy hit Dumb Son of a Bitch in the face with his own food tray and dragged him outside at the owner's request.

Dumb Son of a Bitch's nose is bleeding, not because of the tray . . . no, that's because Me-Crazy slammed the poor guy's face into a BUY THREE SLICES, GET ONE FREE DRINK sign.

"Someone should break this up," Thomas says with an urgency I've never heard from any of my friends.

"He had it coming," Skinny-Dave says. He's bouncing around like he has to piss, and I would know because he has a habit of holding it in so he can just have one great piss later in a staircase of his choosing. Strange kid.

"No one deserves *that*," Thomas says after Me-Crazy punches Dumb Son of a Bitch in his balls repeatedly.

I mean, he's right.

Cars are at a stop now and honking their horns; some drivers get out to yell at Me-Crazy, others to watch the fight. Luckily for this guy, we're close to a hospital because, shit, I'm positive there's no way he's ever had his ass handed to him like he has today. Me-Crazy tackles him against a parked car and before he can smash Dumb Son of a Bitch's head into the window, we hear police sirens.

"Go! Go!"

"Run, fuckers!"

Even if we never touched Dumb Son of a Bitch, we also never tried to stop the fight. There's no way in hell the cops will find Me-Crazy once he goes into hiding, and none of us want to find ourselves in the situation where we're forced to either go to jail or rat out Me-Crazy's identity, so we run. Thomas follows me, and he runs way faster than he did during our race three days ago, and I lead him down into the garage where we camp out behind a silver Mazda.

Thomas asks, "You do this a lot?"

"Not really." It's clear he looks down on us all fighting, so I avoid telling him how we sometimes run into other projects so the cops will look for the suspect—usually Me-Crazy—there instead of our block. "How many fights have you been in?"

"Just one," Thomas says.

"How is that possible?" Even Baby Freddy has been in more than one fight and he's a total pussy.

"I don't go around picking fights."

"I don't either, but I have to fight back if someone comes at me. Right?" I've been exposed to fighting my entire life, and I never really stopped to think that there were alternatives to being laid out. But I like this idea that Thomas grew up never needing anyone to teach him how to make a fist, and I can't help but feel like we're all doing something wrong for always turning to ours.

"Yeah, I definitely don't want to see you beaten to death, but it was kind of a bummer seeing you not care all that much when someone else was getting roughed up," Thomas says, and it's a blow that makes me feel like someone who throws away entire sandwiches in front of a homeless family. But it also makes me feel like someone has my back enough to speak up no matter how I might react.

"I guess being scared of Me-Crazy isn't much of an excuse, huh?"

"It's a hell of an excuse."

No more looking at my fight record like war wounds to be proud of. Seriously, who am I, some super villain who thrives on destruction, like Hitler or Megatron? I can reach my happy ending without all hell breaking loose. "Should we go make sure an ambulance has come to help him out already?"

Thomas stands up and extends a hand to me, just like in the sprinklers last week. I'm nervous of what we'll find when we leave the garage.

☺ ☺ ☺ ☺

DUMB SON OF A Bitch is okay as far as we know. There's no doubt some of our neighbors witnessed the fight too, probably even cheered it on from their windows. But if they were questioned about Me-Crazy's identity, they probably lied to protect themselves. Psychopath or not, he is our own, and we're stuck to him like a conjoined twin who may kill someone in front of us one day. Hell, he might even kill us.

But that was two days ago. Now it's Fourth of July, so we're focused on a day of fireworks instead. Brendan dropped five bucks on white popper rocks and carefully poured them all into an old popcorn bucket. Then he went up to the balcony, and I hung back down by the picnic table so I could give the signal on when to drop them. We tried pulling this prank off last year but Brendan dropped them all like a limp dick, and neither of us had enough money to fill up another.

Baby Freddy comes out of Good Food's. I kick the wall with my hands in my pockets. Brendan turns over the bucket, and all the popper rocks fall to the ground; the blast of tiny sparks and deafening pops scares the shit out of Baby Freddy. I give Brendan an air high five, then a real one when we all join up again.

"One day I'm going to be famous and rich and will never come back to check on you fuckers," Baby Freddy says. He's only a year younger than the rest of us, but we do bully him like he's our little brother.

"Doubtful, if that name keeps following you around for the rest of your life," I say.

"I bet y'all anything. I have faith."

"Faith is just arrogance disguised by God," Skinny-Dave says. It's exactly the kind of thing you expect to hear from a pothead.

Me-Crazy pulls out a few fireworks from his pockets—which, you know, we can all agree is insanely dangerous—and he taunts Baby Freddy with them.

"Let me see those," I tell Me-Crazy, cutting in front of Baby Freddy. I made a promise to myself that I wouldn't just stand by anymore when someone's life was being threatened. I don't want to know what Me-Crazy had to do to convince someone to sell him fireworks.

Baby Freddy asks, "Do you think we can use Thomas's roof to set these off? Our fireworks will be higher than everyone else's."

I invited them all to Thomas's rooftop party on the ninth, although if they don't come it's not much of a party at all because Thomas doesn't seem to have any real friends outside of us. Without them it would just be him, Genevieve, and me.

"His neighbors would be up on the roof too," I say. I think all roofs are out since Skinny-Dave, higher than a pothead on the moon, almost sent a firework blasting straight into someone's window last year.

We decide ground level is best and set up. Fat-Dave stole his mother's cooking lighter; he ignites the first firework while we're all still dangerously close to it. Luckily it soars and explodes in bursts of yellow somewhere above the twenty-seventh floor of Skinny-Dave's building.

We chill back, eating honeybuns and drinking Arizona teas, while Fat-Dave sends more of his fireworks zooming and whistling and exploding into the air.

Thomas finally joins us. He doesn't say a word, just grabs a honeybun and watches the show. I haven't seen him since yesterday morning when I left his house. There was zero sleeping during that sleepover and my body's clock is thrown off now. But it was worth it to be able to play hangman on the wall over his bed, to act like we were spies while we tiptoed from his room to the kitchen so we could warm up Hot Pockets without bothering his mother.

Fat-Dave offers me the lighter. I really wish Genevieve were here to hold my hand right now. There are four fireworks left and I choose the small orange one because the other three look like explosives, and shit, that would suck if they were. I ignite the wick, and the firework takes flight. In that moment, I wish my existence were as simple as being set on fire and exploding in the sky.

13
HEARTLESS

I've been keeping Thomas company during his "Big Job-Hunt Saturday." Things haven't really been going in his favor. His mom told him about an assistant job at this barbershop on Melrose, and even though he didn't really want to sweep up curls while barbers told crude stories about the women they've slept with, he was still bummed when the position had been filled. Worse, it was some smug kid who proudly rinsed a razor as Thomas was being turned away. Afterward we went to a flower shop. Thomas thought it could be a nice meditative place to work, but the florist worried about Thomas's flighty résumé. As did the baker, the fruit-stand guy, the art studio owner, and lastly and perhaps most insulting, the twenty-year-old who didn't think Thomas could bring any depth to his start-up business.

I mean, anyone who thinks you need depth to wrap presents for a pet's birthday is a fucking depthless idiot.

"Fuck it all, Stretch," Thomas says now. He throws his remaining résumés in the trash, spitting on them all, which hardly seems called for, but I'm going to let him have his moment.

"You didn't actually want any of those jobs," I say.

"Yeah, but what if something amazing opened up for me by trying out something I would never go for?"

"There are plenty other jobs to apply to." I wish Mohad were hiring at Good Food's.

"Maybe I can be a pool boy."

"Or a lifeguard," I say. "Or a swimming coach. I'll be your first student."

"You don't know how to swim?"

"Nope. Never really had to know how to, though it would've been nice considering how I almost drowned last summer."

"How the hell did that happen?"

"The water was really cold and I thought I would throw myself into the deep end instead of slowly torturing myself by starting at the shallow end," I say, the panic of that day carrying me away, like an undertow, before I laugh a little. "It was stupid to think I was tall enough to stand up in seven feet of water."

"Pretty stupid, Stretch. What were you thinking when it was happening?"

"I was thinking about how I'd like to draw a comic where the hero is powerful but can't swim and finds himself drowning."

"You weren't thinking about your family and friends? The afterlife? Maybe how you should've taken swimming lessons as a kid?"

"Nope."

"You're heartless," Thomas says. "Is this big drowning scene for the comic you lied about letting me read?"

"I didn't lie! I just keep putting it off because—you know what, follow me." I don't want to be marked as a liar, so we head back to my apartment. I search for my Sun Warden comic as Thomas waits out in the hallway, and I decide I don't want to read this with him on his rooftop. I leave the comic on my bed and open the door. "Get in here," I say.

"I thought you don't like letting friends come over."

"I'm changing my mind in five, four, three, two . . ." I hold off on the last second because Thomas isn't calling my bluff. "Come on, don't make me look like an ass."

Thomas steps inside.

I watch his eyes as he takes in the apartment. I'm immediately self-conscious about the apartment smelling like wet laundry like Me-Crazy once said it did. I can't tell anymore. The first time Baby Freddy came over, he immediately searched for the bedroom—not a big challenge—to see if he could catch a glimpse of the bed we all slept in. The concept was just so weird to someone who had his own bedroom. Brendan never judged, thankfully. And Thomas isn't judging now either. He moves past Eric's video games and over to my collection of comics before turning back to me. "I want your Batcave."

"Shut up, you have your own room."

"I'll trade you."

"If you don't mind rooming with Eric, it's a done deal."

We shake on it.

Thomas picks up the Sun Warden comic, and we sit down on my bed, reading it together. It's crazy rewarding seeing someone laugh at jokes I doubted anyone else would find funny. He's also really impressed with this panel where Sun Warden launches a series of fireballs into the ruby eye of a cyclops, who's dual-wielding mountainous swords. I worked so damn hard on getting that right. He reaches the last panel where Sun Warden must decide on saving his girlfriend or best friend and then looks up. "Spoiler?"

"I don't know what he's going to do." I shrug. "I stopped there."

Thomas thinks for a moment, looking back down at the panel. "Maybe SW could somehow split himself in two, like he taps into a new power because of his exposure to the celestial kingdom. He could save Amelia and Caldwell in one go and then split himself more times. You know, to destroy the dragon with everyone blasting their sun-shots at once . . ."

Thomas continues the story for what seems like another ten minutes, and I pull out a notebook and draw a rough sketch of the diamond-tailed basilisk he wants me to include. When he talks about giving the basilisk the ability to shape-shift into an old man with Alzheimer's who can't recall his villainy, I cut him off and ask him to remind me about that idea for Issue #2.

I'm still writing when he goes to the bathroom to piss, but when he comes back, he's different. I'm mortified that he saw something embarrassing, like my mom's bras, or maybe our hamper just fucking smells. Whatever it is, he isn't going to say anything. He would never do anything to make me uncomfortable, but he doesn't realize I can't sit here and ignore it so I just ask him what changed.

"What happened?"

"The bathtub," Thomas says. "It got me thinking . . ." He doesn't have to go on. The image of someone's dad killing himself will do this to a person, to anyone. "I'm sorry."

"Don't be."

"Who found him, Stretch?"

"My mom," I say. "I don't know why he did it, Thomas. My mom says he was never completely right in the head, like he had a bad temper and stuff, but I feel like he must've had some other life we didn't know about that drove him to do what he did . . ." I stare at my lap, desperately trying to remember everything good about my dad instead of getting pissed and sad again. "We didn't even go to his funeral because how do you look at someone who wanted to get away from you?"

Thomas sits down beside me and wraps his arm around my shoulders. We don't say anything, at least not for a couple minutes, and he tells me about how he still wonders about his own dad. He recognizes that it's different—my father committing suicide, his abandoning him but probably alive—but it's still a loss; it changed everything. He doesn't really have a lot of great memories of his dad, except for this one time when his father took him fishing, but Thomas can't help but think about experiences they could've shared, like driving lessons, hockey games, and sex talks.

"You think we'll be screwed without our dads?" I ask.

"I think we'll be screwed trying to figure out *why* they ditched us without explanation, but I have hope for us," Thomas says. "Well, I'll have hope for you after I teach you how to ride a bike *and* swim. You're going to keep me busy, Stretch."

I smile in spite of myself. His arm is still around me. None of my friends would ever comfort me this way. It's kind of, sort of, definitely different. I'm hardly heartless like Thomas joked. He knows it too.

14
4 A.M. THOUGHTS

Genevieve comes home tomorrow.

Finally.

She's taking a taxi from the airport and she'll be expecting me to be outside her building when she gets there. And of course I'll be there. I haven't seen my girlfriend in three weeks and I miss her a lot. I think it's the anxiety of seeing her that's keeping me awake long after everyone is asleep, even Eric whose double shifts are finally laying him out an hour after he gets home.

I sit up and stare outside the window. It's dead out there.

I have something I want to talk about but it's not the kind of talk I can just have with anyone. It has be the right someone, but that right someone is the reason I need to talk in the first place. I draw instead because putting thought to page helps, it really does.

I draw quick sketches of different things my friends like: Fat-Dave likes wrestling games where he can imagine he's someone fit; Baby Freddy loves baseball more than football, which his father wants him playing instead; Brendan loved being someone's son instead of someone's grandson; Deon loves fighting;

Skinny-Dave just needs a blunt and a staircase to pee in and he's good; Genevieve is at her happiest when she's in front of a canvas, even on the days she can't finish; and finally, Thomas likes boys.

Just as no one ever had to tell me that Skinny-Dave loves blazing, or how Brendan is falling down the black hole of drug dealing because his parents are in jail, I don't need anyone—even Thomas himself—to tell me he's gay. I think he might even like me, which makes zero sense because surely he could do better than a kid with a chipped tooth who's straight and taken.

The thing is, I'm scared for Thomas. Maybe my friends won't care if he ever does decide to tell us, but what if they do? What if they can't accept he's just as naturally interested in other guys like how Me-Crazy and Deon are prone to fighting? What if they try to beat something out of him that won't go away?

I tear out the page from my sketchbook.

I take one last look at my drawing of Thomas kissing a tall guy before I crumple it up.

PART TWO: A DIFFERENT HAPPINESS

1
HIS HAPPY BIRTHDAY

We're in the elevator riding up to Genevieve's apartment, her luggage under my arms. She's pressed up against me and says, "You got to come next year. The instructor taught me so much on shadowing you could use for your comics and also . . ." Her confidence in our future should put me at ease, and it's a reminder that I'm doing everything right. We could get stuck in this elevator right now and I won't freak out, even if she wants to keep rambling on about art camps and colleges and neighborhoods we'll move to and other grown-up shit.

She goes inside her apartment to double-check that her father's not home before inviting me in. She catches me up on who were her friends out there, how much she hated pissing in the woods one day during a long hike, and then tells me, "I have a surprise." I follow her into her bedroom and she pulls out a ten-by-ten painting from her suitcase.

She finished something.

It's a dark-haired girl with silver binoculars gazing up at the attic window of a house. Instead of finding worn and forgotten furniture, she finds a starry universe boxed into the corners of the attic and a glowing constellation of a boy reaching out to her.

"Holy shit, I love this."

I'm sitting down to admire every last detail when she takes it away from me.

She sets the painting down and straddles my lap. She takes off my shirt, plays with my growing patch of chest hair, and skims my jawline with the tip of her finger.

"Missing you was my breakthrough, I think. We can't ever be apart for that long again." She rests her forehead against mine.

"I missed you too," I say, and even though I look her in the eyes, it doesn't feel all that right anymore. I mean, I did miss her—kind of. Not as much I should've, but she was always on my mind—kind of always on my mind.

I flip her over onto the bed. I pull out a condom from my jeans as we strip down. I don't slip it on yet because I haven't quite taken off yet—I'm psyching myself out too much. She grabs me and I close my eyes because if I see her disappointed I'll somersault out the window. The memory of Thomas taking his shirt off, running into the sprinklers, and doing push-ups overcomes me, and as much as I try to push it out of my mind to focus on my beautiful girlfriend, suddenly all systems are a go.

THOMAS IS NOT GENEVIEVE, and Genevieve is not Thomas so this terrible ping-pong in my head over them is bullshit. They both play very different roles in my life. I know this; I swear I do. Genevieve is the girl I love and the one I will always miss more whenever there's distance between us. Thomas is just my best friend, the one I trust a lot, but he won't ever get any secrets out of me that I can't tell Genevieve. So what if Genevieve won't race up bleachers with me or care to count trains go by? So what if sometimes I randomly smell Thomas's cologne on a stranger and instantly relive our hangouts?

If I were faced with Sun Warden's decision—whether or not to save his girlfriend or best friend from a dragon—I'm sorry to change my mind, but Thomas would fall away without me moving a muscle. And I would make that choice without a doubt because the bottom line is that Genevieve is my girlfriend and I'm her boyfriend, and Thomas and I are just friends and that's that.

ALL THIS DOESN'T MEAN I can't celebrate Thomas's existence on the exact day my girlfriend returns after a three-week leave.

He matters too much to be dicked over by friends two years in a row.

Thomas has strict instructions not to come up here on the roof until I go down to get him. I'm the only one who got him a gift, naturally. Well, Baby Freddy stole three bottles of raspberry Smirnoff from his mother's liquor cabinet. (That kid might be a flakey punk bitch every now and again, but he definitely respects any opportunity to get twisted.) I'm hoping Thomas doesn't think my gift is ridiculous or silly like Genevieve did when I told her what it was.

I impulsively bought a few cheap lanterns from a discount store on the way over here, but only two glow his favorite shade of green. We're blasting Brendan's Get Krunk playlist from his stereo dock, and Skinny-Dave is already grinding with our neighbor Crystal, while her friend hovers by the dollar store cakes I bought. I really wanted to get him an ice-cream cake from his old job and make it special, shaped like a director's slate or something, but it costs too much money, which sucks.

"Bangin' party," Brendan says after setting the stereo down. "Didn't know you had it in you after your beach party bombed."

"I was twelve and Orchard Beach sucks. Let it go." I look over. Genevieve is on her second drink. She's been chatting with Me-Crazy for ten minutes; that's an unhealthy amount of time to spend with him alone. "Can you go save Genevieve from Psycho over there?" I walk off and he calls me back.

"Where are you going?"

"I'm getting Thomas." I haven't seen him all day, only spoke with him at midnight last night to wish him a happy birthday, and again a couple of hours ago to let him know we'd be setting up soon. I miraculously shepherded everyone up to the roof without managing to get into a fight with the Joey Rosa kids.

"I hope you throw me an awesome party like this," Brendan says, and it reminds me of that time in fifth grade when he and Baby Freddy competed over who would be my best friend on the school bus. Some friendships can never be as simple as sharing.

I climb down the fire escape and knock on Thomas's window before sitting on the windowsill. He's at his desk, shirtless, and reading something in his journal before looking up with a smile. "Happy birthday, yo. You writing down your words of wisdom for the day?"

Thomas nods. "Nah, I did that earlier. I was reading what I wrote at the end of my birthday last year. I was an angsty little guy."

"Rightfully so. But you got it good upstairs. We probably shouldn't have invited Me-Crazy to a rooftop where he'll be drinking, but we'll cross that bridge later."

"Like when he throws one of us off?"

"I think we're all safe except Skinny-Dave. He really likes throwing him around."

"I owe you a hundred fist bumps for putting this together for me. I can't wait to read my journal tomorrow after I drunk-write my entry tonight." He gets up and walks over to his closet. I look at the posters around his room so I can stop staring at his back. He catches me up about all the great phone calls he got today from his family, and the birthday card from his mother with two hundred and fifty dollars inside.

"Not sure this party will beat a card with that much money."

"BOO!" someone says behind me.

I jump and almost hit my head on the raised window. It takes me a second to register that it's Genevieve. We have been taking a few minutes to come up. Not surprised she's checking on us. Gen looks into the room, and Thomas is standing there, covering his bare chest with a striped tank top, and she looks back at me. "Is party central happening down here now? Let's go up and drink! Wooooo!"

I'm not Genevieve's biggest fan when she's hitting the bottle because she turns into this party girl she always regrets being the next morning. She shifts my head toward her and kisses me intensely, her tongue tasting like raspberry vodka and cranberry juice as she shoves it down my throat. You would think she's expecting Thomas to leave so we can use his bed. She squeezes my hand and leads me back up to the roof. Thomas follows a few steps behind. Some of my friends cheer for Thomas while others keep drinking or spitting game to the other four girls. Thomas points at one of the glowing lanterns, says it's cool, picks it up, and it immediately dies.

Well, that happened.

I offer to get him and Genevieve a drink (well, another drink for her) and leave them chatting.

Fat-Dave walks over to me with a red Solo cup filled to the brim. It spills over his hand. "Cheers to your girl's nice tits!"

"Cheers," I say without a drink. I fill up three cups—20 percent liquor, 80 percent juice for Gen's sake. Then I carry them—two in my hand, one in my mouth—back to Thomas and

Genevieve. I hand them off right as Thomas asks Genevieve, "Are you a witch?" and I'm kind of confused on the crazy turns this conversation must've taken. "What the . . . ?"

"He thinks I'm a witch because . . ." Genevieve races over to her abandoned tote bag on the floor, spilling half her drink along the way, which is for the best. She comes back with a deck of odd-looking cards, wrapped around with a blue ribbon. ". . . of these. Tarot cards. I made these during the retreat. I used strips of bark instead of paper to give them an otherworldly look."

"That was a real witchlike thing to say," I comment.

"Burn, witch, burn," Thomas says with a smile. "Stretch says you used to be really into horoscopes. I'm more of a fortune cookie kind of guy."

"Fortune cookies can be cracked open by anyone," she counters.

"It's about taking a chance," Thomas defends. "It's much easier to follow than all the conflicting horoscopes forecasted everywhere."

She holds in a burp before arguing. "That's why horoscopes are better. If your fortune promises you wealth by the end of the day and you go home poor, then you were lied to. But if your reading from a psychic's website is wrong, maybe the one in the newspaper is right."

This conversation is beyond dumb. Someone shoot me. Now. Twice.

"So why'd you stop?"

Genevieve spins her cup around and stares into the mini-whirlpool before downing it all in one gulp. "Because I was tired of my many expectations not being met."

"Well, I'll have to trade you a fortune cookie for a psychic reading one day," Thomas says.

I swear Gen's face flushes. He's playing the game close to his chest. I normally wouldn't care except it's with my girlfriend.

"You should go get some cake before everyone eats it all," I say. We're skipping right to the eating because this is hardly the "Let's sing 'Happy Birthday'!" crowd.

"Cake? Excuse me," Thomas says, patting Genevieve on her shoulder before racing to the corner.

We follow him and all moan when Me-Crazy dips his finger into the icing and steals a bite. Others grab plates and some just dig in with a fork. Once Me-Crazy grabs a handful of cake, the cake is his and his only. (Sorry, Thomas.) I sit down on the ground, and Genevieve relaxes right into my lap, eating cake and drinking it down with another cup of booze. Part of me would love to volunteer someone else to hold her hair back later tonight, but the part of me who loves her is ready for the job.

Thomas joins us with a pathetic slice of cake. "So I still haven't asked you how New Orleans was, Genevieve."

"That's okay. I still haven't wished you a happy birthday."

I mouth, "She's drunk" to him and he shrugs it off.

"New Orleans was great. I'm hoping to drag Aaron with me next summer. I think I fell in love when I was down there . . ." She puts down her drink and takes my hand, gripping it hard like we're about to arm-wrestle. "In love with the city, I mean, since I have the boy I love here."

"I see that," Thomas says. "Stretch doesn't shut up about you."

Genevieve leans back and kisses me hard again, her tongue completely out of sync with mine. Then she picks her cup and fork right back up, stands, and taps the fork against the plastic like it's going to chime and steal everyone's attention. "Who wants to play a game?"

"Spin the bottle!" Fat-Dave shouts.

Hell no. Seriously, the dudes-to-chick ratio is like the dude-to-chick ratio at a boxing match.

"Flip cup!" Brendan shouts. There's no fucking table up here to play on.

"Kings!" Deon says. Great, a drinking card game without cards.

"Seven Minutes in Heaven!" Crystal suggests, laughing so hard and obnoxiously that she could tumble over the ledge and I wouldn't move a muscle.

"I was thinking Two Truths and a Lie," Genevieve announces to everyone's applause.

How to Play Two Truths and a Lie: everyone shares three stories or facts about themselves and then you take turns figuring out everyone's lie. It's the perfect icebreaker game.

Problem: I don't like a Genevieve who knows this game.

"You start, birthday boy," Genevieve says.

Everyone gathers around while Thomas counts off what he's going to say with his fingers. "Okay, I got it. I worship Walt Disney. I worship Steven Spielberg. I worship Martin Scorsese."

"You don't worship Disney," Baby Freddy says. "Who worships a guy who created princess movies?"

"Who worships another guy, period," Brendan adds.

"You don't worship Martin Scorsese," I answer before anyone else can say something stupid. "You think he's cool but you're not hanging up posters of him around your room." Thomas nods and raises his cup. "So it's my turn now, right?" I ask Genevieve.

She throws back the rest of her drink. "Let's see who knows you best, babe."

I really wish we were playing kings or flip cup or even spin the bottle right now. "Uh . . . I'm great at tic-tac-toe. I love skateboarding. I hate a lot of Spanish music."

"You're Puerto Rican so you definitely love Spanish music," Deon says.

"Yeah, and you probably shake your hips to it while skateboarding," Skinny-Dave says.

"You're not great at tic-tac-toe," Genevieve agrees less offensively.

"You don't skateboard. You skate on rollerblades," Thomas says.

I point at him and click my tongue. "He's right." I turn to Skinny-Dave. "When the fuck have you seen me skateboard around the block?"

"No way you're good at tic-tac-toe!" Genevieve shouts. "I beat you all the time."

"He beat me every time we played the other night," Thomas says.

Genevieve rakes her hand through her dark hair, and she looks super ill, like she could throw up any minute now. "I guess it's your turn again, Thomas."

"No, please. You go."

She covers her face with her hand. I think she does this so we can't detect any lie. Or she's actually about to throw up on me. "I'm ready. I grew up wanting to be a ballerina and an actress and a nurse." For a drunk girl, her tone remains so steady I think every single one can be true. Everyone's about to start shooting guesses when she holds her hand out. "Let Aaron go first. Which is the lie, babe?"

"You never wanted to be a ballerina. Come on, that was easy."

"Yeah," she says to my relief. Bluffing FTW.

I'm about to offer my turn to someone else when Genevieve stands up, a little wobbly. She raises one arm above her head and trails one leg up the other until she kind of resembles a flamingo—a wasted flamingo. "I wanted to be a ballerina badly. Owned tights and everything." She stumbles and Baby Freddy catches her. "I was never good enough so I mock the girls who are." She sits down next to me and nudges my shoulder with hers. "I guess you forgot."

Skinny-Dave and Fat-Dave hiss like something is sizzling, and Me-Crazy chimes in with, "You got burned!"

I glance at everyone clockwise . . .

Brendan unties his shoelaces so he can tie them again.

Thomas pulls out his phone and I bet anything he's typing nonsense to no one.

And everyone else is just drinking or looking like they feel very fucking sorry for me. Maybe they feel sorry for her.

"It's only a game," Genevieve says, shrugging. "Thomas, you should totally open up Aaron's present."

Holy shit, my girlfriend has the biggest balls ever.

"Present time!" Thomas shouts, killing zero tension.

Crystal's drunk friend tosses Thomas the gift-wrapped present.

"It's nothing big," I say.

Thomas unwraps it and rocks forward laughing. "This is awesome!"

"It's a toy," Genevieve says.

"It's Buzz Lightyear!" Thomas breaks Buzz free from the box and presses a button on his wrist; red lights blink.

Fat-Dave asks, "From *Toy Story*?"

Me-Crazy says, "Me-Crazy likes the talking piggy bank."

Thomas goes into the whole story about how his asshole father said he would give him Buzz Lightyear for his ninth birthday and just drove away. "I've been waiting for this guy for so long. Thanks, Stretch." He reaches over and we fist-bump. "Nope. Not good enough. Get up."

I stand and he full on hugs me, none of this one-arm hug with a pat-on-the-back nonsense.

Reasons Why I'm Feeling Warm Right Now:

1. I downed my drink pretty quickly on a fairly empty stomach.
2. Everyone on the roof is staring at us.
3. My unspeakable truth.

"No homo."

"No homo," I say back.

Everyone resumes drinking but Thomas sticks around. "Stretch, seriously: best birthday since I celebrated my sixth birthday at Disney World. Getting me Buzz Lightyear just made you beat Mickey Mouse."

"I mean, Mickey Mouse never stood a chance, did he?"

"I have an idea on how I could top this night on your birthday."

"It's not a competition, dude."

"Game on," Thomas says with a smile. He leaves to grab another drink.

Maybe an hour or so later, the bottles are all empty and everyone clears out. I stop helping Thomas clean up because Genevieve is pretty damn drunk and needs to get home, so we bounce.

I've been trying to hail her a cab for a couple minutes now without much luck.

If the tension between us were a person, I would snap its neck and kick the corpse for good measure.

"I'm losing you again," Genevieve cries.

"No you're not, Gen—"

"Yes I am! Yes the fuck I am!" She's crying harder and I don't know what to say. A cab pulls up and she opens the door.

"Do you want me to go with you?"

"You shouldn't have to fucking ask if you should fucking take me home, Aaron!" I try to follow her into the cab but she pushes me back. "Not tonight. I'm going home alone to go punch a pillow or something. We can figure this out tomorrow." She closes the door and the cab takes off.

I should chase after the cab. But the impulse isn't there. In my head, I play a round of One Truth and a Lie.

I need Thomas to be happy. I need Genevieve to be happy.

I can't keep lying to myself about the truth.

2
THE WAR INSIDE ME

It's been nonstop raining the past couple of days, which sucks for a lot of reasons. Genevieve has been using it as an excuse for why she can't hang with me, even if I know it's because she wants more time away from me. I can't play any card games with Thomas on his rooftop, or go on any job-hunting adventures with him. And I can't stay outside and lose myself in a game of manhunt or Skelzies or anything without risking pneumonia. If there's anything worse than being stuck in the smallest home ever with thoughts I shouldn't be left alone with, it's being stuck while coughing all over my brother's stuff, who will in turn get sick, and then cough all over my stuff . . . and will get me sick again in a cruel, cruel cycle of screwing each other over until we're both so immune we could eat candy off the floor of Washington Hospital's ER.

But Mom has tasked me with post office duty today.

My little cousin's birthday is tomorrow, and she needs me to overnight a gift to Albany. The umbrella I leave with gets its ass kicked by the wind within two minutes, and while paying twenty dollars for an umbrella has always seemed excessive to me, having to buy a new five-dollar umbrella every single time it rains just seems like shitty math on my behalf.

I walk the block to the post office, my bad mood growing heavier like a backpack of big-ass bricks I'm calling "THE WAR INSIDE ME." The heaviest bricks are "GENEVIEVE HATES ME" and "I DON'T KNOW WHAT TO DO WITH THOMAS" and "I STILL MISS DAD."

The last brick weighs the most right now. This is the first time I've come near his old workplace since we lost him. When I was a kid I'd pretend I was a security guard outside the bedroom door, and only Mom would entertain my high-five fee if she wanted to enter, whereas Eric would storm past me.

The package is getting wet, and I'm risking pneumonia, so I rush inside before I can change my mind and walk the twelve blocks to the second-nearest post office. The line isn't too bad. No one here recognizes me as the kid of the security guard who killed himself, so that's a plus. The clerk hands me my receipt and on my way out, I spot Evangeline sitting down on the wooden bench by the envelopes and stationery, writing a postcard.

"Evangeline, hey," I say.

She looks up. "Hey, kiddo. What brings you here?"

"Mailing some plush giraffe to my little cousin for her birthday. Who you writing to?"

"I broke some hearts back in London and promised to keep in touch. Didn't give them my email either. It's better this way." Evangeline shows me all of the ten postcards she's sending out. She signs her name and writes today's date on a Yankee Stadium postcard. "Phillip was a sweet one, but his brother was falling for me too. I couldn't come between family."

"So the brother isn't getting a postcard?"

"No, I've already shipped him a letter asking him to stop writing me." Evangeline makes room for me on the bench and shuffles all her postcards as she tells me, "Anyway, thought I would hang around here and get these sent out before the siren song of unread books back home captures me. How are you doing?"

"I'm really wet."

"Another reason I'm hiding out here."

I'm not sure why I feel the sudden urge to confess to my former babysitter, but maybe it's because she's both a stranger and someone I trust. "I'm really missing my dad pretty hard this week. I just don't know why the hell he would leave us, you know." I breathe in and out, in and out, in and out, trying to push the anger back down, but instead it beats me and I spit out, "It's affecting my relationship with Genevieve, who thinks she's losing me and . . . I don't know."

"*Is* she losing you?"

"I think I'm kind of, sort of, definitely losing myself right now."

"In what way, kiddo?"

"I don't know. Maybe I'm just growing up."

"You mean you're done playing with Teenage Mutant Ninja Turtle toys?"

"They were action figures, Evangeline." I feel a little better talking to someone outside the universe of my problems. But I don't know if I want to fill her in on how someone who doesn't have much direction is seriously disorienting me. "I should probably get home and see if Genevieve is in the mood to answer my calls. Or go fucking punch myself if she isn't."

"Language," Evangeline says.

"The babysitter never died in you, did it?"

"Afraid not, kiddo."

She mails out her postcards and walks me back home under her large yellow umbrella. I don't even change into dry clothes before jumping onto my bed and calling Genevieve. I'm not really sure I even know what I would say, but it still sucks when she doesn't answer.

3
SIDE A

If I could afford a Leteo procedure, I'd give Genevieve the money so she could forget me, but since that's never going to happen, I'm outside trying to sketch what our future will look like if we stick together. The page is still blank. It's been a week since Thomas's birthday, and despite another awkward phone call last night, I'm still pretty sure Genevieve doesn't believe I love her anymore.

I put down my notebook when I see Me-Crazy coming through the gates, his head craned back and fingers pinching his bloody nose. Brendan, Skinny-Dave, and Baby Freddy are all behind him. I rush over. "What happened?"

"Nosebleed," Me-Crazy says, laughing.

"Nosebleed after beating down some Joey Rosa dick suckers," Skinny-Dave says, hopping up and down and smacking his fists like he was a part of the fight. Whenever we brawled with kids from the Joey Rosa Projects, he always bitched out and hid in bodegas or behind trash cans.

"What the fuck did they do to you?"

Brendan sits Me-Crazy down on the bench. "We were walking

by when the usual suspects ran their mouths because we partied on your boy's roof. Danny blew a kiss at Me-Crazy and got his shit rocked."

"Me-Crazy wrecked them all!" Skinny-Dave shouts.

Baby Freddy and Skinny-Dave are walking to Good Food's to grab some tissues, and I hear them recapping their favorite part of the fight—when Me-Crazy made Danny kiss the bottom of his boot—seven times. I don't even think Danny is gay, but that kind of stuff just sets Me-Crazy off like little white party poppers. He's fucking insane, but at least he's on our side.

And here's one of my problems: if I don't choose Genevieve, I'll find myself on the receiving end of a boot to the face.

BEFORE I HEAD OUT to meet Genevieve, I suddenly have a big to-do list. It ranges from balling up socks to color-coding my comics to add some life to my corner of the living room. But I snap out of it because I'm excited to see her, or at least I'm telling myself I am, because it's how I would've behaved if I were going to see Thomas.

On the phone last night, Genevieve mentioned there's a flea market opening up today, and I invited myself along because that's what a good boyfriend does.

When I see her, I make it a point to tell her something really nice about herself, like how much I love the constellation of freckles running down from her neck to her shoulder blade. I'm trying to prove to her that she's my universe and I orbit within her, simple as that. I learned how to be this way because of my friends. Not directly, of course, since Brendan blasts his way through girls, and Skinny-Dave is always texting multiple prospects simultaneously, but anti–role models are just as enlightening. And at the very least she seems to appreciate the effort. Or she pretends she does.

The flea market is packed. We pass by boring vendors selling buttons, shoelaces, tube socks, and underwear. She tries on some emerald earrings by one table and I walk off a little bit to find a comic worth buying. I check out the next table and there's a sign that reads VINTAGE VIDEO GAMES. They have the old Nintendo cartridges for Pac-Man and Super Mario Bros. 3 and Castlevania, all priced for twenty dollars or more with a marker. I nod at the guy in the Zelda shirt and move on to the next table with all these fridge magnets. I consider buying one for Thomas. But that would just be an excuse to go see him, so I don't, even though there are words crawling around my brain that I want to come out and say.

I turn and Genevieve isn't at the jewelry table anymore. I tiptoe and find her waving me down. I make my way to her and she's holding a blue moleskin sketchbook. "What do you think? I want to make sure you actually like it before I surprise you with it."

"I don't need a new notebook," I say. I still have enough spiral notebooks with loose leaf I haven't used up yet.

"But do you want a new one?"

"No thanks." I know she's not some rich girl, but she's definitely much better off than I am with her own bedroom and weekly allowances. She doesn't really understand Want versus Need like we do at home; just because you can afford something doesn't mean you have to have it.

Things I Want: new video games; trendier sneakers; a laptop with Photoshop; a home with enough bedrooms so friends can stay over.

Things I Need: food and water; coats and boots during the winter; a home to come home to, no matter how small; a girlfriend like Genevieve; and a best friend like Thomas instead of a sort of best friend like Brendan.

Genevieve grabs my hand and I fake a smile. I notice she's still a little unhappy herself.

😃 😃 😃 😃

LATER THAT NIGHT, THERE'S a knock on the door. Eric's about to leave for his overnight inventory shift and Mom is laid out from her double. I sometimes catch myself mistaking a knock on the door for Dad without his keys. It'll be a while until I shake that off, I think. Normally my friends call for me outside the window. I pause my game and pray it's not someone ding-dong-ditching me because so help me God . . .

I open the door and it's Thomas. "Hey," he says with a smile.

I smile back.

"You game to come over tonight?" he asks after I say nothing. "I've made progress on my life chart and thought we could catch up. Been a while."

Yeah, eight days since I last saw him and ten hours since we last texted. I should really stay home and rest because I'm spending the day with Genevieve again tomorrow. But if I stay, I'll be up all night anxious over how I could've been helping him figure out who he is so he isn't walking around blind and lost. "Yeah, I'm down. Give me a sec."

I go back inside to turn off the Xbox, and Eric is eyeing me like he knows all my secrets and lies; it's the same look he had the day I left home to go have sex for the first time. I let Mom sleep since I'll be home before she even wakes up during the middle of the night to pee. To avoid all our friends in the court, I lead Thomas out of the back staircase. It smells like recently lit weed. I put a hand on Thomas's chest to stop him so we can listen out for anyone down there.

When I don't hear anything, we go down and bump into Brendan and this girl Nate. Nate's real name is Natalie but she's been reinventing herself as a dude for the past four years with thick braids, fake gold medallions, fitted hats, and basketball jerseys. Brendan looks at Thomas but asks me, "What you doing here, A?"

"Heading out." I see the packet of weed in his hand. "You?"

"Business," Brendan says.

"You would've been busted if I was a security guard," I say.

"Nah. Their loud-ass keys always give them up."

"I could've been someone who would've snitched."

"My grandfather doesn't care what I do to bring home paper," Brendan says, rubbing his fingers together. "I should finish up here."

"Yeah," I say.

When we leave, I hear Brendan ask Nate something: "You sure you don't like guys?"

We stop into Good Food's and Thomas buys Pop-Tarts, sour candy, and enough bags of potato chips for a party of six. It's nice out, so we go up to his roof and play cards. It's a little dark, but Thomas saved a green paper lantern from his birthday that miraculously still works. I tear into the sour candy and ask him, "So what's new with your future?"

"I figured out something big. About who I want to be." Thomas downs his Top Pop and burps. "Or more like who I don't want to be."

I don't know if it's the sugar, or where he could be going with this, but I'm a little shaky. "And who's that?"

"I don't want to be a director," Thomas says—exactly the kind of thing you expect to hear from someone who is so young and lost. "I just don't think I'm as passionate about it as I thought I was. Think about it, I haven't ever filmed anything or even put up a video on YouTube. All I do is look up directors and watch movies as if that's all it takes."

"But you've been writing scripts," I say.

He shrugs. "I don't have any real stories to tell. I can write all the scripts I want, but I'm only seventeen and haven't lived anything interesting enough to write about. When your life sucks, your story sucks."

"Sometimes your story is worth reading about because your life sucks," I say. "And I don't think your life sucks."

"Sure it does. I don't know what I want to do when I'm older. You're my only real friend. My mother is always working and never has time for me, and my father might be dead for all I know." Thomas immediately looks up at me, horrified. "I'm sorry. That was such a dickhead thing to say."

I want to tell him that it's okay, that it's not like my father killed himself because of me, but that will only sound like his father left because of him. So I say nothing. It's quiet except for the wind. I throw a rock back onto the ground. "I think it's okay for you to be confused by things right now, Thomas. We're young and figuring shit out, but our lives don't completely suck. Take it from the kid whose bedroom is the living room."

"I just want the future figured out, you know?" He grins. "Maybe we should invite your girlfriend up here with her tarot cards to lay it all out for us."

"I'm not sure how much longer we'll be dating," I say, looking down.

"Why's that?" Thomas asks, and I can see from the corner of my eyes that he's lowered his head too.

"Things aren't what they once were. And I think I'm going to take a page out of your book and put some distance between me and her." I'm tugging at my sleeve now, something I used to do as a kid whenever I got really nervous. "I love her, and I want to know her forever, but we don't fit."

"I get that."

I'm staring very hard at my hands now. "I feel weird talking like this. Do guys do this kind of thing? Hang out and talk about love?"

"You ask that like you haven't been a guy your entire life.

Some dudes make their mind a prison. I like living outside of bars. If we're different, that's fine with me."

He's right. I will dare to be different. I will prove to everyone that the world won't turn to ash or spin out of control or be swallowed alive by a black hole. But someone has to man up first to get this ball rolling.

"There's something I want to tell you but it has to stay between us," I say. The words almost sound like they're being spoken by someone else. "And you can't go running away."

"Please tell me you have a superpower, like you're actually a descendant from aliens or something. I've always wanted to be the best friend in a superhero movie who keeps the superhero's secret," Thomas says. "Sorry, too many movies. Of course you can trust me, Stretch."

"There's two sides to this and I'm not sure I'm ready to tell you both yet. But I want to soon."

"Okay. So tell me Side A now. Or whenever you're ready."

I look down again and massage my temples, my head ready to explode from what I'm about to admit. "Look, you're my best friend and everything, but if what I'm about to tell you is too much for you, it's fine and—"

"Shut up and talk to me," Thomas interrupts.

"That's kind of a mixed signal." He stares at me with shut-up-and-talk eyes. "Okay. No wasting time. I'm going to come out and say it. I think I might . . . maybe . . . kind of . . . sort of . . . possibly . . . be . . ."

" . . . Is this fill-in-the-blank?"

"No, no. I can say it. Let me say it. I'm going to say it. I think I might . . . kind of . . . sort of . . . possibly, no, definitely . . ." I can't spit the last word out, the unknown of everything that will come after choking me.

"Maybe it would actually help you if I guessed. Should we try that?"

"Okay."

"You're a virgin."

"Nope."

"You're a descendant of aliens."

"Still no."

"I'm out of guesses. Let me tell you something about me: I don't care if you're a gigantic virgin who's part alien. You're Stretch and nothing you say is going to change that."

I hide in my hands, and then dig my nails into my head as if I can tear off my face and unmask the person I'm trying to reveal. "Okay, yeah, I kind of, maybe, sort of, might . . . I think I might . . . I like guys, okay?" And then I sit here, unable to take the words back. I wait for the world to spin out of control, or worse, for Thomas to get up and walk away.

"That's it?"

"Kind of maybe sort of."

"Okay. So what?"

I look up and the sky isn't bleeding. I hear cars honking and drunk people shouting. Birds are still flying and stars are coming out of hiding, like me. Kids my age are having their first kisses right now or even taking it a step further. Everything, life, is continuing. "You don't care?"

"I care about you but I don't care about that. I mean, I do care but I don't care in that way you think I care." Thomas scratches his head and whistles. "You know what I mean, right? I don't care that you're gay."

"Can we maybe use a different word? I'm still wrapping my head around this."

He gives me a thumbs-up. "Dude, this is your business. If a code word makes you feel more comfortable, I'm in."

"I don't have anything in mind."

"How about dude-liker? It sounds pretty matter-of-fact."

"Yeah," I say. It sucks how a word that's supposed to mean happiness can somehow feel warped.

"It's your call, dude-liker. So no one knows?"

"Just us," I say. "Not even Gen. I'm going to figure out how to handle that when I understand what's going on with me. Maybe it happens like this for all dude-likers, where one day you're a girl-liker and the next day you're not. I guess maybe I could be a girl-slash-dude-liker, but I don't know."

Thomas readjusts himself, coming a little toward me or maybe just leaned my way for a second. "So what do you think changed everything?"

You did, I want to say but don't. It's quiet. This silence makes me uncomfortable, like I'll never be comfortable again. If I play my cards wrong, I'll not only lose my privacy, but maybe rob myself of my happiness, too. "I've been thinking about my happy ending even more than usual, probably because you're trying to engineer yours right now. I don't think I'll ever be happy until I figure out who I am and it comes down to me not being a hundred percent happy with the life I have."

"Do you mind being a dude-liker?"

"I don't know yet. Obviously I'm scared for my throat being a dude-liker around here, but I'm not exactly rushing to tell everyone tomorrow. I also don't think I'll be campaigning anytime soon with other dude-liker-friendly organizations. I mean, if they can create a future where I can get married to another dude without it seeming like a big deal, then good on them. I'll remember to send a fruit basket or something."

Thomas laughs and I know this is it, this is when he confesses that he's been pranking me and dropping signs he likes guys too just to get me to say it. "F-fruit b-b-basket. Pun intended?"

"You're an asshole and I hate you."

He's rocking back and forth and when his laugh finally winds down—though I wouldn't have minded watching him for a few more seconds—he says, "So what's next? Are you on the hunt for a guy in your happy ending?"

"I have zero clue."

Thomas inches toward me, for sure this time, and folds his hands in his lap. "Well, this all kind of reminds me of that blackout a few years ago. Remember? I was outside when it happened and it was so dark out I could barely see my own hand, let alone what was up the street. But I kept going forward, step by step, until I reached a familiar corner. Sometimes you just have to push ahead to find what you're looking for."

"Do you still have the fortune cookie you ripped that off of?"

"Nah, had to get rid of the evidence."

I smile, and like earlier, it feels legit, because it always is with him. But there's still a sinking feeling in my chest. I don't know what else I can say to him that'll make him feel comfortable enough to do what I just did. Since he doesn't ever lie, I wonder what he would say if I just directly asked him if he likes dudes too. If he says no, I would know that he is capable of lying. But if he says yes, I don't know how I would feel by dragging it out of him like that.

"Maybe you look distressed or maybe I'm a mind reader, but I want you to know that nothing is different, Stretch. Sure, you do things differently and that's okay. Nothing is changing," Thomas says, and he wraps his arm around my shoulder as if this were ordinary. This is the guy who makes me happy.

"Thanks for being telepathic," I say. I pat his knee. "So I guess this means I'm no longer allowed to call 'No Homo' anymore, right?"

"It doesn't matter." Thomas laughs and I want every night to be like this, where we can just laugh against each other without it being weird.

But for tonight, this is enough. From the shapes cast by the green paper lantern, you would never know that there were two boys sitting closely to one another trying to find themselves. You would only see shadows hugging, indiscriminate.

4
REMEMBER THAT TIME

Instead of manning up, I've been standing outside in the pouring rain for the past twenty minutes under Genevieve's window. A cab with an ad for the Leteo Institute drives through a puddle and soaks my jeans. I really, really wish Genevieve could just forget me.

And I really, really wish I had another pair of pants right now.

I finally go upstairs and leave my sneakers outside the door. I almost slide across her hallway in my wet socks but she holds my hand and keeps me steady. I almost come up with a bullshit excuse about how we should stay out in the living room so I don't get her bed wet, when I actually have other reasons not to go in there, but she leads and I follow.

"The flea market is totally closed today," Genevieve says. She helps me out of my hoodie and pinches my nipple through my white shirt. It tickles but I barely laugh. "Bright side of having a terrible father is he's never around." We sit on her bed. She kisses me and I know I should push her off but I don't. "I love you," she says, and before there's an awkward silence where I don't say it back, she adds, "Remember that time your soaking-wet jeans ruined my bed?"

The game has lost its spark, and maybe it's because of my low spirits, but it's also very likely because it's kind of, sort of, definitely ridiculous to ask me to remember something that is happening right now.

I'm being unfair.

I sit up, cross my legs, hold her hands, and play along. "Remember that time we bought water guns last summer and I chased you around Fort Wille Park? And you kept calling time out and sprayed me whenever I stopped?"

She sits up and tangles her legs in mine. "Remember when we kept riding the subway back and forth last February because it was too cold to go outside?"

"Which was stupid because it was even colder when we finally got off at one in the morning," I say, recalling how the cold was killing us, me especially since I had wrapped my jacket around her. "Remember that time we were writing each other messages in a crossword puzzle during study hall and it got taken away? I lost the evidence on how you misspelled *tornado* with an *e*."

Genevieve punches me. "Remember that time we texted each other using only song titles?"

"And how about that time it started raining when we were rowing the boat in Central Park and I started panicking?"

Genevieve laughs. While playing this game might be even worse than being intimate with her, it's both the right and wrong time to stroll down memory lane. "Remember that time we time-traveled together on my birthday and you told me you love me?" She climbs into my lap and feels up my arms.

We look into each other's eyes and when she leans in to kiss me, I let her because this will be the last kiss we share whether she knows it or not. Then she rests her chin on my shoulder and I hold her, hard.

"Remember that time I was a better boyfriend who gave you happy memories like these?" I feel her try to pull back, so she can meet my eyes again and tell me that I'm a good boyfriend, but I continue holding her because I can't look her in the face and do this. "I'm not the guy we're remembering anymore."

She stops resisting. She holds me tighter too, her nails digging into my arms. "Are you . . . ? You are. Aren't you?"

She's gotta be asking me if I'm breaking up with her, but I consider the chance that she's asking me if I'm a dude-liker.

I know this: the part of me that was playing straight for so long wants to lie and tell her that I can transform back into the person she needs me to be, except that's not who I am anymore or who I ever should've been. So I just nod and say, "Yeah." I'm about to apologize and try to explain why, but she breaks free from my hug and sits at the edge of her bed with her back to me.

Genevieve was the girl who brought me home after my dad killed himself and let me cry in a way I never would've in front of my friends. She tutored me in chemistry when I was failing, even though I was always too absorbed by her to actually pay attention. When her father started bringing home younger girls for the first time since her mother died, I distracted her with weekend outings, like a trip across the Brooklyn Bridge and people watching in Fort Wille Park. And now she's the girl who won't let me hug her.

"It's because of him," she says.

I bullshit her: "I don't know what you're talking about."

She's crying and doesn't let me see her face, like usual, and she throws me my hoodie. "You can go."

So I do.

5
ANOTHER FIGHT

How to Play Skelzies: Some people draw their Skelzies boards with chalk, but we properly outlined ours with yellow paint against the black asphalt ground years ago. There are thirteen numbered squares—Box #13 in the center—and you have to flick a cap across the board in numerical order. First person to hit all thirteen wins.

Making the caps has always been the coolest part. Whenever we go through gallons of milk or water in our homes, we keep the caps (or sometimes steal them right out of store fridges) and pour an even amount of candle wax inside so they have some weight and don't blow away whenever the wind surprises us. My mom likes skim milk so my cap is blue with yellow wax from one of her Santeria candles.

I'm playing with Baby Freddy (green cap, red wax), Brendan (red cap, orange wax), and Skinny-Dave (blue cap, blue wax).

Thomas should be joining us soon.

Baby Freddy is on his knees and elbows, measuring the distance between the starting line and Box #13; if you get in the box on your first move, you automatically win. He flicks the cap and it falls short. Brendan flicks his cap next and it's like a comet both in appearance and its glide. He lands in Box #1, then Box #2, and misses Box #3.

"Yo, A. I was trading in some games yesterday and guess what I found? Legend of Iris!"

I laugh. We bought it when we were twelve because there was a rumor that the developer—some beautiful girl in her late twenties—hid a picture of her ass in the game as some sort of erotic Easter egg. We played for hours, using cheat codes to speed the game along, but no dice. "The Great Ass Hunt of Sixth Grade. Good times."

"Yeah."

Here's the thing: I remember genuinely being a girl-liker when I was younger. I asked girls out on dates, was offered a blow job at fourteen if I pretended to be this girl's boyfriend to get her ex jealous—which I did, but pussied out when she unbuttoned my pants—and I only focused on the girls when watching straight porn. In January I was freaking out about what to get Genevieve for Valentine's Day, only for her to tell me a couple weeks later she doesn't believe in celebrating it. Major relief, but also super real.

I play my turn after Skinny-Dave goes and it's a direct hit with Baby Freddy's cap, sending it out of the board. I go again and miss Box #1.

By the time Thomas shows up, Brendan and I are on our way to Box #7. After my turn, we fist-bump and I hand him the cap I made for him (green top, yellow wax).

"Can I jump in, guys?"

"No way you'll catch up," Brendan says.

"Is that a challenge?"

"Sure. Maybe you'll beat Skinny-Dave, at least."

Thomas lines his cap to the left of the starting line, flicks, and lands right in Box #13.

Brendan kicks his cap. “That’s motherfucking bullshit.”

“We don’t have to count it,” Thomas offers.

“New game,” Brendan calls out as he retrieves his cap. He makes Thomas go first and I feel like Thomas might’ve missed Box #13 on purpose this time around.

I go next and get as far as Box #4 before missing.

Thomas asks, “How’d Genevieve take the news yesterday?”

Brendan is about to flick his cap when he looks up. “What news?”

“I sort of broke up with Genevieve.”

Brendan stands. “You’re shitting me.”

“What? No. Things are still crazy at home and—”

Brendan picks up his cap and hurls it. “Why the fuck does this kid know before us? What makes him so fucking special?”

“Stop playing like you’ve been around to help me figure my shit out.”

Before I can do anything to stop it, before I can actually register that this is happening, my sort of best friend, Brendan, charges toward my best friend, Thomas. Brendan snuffs him in the chin and lays into him. “Get—out—of—my friend’s head!” Before Brendan can land a sixth punch, I tackle him to the ground and pin him down, my arm against his throat.

“Leave him alone!” I’m breathing hard. I press down on his throat harder when he tries flipping me back with his legs, an old wrestling trick he used to be great at. I bet he’s regretting teaching me how to fight. I get off and check on Thomas while Brendan catches his breath. Thomas isn’t bleeding, but I can tell he’s doing his best not to cry.

“You’re okay, you’re good,” I tell him.

I help him up and he wraps his arm around my shoulders. Baby Freddy and Skinny-Dave kneel by Brendan and they all watch us walk off.

“I’m sorry,” Thomas tells me. “I didn’t know you hadn’t said anything—”

"Stop. It's not your fault. He's a fucking asshole."

He rubs his face and his eyes squint; a tear escapes. "You didn't have to take my side, Stretch."

I kind of, sort of, definitely always will.

6
SIDE B

Defending Thomas yesterday was instinctive, but not easy. If someone were to write my biography, there would be many stories about Brendan and Baby Freddy and Me-Crazy and the rest of the crew. They're my history. But I slept okay last night knowing I chose the person who agrees with the happy ending I'm building toward, not the ones who would punch in a face to demolish it.

I brought beer over to Thomas's house earlier today. Perk of being a cashier at Good Food's is how I get away with checking people's IDs but no one has to check mine when I cash out. I sit up against his bedroom wall, chugging back the rest of my third Corona as Thomas twists his fourth PBR open. I get another too, not just to catch up, but because I need a drink when I catch Thomas icing his bruised eye with the freezing can.

"I'm sorry for the thousandth time. I don't know what got into him."

"He thinks I'm stealing you away from them," Thomas says, like it's okay he got snuffed because my friends are jealous of all the Aaron Time he gets. "Do you ever think you'll tell them? Side A?"

"Maybe one day I'll move away and send a postcard saying, 'Hey, I like guys. Don't worry, I never liked any of you because you all suck.'"

Thomas looks left and right, then over his shoulder, and peeks out his window. "Sorry, just making sure Brendan's not hiding around here to punch me before I ask this next question." We both laugh. "You think you'll ever tell Genevieve?"

"I don't know. I haven't even heard from her the past couple of days. I have words I can say, I guess, but I'm scared she'll take it as a blow, like she turned me this way or something."

"I'd pay to be there for that conversation."

"It won't be for another few eons, so hang tight."

"Who's your celebrity crush?"

"What?"

"I'm trying to help you get more comfortable with everything."

"Okay, then. Emma Watson," I answer. He raises a large, skeptical eyebrow. "Look, she was awesome as Lexa the Enchantress in the Scorpius Hawthorne movies, and if she wanted to marry me, I would magically be straight again. But on the dude side of things, I'm going to have to go with Andrew Garfield. Slinging around with Spider-Man would be badass. How about you?"

"Natalie Portman really won me over in *Garden State*. I even loved her in *Star Wars: Episode One* . . . She was the only good thing about that trilogy," Thomas says.

Not exactly what I was hoping to hear, but I've got three and a half drinks in me on an empty stomach, so I'm feeling ballsy. "Who would your guy crush be?"

"Like if I had to go gay for someone?"

"Yeah."

"Hmm." Thomas lays back and rests his head on his pillow, kicking his knees up. He chugs his PBR like a funnel, until it's empty. "I gotta go with my dude Ryan Gosling. He has swag and I couldn't help but want to *be* him after watching *Drive*."

"I would ride shotgun with him," I agree.

"PBR me."

I toss a can to him like an overhead basketball pass and we cheer when he catches it. He opens it and beer sprays all over him. I'm drunk-laughing on the floor, which is the same as regular laughing, except it's obnoxiously louder and only happens when you're drunk. Thomas is drunk-laughing too while he changes into a new shirt. He's got to know always watching him change is killer on me, a turn-on with no payoff. He puts on a yellow sleeveless shirt.

"Get up. I'm going to teach you how to fight."

"No thanks, Stretch."

"Unless you're bench-pressing girls all the time, you're wasting your muscles."

"I've seen wrestling."

"Wrestling's fake. Come on, get up." He puts down his PBR and joins me in the middle of the room. "Awesome. Next time Brendan or anyone comes at you, you're going to lay them out."

How to Street Fight: You are your own weapon, but if you happen to have some brass knuckles or a baseball bat in a particularly nasty fight, more power to you.

"Okay, for starters, we're going to—" I cut myself off and trap him in a headlock. "Never wait for someone else to swing first." I let him go and he wobbles. Before he can protest, I swing and stop an inch from his face. "The nose is a good spot to aim for because even if you miss, you have a good chance at clocking them in the jaw or eye. But if you're dead set on breaking the nose, a head-butt is the way to go." I grab his shoulders, lean my forehead against his, and stare into his somewhat intoxicated eyes as I fake a head-butt into his nose over and over.

"That's a lot of violence to absorb in one minute," Thomas says. "I think I'm good for the night."

"You'll be good when—" I swing at him again, but this time

he catches my wrist with one hand and grabs my leg with the other, pinning me to the floor.

Thomas smiles. “I told you I’m good for now.” He pats my shoulder and sits across from me on the floor.

“We’ll go for Round Two later on. I’m just happy you’ll be able to put those muscles to use. Maybe I should work out more too, at least for the look.”

“I’ll be your friend, muscles or not,” Thomas says.

“I’m going to tattoo that promise on you as a reminder,” I say.

“I’m never getting a tattoo. What if I decide I want to take up underwear modeling? I can’t have YOLO running across my heart,” Thomas jokes, or at least I hope he’s joking.

I get up and grab a marker from his desk. I sit down next to him and palm his shoulder. “You’re getting a tattoo right now. What do you want?”

“No way,” he says, laughing. I know he wants one.

“Come on. If you don’t end up as an underwear model, what tattoo would you want?”

“I’m scared of needles.”

“This is a marker.”

“Fine.”

“How about one of your little fortune cookie quotes?”

“Surprise me.”

I hold his wrist, steady his arm, and begin drawing a stick figure holding a movie slate; it’ll one day be very meta, if meta is still a thing. My scar is pressed against his forearm, and if I had as much hope in life back then as I do now, it would’ve never existed in the first place. This all feels so right and I like my chances with telling him Side B. “Thomas?”

“Stretch?”

“Were you shocked? When I told you Side A?”

“A little. You’re just so different from any other friend I’ve ever had, and it’s also why I wanted to be your friend in the first place," Thomas says. It's funny that he says this while I shade in his stick figure's eyebrows, one of my favorite things about him. "But when you told me, I didn't care. I was honored you trusted me."

"Of course. You're my favorite person," I say without a doubt. Thomas isn't just someone I want in my life—I need him to stay happy, to keep the death out of my life, to make being who I am easier. "It sounds stupid, but I think you're my happiness." I rub his shoulder. When he turns to me, I trace his eyebrows from one to the other, and I lean in and kiss him.

Thomas pushes me off and gets up. "Dude, I'm sorry. I'm straight, you know."

Hearing those words, that lie, feels like every wrong thing in the world: heart attacks, gunshots, starvation, fathers who leave you on your own. I blink to fight back the tears. "I thought . . . I thought that you . . . Sorry, fuck. I've just had too many drinks." I feel like a fucking idiot. "Fuck. Sorry. Fuck." I look up at him and he's covering his mouth. "Say something."

"I don't know what to say. I don't know what to do."

"You can forget about it. What I did and what I said. I can't lose my favorite . . . I can't lost my best friend."

"Yeah. I can forget, Stretch."

"I'm going to go home. Sleep off everything."

"It's raining." He says it so matter-of-fact that his words loop through my head again as if they should've been obvious: *I'm straight, you know. I'm straight, you know. I'm straight, you know . . .* "Do you want an umbrella?"

"It's just rain."

He tells me something, but I can't hear him over the echoes. He reaches out for my shoulder and pulls back. "I'll talk to you later."

I feel his eyes on me as I let myself out of his window, almost knocking his Buzz Lightyear toy off the ledge. I reach the bottom and turn around to see if he's been following me. But he's not there, not even looking out his window.

I'm alone.

Garbage tumbling by creates hurtling shadows underneath streetlamps. I stop at an almost even distance between my house and his, feeling like I belong nowhere now. I collapse onto the curb and just sit there under the expectation Thomas will come for me. And the reality is killer.

7

LATE NIGHT/ EARLY MORNING THOUGHTS

12:22 A.M.

The moon needs to get the fuck out of my face.

We don't have blinds, of course, and I can never keep my back to the window because Eric's side of the room is always glowing from late-night gaming. I sit up and see Brendan, Skinny-Dave, and Me-Crazy passing a cigarette around on the jungle gym. I fall back down so they don't throw a handball at my window.

I reach for my sketchbook and see the black ink from the marker on my fingertips.

I can't draw right now.

☺ ☺ ☺ ☺

1:19 A.M.

I can't even remember what I like about Thomas.

I latched on to the first person who always had a smile for me and who didn't run away when I told him my secret. Everything I felt was an illusion, nothing more. He reminds me of when I turned fourteen and my family stopped caring about my birthday as much, when my friends made fun of me for wearing the same shirt two days in a row even though it wasn't dirty.

His eyebrows are ungodly large, a couple of his teeth are crooked, and he's mastered the art of lying so well he made me believe he doesn't lie, when actually, the best liars are the ones who fool you by claiming they never lie at all.

(2:45 A.M.)

I never forgot what I like about Thomas.

I'm the liar, not him. I lied to Genevieve, to my friends, to everyone. But I've pushed my limit and here's the truth: this is the most painfully confusing time in my life and he's the first person who said all the right words to me and reminds me of the first days of summer where you leave home without jacket, and my favorite songs playing over and over. And now he may never talk to me again.

(5:58 A.M.)

I remember this time last year, whenever I was in insomniac mode, I could put on my shoes and go visit my dad down the block at work. I remember this time two months ago, I could call Genevieve who would wake up to talk to me. I remember this time last week, I could go outside and talk about nothing with Brendan and the guys if they were still out. I remember this time yesterday, I could be sleeping over at Thomas's house without it being weird.

I have lost all these people. I'm left with a brother who snores. I'm left with post-programming infomercials about acne medicine, suicide prevention lines, and animal charities. I get up to turn off the TV before reruns of old and unfunny comedies come on, but one final ad catches my attention.

Leteo. It promises forgetting and moving on.

I sneak into my mom's room and steal her pamphlet.

8
MEMORIES AND SUCKER PUNCHES

I want to undergo the Leteo procedure.

It was originally just an insane thought, the kind of thoughts one has at 6:00 A.M. after a sleepless night when life is sucking, but I spent my weekend researching all things Leteo and there's actually hope for me. The main red flag is all the controversy surrounding the unsuccessful procedures lately. But I discovered for every backfire all over the country in the past month, there were twelve successful alterations. If others believe this procedure is worth the risk of ending up brain dead, I can't help but agree that it's probably better than me trying to you-know-what myself again out of pure defeat.

Leteo is this place of second chances. I read a lot of the stories provided online through Leteo's site, all names and intimate details redacted, of course.

A soldier known only as F-7298D was crippled by post-traumatic stress disorder until Leteo stepped in and buried the worst of his memories. Now F-7298D isn't suffering from disturbing dreams and sleeplessness. A mother of twins, M-3237E, was afflicted with agoraphobia after witnessing a bomb go off during a marathon. Leteo hid the memory away so M-3237E no longer fears the outdoors and can open more doors for herself and her children.

And they take care of kids like me, too.

A seventeen-year-old girl, S-0021P, was sexually abused by her uncle and even though he's in prison, she began burning her thighs. Leteo gave her the power to move on and trust her family again by suppressing past events where she blamed herself for leading her uncle on. Another seventeen-year-old, J-1930S, suffered from crazy panic attacks and always assumed the worst scenario possible if his family wasn't home when he returned from school. Leteo figured out the source of his problems and healed him.

Leteo takes our stories seriously.

But that's not what has me itching for the procedure.

I stumbled on a story of a fifty-year-old father in Russia, A-1799R, who realized he spent half his life being someone he isn't, and a quarter of that time married to a woman he doesn't love—can't love. But he couldn't uproot his family, couldn't abandon them or abandon Russia for a more accepting country, so he flew out here and asked Leteo if they could make him straight. And Leteo played with his head and did it. I followed that article to another about a nineteen-year-old teenager, P-6710S, who wanted to escape bullying and this feeling of wrongness. After her parents tried everything in their power to make her feel accepted, they turned to Leteo who "straightened her out."

I don't want to be me.

I don't want to second-guess if my friends are going to be okay with me being me, and more importantly, I don't want to see what happens if they're not. I don't want to be someone who can't be friends with Thomas, because if there's anything worse than not being able to be with him, it's knowing our friendship will ultimately have an expiration date if being around him becomes impossible.

I know not being me will be a lie, but I know I'm doing myself a favor in the long run if I can somehow book a Leteo procedure. Because as I stand now, I have so much bullshit to look out for.

Happiness shouldn't be this hard.

THE DOWNSIDE TO THIS whole Leteo pursuit: you need an adult if you're a minor seeking a consultation. I'm already down one parent, and I'm sure as shit not asking Eric to accompany me, but this means I'm going to have to tell my mom what kind of Leteo procedure I want, which sort of feels like when she used to take me to the barbershop and would tell the barber what kind of haircut I wanted. Except Leteo isn't a barbershop—it's more of a tattoo removal clinic, if anything—and this means I gotta tell her everything.

I run to catch her at Washington Hospital before she can leave for her night shift at the supermarket. Considering she's only right across the street, this is hardly the most difficult thing I've done today. No, that would've been when I was working a morning shift at Good Food's and I smelled Thomas's cologne on a customer and my heart just fucking hurt. Surviving that was today's battle. I'm done fighting.

I get to Mom's office where she's ending a call with someone. "Aaron . . ."

I close the door behind me and sit down. The truth is kind of, sort of, insanely crushing—but if I tell her and she gets behind my plan, which she will because she wants what's best for me, then I can make a happy liar out of myself. Best of all, I'll probably forget this awkward moment ever even playing out.

"What's wrong, my son? Are you feeling okay?"

"I'm okay," I say, and okay feels like too strong a word because I'm not even that. It's all hitting me hard right now—the rejection, the fear, the uncertainty. So thank God I'm here with my mom because I might need one of her hugs that always made me feel better as a kid, like that time I got in trouble with security for running in the hallways, or when Skinny-Dave's father made fun of me for being a waste of height during a basketball game, or every other time I was feeling ashamed or worthless.

"Talk to me," Mom says, sneaking a peek at the clock on her monitor screen. I know she's not rushing me, especially when she has no idea what the hell I want to say, but our bank status is no doubt still on her mind as it has to be.

"I want a Leteo procedure."

I have her full attention again. Her stare is so intense I look around her desk, wondering when she took down the photo she had of me as a kid on Dad's shoulders with Eric in his lap, the three of us in my grandpa's recliner chair. "Aaron, please, whatever it is—"

"No, Mom, listen, because time is very important here and I'm already feeling crazy and scared of what might happen if I can't have this procedure."

"What could you possibly want to forget?"

"I hope this isn't hard to hear, but I sort of have—had something . . ." I thought I would spit it out, but no matter the possibilities of forgetting this moment, living in the now with this weight still feels pretty impossible. "Um, I had something going on with Thomas. Maybe you guessed that because you have eyes."

She rolls her chair over to me and grabs my hand. "Okay . . . but what's wrong?"

"Me."

"You're not wrong, my son." She gives me a side hug, resting her head on my shoulder. "I don't know what you were expecting would happen. That I would hit you with a belt? Maybe rub some cleansing oil on you?"

"I wish you could." I cry, because there's nothing like my mom telling me I'm okay the way I am to really scare me about living with this heartache forever. "I want a reboot, Mom. It's not working with Thomas. I know I said I would be more open after what I put you through in April, so I'm telling you now: this whole thing with Thomas was a major awakening for me. But he's still sleeping and I'm not sure I can do or say enough to wake him up."

"What are you asking of me?"

"To make me right."

She's sobbing a little too, and she squeezes my hand. "Thank you for being honest with me, Aaron. I have said it before and I'll say it always, but I'll love you however you are. You're being impulsive about Leteo. We can talk this over or schedule another appointment with your therapist—"

"Dr. Slattery is a joke! He's a waste of your money! Leteo is the real damn deal, Mom. They say you can't choose whether or not you like boys or girls, but you can help me get back on the right track." I move out from under her head because she's making me feel like I'm begging for a new Hess truck at Christmas. Kids my age can be impulsive, I get that, but when your son who almost killed himself asks for a better life overnight, your job as a parent should be as simple as signing on the dotted line.

"No, Aaron." She lets go of my hand and stands. "I have to go to work. We can talk about this later tonight and—"

"Forget it." I storm out of her office, speeding up when she calls my name over and over. I only wipe the tears from my cheeks when I reach the street corner.

I pull out my phone. I really want to call to Thomas or Genevieve but I can't. I can't hit up Brendan either because I'm pretty sure he's pieced together all the Thomas-shaped pieces of my cataclysmic puzzle. The same goes for the other guys. I go through my phone book, scrolling past Baby Freddy, Brendan, Collin, Dad, Deon . . .

I call Evangeline. She doesn't pick up.

I sink against the wall, wondering where the fuck my place is in this fucking universe that fucked me over. Thoughts I shouldn't be thinking creep up on me. They're telling me to seek out oblivion where rest and happiness await. I cry harder because it's not what I want, but once again I am beginning to feel like it is the only solution.

My phone rings. It's not Thomas or Genevieve but it's the next best hope. "Evangeline, hey."

"Hey, kiddo. Sorry I missed your call."

"Don't worry about it. I need to ask for a favor." And in that moment, I realize that one lie will help me reach my life of lies, my only way out. It's not like this lie would hurt anyone. "I've been talking with my mom about getting some Leteo work done but she can't come with me. Are you around this afternoon?"

She's quiet for a bit. "I'll meet you in an hour. Grab a spot in line, okay?"

There's a chance for my happy oblivion, after all.

I'VE BEEN IN LINE on the corner of 168th Street for close to an hour now, waiting to get into the Leteo Institute. I got bored and asked the older man in front of me what he was here for, and he told me he wanted to forget his cheating ex-wife before he kills both her and the twenty-year-old she slept with.

After that, I let a couple of people skip me.

When I finally get inside, I grab a ticket, and sit down in a waiting room as big as the one at the DMV.

On every wall there are two TVs, all rolling out the same Leteo videos.

QUESTION: How safe is this procedure?

ANSWER: Very safe. Our nonsurgical approach allows all memories in the blueprint to be targeted and altered with molecular precision. Our new FDA-approved pills are absolutely painless.

For side effects, please review the brochures, available at all HELP windows.

QUESTION: Where does the name Leteo come from?

ANSWER: Leteo is the Spanish translation of Lethe, the mythological river of forgetfulness in Hades.

QUESTION: Who is the brain behind Leteo?

ANSWER: Dr. Cecilia Inés Ramos, PhD, MD, a Nobel-prize winning neurosurgeon, developed the procedure. Dr. Ramos unlocked the science of alteration while researching psychological disorders. She has a unique personal connection: her sister suffers from paranoid schizophrenia. In the struggle to improve the quality of a beloved sibling's life, Dr. Ramos uncovered opportunities to fold memories over each other. Leteo grew from there. Dr. Ramos resides in Sweden. You can learn more about Leteo's origins in her scientific journals and more about Dr. Ramos in her biography *The Woman Who Made the World Forget*.

QUESTION: How much does it cost to forget? Will my insurance cover this?

ANSWER: Costs for procedures vary per alteration.

For a list of medical plans we are currently accepting, please review the brochures, available at all HELP windows.

QUESTION: Can patients remember what they've forgotten?

ANSWER: Yes, buried memories can resurface. This is known as "unwinding." They are typically triggered by detailed reminders, often care of loved ones, of exact moments or traumas. Specific scents, sounds, or images can also trigger an unwinding.

QUESTION: How long are patients put under for the procedure?

ANSWER: Length of time varies per alteration. Some patients stay overnight and others are released sooner.

QUESTION: Is this procedure total bullshit?

ANSWER: No, this procedure is NOT total bullshit.

Okay, the last one is in my head, but it's exactly the wise-ass type of question I would've submitted back before Kyle pulled this little magic trick on himself. The ticket queue is only on 184 and I'm 224. At least that will give Evangeline some extra time to get off the line outside and in here. Seriously, the amount of lines in this place alone makes me think that if you knock one person into another, it'll create a crazy domino effect and we'll all be amnesiacs by the time the last person falls.

☺ ☺ ☺ ☺

"THERE YOU ARE," EVANGELINE says, sitting down beside me. She's in this silk vest that reminds me of the one Genevieve wore on a movie date last year. But she's still the same old babysitter I knew. "Care to catch me up?"

"Everything's a shit show. That's pretty much it, Evangeline."

"Language," she says. "Talk to me." Her eyes dart around the room. I can't blame her. Mine did, too.

"When I was younger, did you ever think that I might be . . ." I thought I'd be able to spit this out. "Did you ever think that I might like other guys?"

"Not at all. Why do you ask? Do you believe you might be gay?"

"I am . . . but I don't want to be. I want to be made straight."

"Why do you believe being gay is the root of your problems?" she spitfires. I almost feel like she's judging me.

"I had a girlfriend who loved me and good friends. Now I don't. And that all changed when I met an idiot with zero direction in his life." I'm trying not to sound defensive. If this procedure means I can forget my feelings for Thomas and the pain that would come from a goodbye, I need it. "I'm not happy with who I am. That's enough, right?"

Evangeline searches my face. "Listen, kiddo. Even if what you're asking of me is possible, and if you had every last penny needed to cover the costs, this isn't a facility you can simply walk into and schedule work to be done this weekend. Your mother needs to sign off on everything, for starters, and they would force you to speak with therapists over a stretch of time first to determine if your feelings can be resolved over time."

I don't answer.

She massages my shoulder, and I flinch because it's the same thing I did to Thomas on Friday before kissing him; this is one of many memories I need to live without if I'm ever going to be able to live at all. "I know the pain you're going through, Aaron," she says.

"Yeah, because you're older, and I'm just a fucking kid, right?"

"Language," Evangeline mouths.

We sit in silence while I wait for my number to be called. Then she straightens. Someone is waving to her from the other side of the room.

"Do you know that woman?" I ask.

"Stay here," she whispers. "Don't leave."

Yeah, like I'd leave the place that has my ticket to Elysium, a place of perfect happiness. I watch as she checks on this woman before returning my attention to the FAQ slides. Evangeline is back at my side a few minutes later and I ask her again if she knows that person.

"Sort of. She interviewed me for an assistant job at Hunter College's Department of Philosophy. Didn't realize she was pursuing a procedure. Apparently she's on her sixth and possibly final appointment to have memories altered about her husband's affair before he died so she could remember the good and only that. Funny, huh?"

"More like messed up," I say. Guess philosophers are pro-Leteo. My number is finally called and I speed-walk to the HELP window, almost knocking into a crying man.

A brunette in a gray lab coat—Hannah, according to her name tag—clears the screen on her sleek tablet and smiles at Evangeline and me. "Hello. Welcome to Leteo. How can I help you?"

There must be cameras on her because no one working a customer service counter is ever this nice.

"I don't have an appointment or anything, but I want a procedure."

"Absolutely. May I see your ID?"

I pass her my ID. The photo of me is in desperate need of a haircut.

Hannah punches in some keys at a crazy speed and after some chimes, she looks up at me again. "All right, Mr. Soto, what distresses bring you to Leteo today?"

"I'm not feeling very happy," I say, and then I do something that is really downright despicable of me: I place my arm on the counter and I make sure she can see the smiling scar on my wrist in the hopes she'll take me seriously.

"For how long have you been feeling this way?"

"A while."

"Could you be a little more specific, Mr. Soto?"

"A few days, really, but it's been building for months."

"Did any event precipitate these feelings?"

"Yes."

"Could you be a little more specific, Mr. Soto?"

"Are you going to be the one who handles my altering?"

"No, Mr. Soto, I'm simply collecting information for our technicians."

"I'd rather keep my secrets as secretive as possible, if possible," I say.

Hannah turns to Evangeline. "Are you his relative?"

"Family friend," Evangeline says.

Hannah plays with her tablet some more. "I can schedule a consultation for Mr. Soto with our team for the twelfth of August at noon." She reaches into a drawer, pulls out a folder, and slides it toward Evangeline. Before I can demand to be seen sooner, she says, "I'm afraid that is the earliest we can do at this time. We look forward to seeing you in August." She calls the next number, and Evangeline leads me outside.

I'm in a daze, looking up at the squat building in the summer heat, not sure how to process what exactly happened just there.

"I'm sorry that didn't go the way you wanted it to," Evangeline says, looking pretty defeated herself. "This will give you some time to make sure this is what you really want."

"It's not only what I want," I say. "It's what everyone wants."

😃 😃 😃 😃

I HIDE THE FOLDER under my mattress like it's porn or something, and I go outside to grab an iced tea at Good Food's. I'm about to pay Mohad when I catch Brendan in the pastries aisle stuffing coffee cakes into his pockets.

"Do you need a dollar?" I ask, and he jumps. "I can spot you a dollar if you promise not to hit me."

He doesn't flip me off or tell me to go fuck myself, so I walk over and hold out the one-dollar bill.

"I have money," Brendan says. "I'm trying to save up."

"Okay."

"You going to snitch and get me banned?"

"Not if you let me buy that for you. Truce?"

Brendan smirks and hands me the coffee cakes. "Truce."

I buy everything at the counter from Mohad. I feel something like hope as we leave the store together. There's always an awkward silence after our fights. It happened in third grade after he dissed me in front of the entire class for sleeping in the same bed as my parents; it happened again on Christmas morning a few years ago, when he stole a controller my mom had gotten me out from under my tree and claimed his father had gotten him the same one. And even though Brendan was the one who attacked Thomas, I'm guilty for not choosing his side.

"I'm sorry," I say.

"My bad too." Brendan tears open the coffee cake and asks, "You want to play manhunt? I was thinking about getting a game going."

We go to the first court where everyone is gathered around the Skelzies board. They're talking about how to get a girl wet with only their fingers and how you don't need a condom if you're hitting it from the back. I don't try to fake a laugh or chime in. I wouldn't do that, anyway, and this way it's natural: I can look and feel the same, like I'm still one of them. Brendan nods, as if to say I'm cool again, and all is good.

"Fuck Skelzies. Manhunt time. Aaron already volunteered to be hunter."

"Asshole," I mutter as everyone runs off into different directions.

I check underneath cars for Skinny-Dave, but he must actually be sober because he wasn't dumb enough to hide there today. I do a quick sweep for where Me-Crazy might be hiding down here. No luck and I'm cool with maybe never solving that mystery because spending more time with that insane bastard isn't high up on my to-do list.

I get back to the courtyard and spot Fat-Dave up on the roof and he moons me. I flip him off. I see Nolan and Deon and chase them as they run out of the gates. They split up right when I see Thomas walking toward me, and for a second I think about catching him until I remember he's not part of the game.

He's actually here.

Thomas quickly says, "I know things are weird even though we didn't want them to be." He looks me straight in the eyes, and I try and catch my breath. I don't know whether to float or sink yet. "But you're my best friend and I miss having you around. I know you don't actually have a thing for me. Drinking confuses people like that, so we'll call the whole thing taboo and not talk about it for the next ten years or so. Let's hang and talk about Sun Warden while I apply to a job to—"

"Why can't I like you?"

"Because it wouldn't work out in the long run," Thomas says.

"Because I don't fit into your little hierarchy of needs?"

"Because I'm straight. Stretch." His voice has an edge now. "I thought we wanted to forget it ever happened."

"Yeah, well. Forgetting isn't as easy as you're making it sound." My throat tightens. "I can't sit around you and act like nothing happened, or to wait around for you to figure things out."

"There's nothing to figure out," Thomas says. "I know I can be really confused about what I should be doing with my life and how I feel like I don't belong, but I have no doubts about what gets my heart going and my dick hard. That's not meant to be a blow to you, Stretch, but it's just the way I'm wired."

"I was like that once. I denied it, but then I met you over there by that fence and it flipped around everything I ever thought about myself. I didn't want to be unhappy so I stopped dating someone I can't actually love. I get it if you need more time."

"I can't live up to this fantasy playing out in your head," Thomas shoots back.

Without thinking about it, I hug him and hold on to him even though he's not hugging me back. "I can't promise I'll wait."

I don't think the pain will vanish the way Evangeline thinks it will. I'm sure waiting for unfulfilled expectations will only make weeks feel like months, months feel like decades, and decades feel like my end of days. If there's no happiness waiting for me there, then I lived a life without laughs and smiles and that's not living at all.

I turn my back on him.

I move back into the complex and walk across the third court when two big hands grab my shoulders. I half expect it to be

Thomas spinning me around to lead me somewhere private, but instead I find myself falling forward and rolling into a pillar by my building. Fear chokes me. I doubt it's those bastards from the Joey Rosa Projects because I had nothing to do with Me-Crazy beating their boys down.

This attack is personal. These are my friends. I pick myself up. It's Me-Crazy, backed by Brendan, Skinny-Dave, and Nolan—too many to outrun.

"Fight back, faggot," Me-Crazy challenges, rolling his eyes back until they're just white. He's going to start pounding on his head any moment now and I'll be laid out.

"What the fuck is your problem?" I ask him.

"Me-Crazy saw you hugging your boyfriend," Me-Crazy says.

Nolan chimes in, "Why you playing with other dudes? You had a bomb-ass girlfriend, and Bren told us you stopped hitting that."

"It's for your own good," Brendan says, too ashamed to look me in the eye like the man he wants me to be and thinks he is. He cracks his knuckles and rocks back and forth, and I almost laugh at how ridiculous he looks.

I get in his face, so close that I could kiss him and really piss them all off. "Come on, guys. Try and beat it out of me."

The rules of the street aren't clear, but I've known people—Brendan, actually—who walked away from a serious beat-down from our rival high school because he kicked one guy's ass and earned everyone's respect. Maybe if I fuck up Brendan, or Skinny-Dave who looks too high for his own good, that'll get them to back off.

Brendan shoves me. I recover. I shove him back and slam into him with the hardest head-butt I can swing without knocking myself out. Brendan, somewhat dazed, fakes right and swings a hard uppercut into my chin with his left. I kick him in his knee, hard like he taught me, and he collapses so

I knee him in the nose. Then Skinny-Dave comes at me with a sucker punch, but it's Me-Crazy who actually tackles me down to the ground and I know I've lost. I can't move out from under his grip. Now it's all pain. Resisting gets harder and everything becomes dimmer and blurrier with each punch to my face and each blow to my chest. Me-Crazy is roaring while he strangles me, and Skinny-Dave and Nolan stomp me out.

I shout and twist and cry and guard my face with the one arm I manage to get free. Me-Crazy gets off of me and I think it's over. I'm so dizzy. The ground I'm crumbled on is spinning around, first one way and then another. I don't even bother trying to crawl away. I feel like I'm falling . . .

No, someone is picking me up. I confused up with down. But the terrifying sensation of Crazy Train Mode is insanely familiar. He runs with me over his shoulder, and I hear Brendan yelling at him to stop, that he's taking it too far, but Me-Crazy keeps running. I don't know where we're going until we crash through the glass door of my building and I'm sprawled across the lobby floor.

There's an explosion in the back of my head, a delayed reaction. Blood fills my mouth. *This is what death feels like,* I think. I scream like someone is turning a hundred knives inside of me, spitting up blood as I do. And I'm not crying because of the attack. I'm crying because there's new noise in my head, and it builds from a couple faded echoes into an uproar of jumbled voices—all the memories I once forgot have been unwound.

PART ZERO: UNHAPPINESS

HERE TODAY, GONE TOMORROW

(AGE NINE)

It's way past my bedtime but I can't sleep because of a really real nightmare—myself.

There's been enough crying in my family lately but I can't control myself. Mom tries to calm me down in the kitchen with cranberry juice. It's stupid, but I cry harder because I'm jealous of Brendan and how his house is better with better juice and better video games because his parents have more money than we do.

Mom hugs me to her shoulder as I sit on the kitchen counter. "Baby, you can tell me anything. I love you as you are."

I don't want to tell anyone, but I'm scared something will happen to me if I don't.

"Baby, my son, you are safe. Nothing bad will ever happen to you, I promise."

"I think I'm . . ." I take a deep breath. "I can't say it. I'm too scared."

Eric pops up from around our old and busted stereo system and shouts, "You're gay! No one cares!"

"NO! NO! I'm scared I'm going to become crazy like Uncle Connor and eat too many pills and die." I punch this plastic bin where we keep packets of salt, pepper, and ketchup Mom pockets from restaurants and everything spills onto the floor. "You're an asshole!"

I got my bad temper and bad mouth from Dad. I jump off the counter to punch him in his stupid face but Mom drags me back.

"Aaron! Aaron! Stop! Eric, back to bed *now*!"

Eric doesn't taunt me like he usually does whenever Mom or Dad or my cousins hold me back from fighting him. He shrugs. "I'm only trying to help, freak."

Freak. Freak. Freak. Freak.

(AGE TEN)

MOM BOUGHT US THE newest PlayStation for Christmas, plus a discounted X-Men game because she had a little extra money left over. We're playing and Eric chooses Wolverine because he likes playing as the main characters. He calls himself a "one-man army" since he's always good with them. I choose Jean Grey because she can transform into Dark Phoenix and becomes extra powerful. She has this really cool flight-and-fire trick I saw in the video's game demo at the store.

"Stop choosing the girl characters! Be a boy!"

I choose Cyclops instead.

☹ ☹ ☹ ☹

(AGE ELEVEN)

THE SUPERINTENDENT BRINGS HIS wrench out at 11:00 A.M. like every summer and jerks open the fire hydrant. Jets of water blast free and some kids stop to take off their shirts while others charge straight in to cool down.

Brendan takes his shirt off.

He's been my best friend since first grade and I see him all the time but I don't stop looking at him until Baby Freddy tells me we're playing tag and I'm it. I only chase after Brendan, like a magnet. When I finally catch him, I tag him on his bare shoulder, and my hand stays there a little longer than it needs to.

☹ ☹ ☹ ☹

BRENDAN FINALLY COMES BACK from visiting his family in North Carolina this weekend and I'm so excited. While he was gone, I really got into comic books to pass the time that would've been spent playing with him. I even draw one just for him.

It's a Pokémon comic with its pictures colored in by pens. There are a lot of eraser streaks from my outlining stage but he won't care. It's about Brendan becoming a Pokémon master and shows how unstoppable he is throughout all his gym battles.

I hope he likes it.

☹ ☹ ☹ ☹

(AGE TWELVE)

MRS. OLIVIA TAUGHT THE class about Shakespeare and all his plays today.

I'm on the couch next to Dad while he watches basketball with Eric. The game is really boring. Since learning about theater and our school's drama club, I want to become an actor who will star in really cool action movies like *Scorpius Hawthorne* with sword fights and magical battles. I would rather watch movies than a bunch of sweaty guys trying to put a ball through a hoop so I can study how to be an actor, especially since so much has changed since Shakespeare was alive. (If he was ever really alive. I think he might be made up, like Santa and Jesus but grown-ups tell you he's real.)

"Dad, did you know that men used to play the roles of women in Shakespeare's plays? That's pretty funny, right?"

Dad turns away from the game for the first time all night. "You're a boy," he says. "Don't ever act like a girl."

(AGE THIRTEEN)

BRENDAN RUNS UP TO me. "Yo! Yo! I just got my first blow job!"

I get a little heated. I'm just surprised, you know. "Whoa. Awesome. From who?"

"Some girl who's friends with Kenneth and Kyle. She thinks Kyle is cuter because he's coming into his mustache, but I talked a good game and got her into my pants. I am a god!"

I pat his back. "Good job, dude. Good job."

Brendan sees Baby Freddy coming out of our building with his baseball equipment. "Hold up, let me go tell that little shit." Brendan runs off and I feel a little sick.

(AGE FIFTEEN)

THERE'S DEFINITELY SOMETHING GOING on between us: we spend all of Earth Science passing illustrated notes back and forth instead of listening to Ms. O mispronounce minerals with her thick Puerto Rican accent; we always come up with bullshit excuses to keep hanging out after school; we trade stories at this pretty cool chicken spot; we go to the movies and throw candy and chocolate into our buckets of popcorn; we rest our arms next to each other's. Mostly we play around a lot in the park, just the two of us, like a secret. A secret we suck at hiding because everyone already suspects we're dating, but I'm still pretty damn shocked when I hear: "You should be my boyfriend."

I gotta admit, I thought I was doomed to a life of hookups like Brendan and Skinny-Dave. Or more like Baby Freddy who always chases and never catches anything. I never thought someone would give me the hand-holding treatment. This must mean that I was wrong about everything I thought about myself. I scoot a little closer to Genevieve on the park bench. I squeeze her hand and say, "Sure. I'll give being your boyfriend a shot."

I DON'T UNDERSTAND.

It all felt so right in that moment I agreed to date her. I was the straightest guy I knew, but when I got home that night, I was still thinking about other guys. Not Brendan anymore; I got turned off from him after hearing him talk about sleeping with girls as conquests. No, I think about the dudes I see undress in the locker room at school, the ones sitting across from me on the bus staring at nothing and likely thinking about their normal crushes.

I don't think about Genevieve. She's staring up at me now like I'm all she thinks about, like I should be inching toward her lips, as she is mine. I go for it, to prove myself wrong. I turn at the last second and we bump heads.

"Ow!" Genevieve laughs. "Watch it, dumb-idiot."

"Sorry." I rub my forehead.

"Take two?"

I nod and she jokingly backs away as if she were in danger of another head-butt. She pulls me toward her and when she turns left, I freak out and turn left too and we hit each other again. Maybe this time she'll take it as a message from the universe that I'm the wrong boy to be kissing.

I know I can't possibly be fooling her, or anyone, and that's my problem—without her, I definitely won't be fooling anyone. I pull her to me, and this time I get it right, and when it's done I laugh, which probably wouldn't make anyone feel good. But Genevieve smiles—and then punches me in the arm.

"I suspect I'll be hitting you a lot."

☹ ☹ ☹ ☹

(AGE SIXTEEN—OCTOBER, NINE MONTHS AGO)

I'M IN THE SCHOOL library rereading *Scorpius Hawthorne and the Legion of the Dragon* when I catch him looking at me from the fantasy section. Collin Vaughn is another junior, and he's what I like to call an almost-jock: he hasn't been able to get on the basketball team since freshman year but acts superior anyway during gym class.

Collin walks over with two books and pulls out the chair across from me. "Cool if I sit?"

"Cool," I say. "I see you reading these fantasy books and comics a lot during class and lunch." His brown eyes wander to my Scorpius Hawthorne book. "Are these any good?" He slides over *The Hitchhiker's Guide to the Galaxy* and *The Hobbit.*

"*Hitchhiker's Guide* is really fucking funny," I say.

The librarian rolls her eyes at me before returning to her trashy-looking romance novel.

"I haven't read *The Hobbit*, but the movies are epic," I add.

He knocks on the Scorpius Hawthorne book. "Ha. I haven't read *these* books, but saw the movies."

Some people are obsessed with the works of Jane Austen or William Shakespeare or Stephen King, but I grew up with the demonic boy wizard, so whenever someone my age tells me they haven't read these books, I imagine a Reaping spell being fired into the sky because a childhood is dead. "Why the hell not?"

Collin smiles. "Never got around to them."

"But you willingly walked into those movie theaters and kicked your feet up?"

"Aren't they the same thing?"

"You are the worst," I tell him. "If I bring you the first Scorpius Hawthorne book tomorrow, will you read it this weekend?"

"I'll give it a shot. Meet back here tomorrow?"

"We'll keep meeting back here until you can recite The Seven Laws of Hybrid Magic."

☹ ☹ ☹ ☹

I'M ACTING LIKE I'M reading the final pages of *Legion of the Dragon* when Collin comes into the library looking for me. He sits right across from me, not asking this time, and says, "You got the goods?" It's a tone someone might mistake for drug dealing.

I slide the backpack over to him. I packed the first two Scorpius Hawthorne books plus *The Once and Future King*, *A Game of Thrones*, and a couple comics in case he's in the insanely minuscule percentage of the universe that doesn't like the demonic boy wizard who inspired a fucking amusement park and seven films. "I tossed in some classics too. What got you into fantasy?"

Collin opens the backpack and opens the first page of *Scorpius Hawthorne and the Monster's Scepter*; if this Leteo Institute weren't bullshit and I could get a free procedure, I would definitely have my memory of ever reading this series buried so I could relive these books again for the first time. "I like pretending, I guess." The pages are yellowed and he sees my illustration of the horned Alastor Riggs, the Overlord of the Silver Crown School. "You draw?"

"Yeah. It's a thing I do," I say. I normally don't think I'm an awesome artist, because one should always exhibit some modesty, but Collin studies my drawings like he would bid high for them in one of our dumb school auctions. "You should be honored I'm loaning you my original and sacred copies, but I should warn you that I will destroy you like a Bone Grinder if you ruin them."

"I actually get that reference," Collin says, and it makes me feel like there's still hope for him. "Those are the trolls from the first movie, right?" He just compared a skinless demon to a dumb troll—hope killed.

☹ ☹ ☹ ☹

A COUPLE OF WEEKS later, Collin hands me back my copy of *Scorpius Hawthorne and the Hollows,* the final book in the series. Inside is a note asking me to check yes or no without a question. But I know what he's talking about and it doesn't scare me like I thought it would if this day ever came.

I check yes and slide it back across the table.

Collin reads it, folds the paper into his front pocket, nods and says, "Cool."

After school there's a basketball game and I tell Genevieve I'm going to hang back and watch it. She thought it was weird, but wasn't too bothered by it because it gave her a little extra time to focus on her homework without me calling to distract her. Collin told his girlfriend, Nicole, that he wanted to see if any of the players who made the cut are actually worth anything.

But we don't watch the game.

I chase him up the staircase to the top floor and, out of breath, I ask him, "Why me? And don't try and shrug your way out of this one, or tell me I'm cool."

He shrugs.

I fake going downstairs.

He grabs my arm. "Because I could tell you were different without it being obvious to everyone else you were different, okay? Someone would have to sit down and get to know you to actually figure it out, if that makes sense. And I like what I've seen so far. That do it for you?"

"Sure, even if that speech was a bit much."

"Asshole. Your turn: Why me?"

I shrug, get in his face, and tell him he's cool. We both look downstairs at the same time to make sure no one's coming up, and then we turn and kiss.

(AGE SIXTEEN—NOVEMBER, EIGHT MONTHS AGO)

"I'M TEACHING YOU HOW to ride a bike," Collin says as he wheels over a beat-up ten-speed with a popped chain toward me. "You're sixteen and officially ten years too old to wait around for your daddy to teach you." He kneels over and fixes the chain; I can see the skin of his lower back.

"Maybe I'm too old to learn."

"No, you'll never get a driver's license if you can't even ride a bike. Come on, you can act like it's Scorpius's broom. The Red Sprite, right?"

"Sold."

I get on and Collin tells me the basics. I expect him to hold my back or my shoulder but we're in his neighborhood and his friends are around. I pedal and fall over, almost banging my head into a fire hydrant. He extends his hand to me and asks, “Any chance I’m forgetting a broom with training wheels?”

☹ ☹ ☹ ☹

COLLIN HAS ALREADY LOST both of his virginities.

He got it on with this girl Suria when he was fourteen, after she gave him a hand job under the bleachers in the gym. Then he let this guy plow him last year when he was vacationing in the Poconos.

I still have both of my virginities to lose. I’ve only gotten as far as groping with Genevieve. I want to take it to the next level with Collin.

We recently tried doing it in a nearby building’s staircase, but didn’t get very far undressing ourselves before we heard someone coming down. The same deal with this abandoned porch up on the balcony a few nights ago, which was really risky, but worth risking, I think. We’ve ventured far away from my block and stumble on to a hiding space behind a wired fence, in-between a meat market and a flower shop, businesses of death and life.

“It smells like dead cow,” I say. “But kind of nice too. Weird.”

“Jesus, do you want me to go get you a flower?” Collin asks, flipping me off. We always flip each other off because it’s how we remain guys, you know. Collin steps over a rusty bike without wheels, leaving me to wonder the next time he’ll try and teach me how to ride a bike, and he wrenches the bottom of the fence until it folds back enough for us to crawl through.

It’s dark out and we’re so far away from our friends on the block and our girlfriends at home. I bet the fucking moon can’t even see us right now. I shove him and he shoves me back. I tackle him against the wall, unbuttoning his shirt, and it's all condoms and awkward memories from there.

☹ ☹ ☹ ☹

IT'S CHILLIER TODAY, SO we can't have sex when we go to our spot. We decide to leave a physical mark instead. I borrowed some cans of spray paint from Genevieve she had left over from an assignment a year ago. I was happy as hell when Collin agreed to this because it meant we shared something beyond sex.

Collin sprays a black-and-blue world onto the dirty wall. I hear police sirens so I have to think quickly in case they're coming for us. I streak a green arrow over the world. It looks like the universal icon for boys, which makes sense because we're men no matter what we do together. Collin adds a crown and makes us kings.

The sirens fade into the distance so we hang around and keep decorating—for lack of a straighter word. He sprays some weird, shapeless creature on the other wall. "Hey, can I borrow a kiss?"

"Nah."

"Okay, let's try this again: kiss me or I'll spray you," Collin threatens.

I smile. I walk toward him and he aims the can at me. "Don't fucking do it, Collin Vaughn." I back up and a spray of blue hits me in the chest. "You motherfucker." I pick up a can and spray green all over his back while he runs around. The war goes on for ten minutes until we're both covered in blue and green and black and I have no idea how I'll even begin to explain this to my parents.

☹ ☹ ☹ ☹

(AGE SIXTEEN—DECEMBER, SEVEN MONTHS AGO)

KENNETH WAS FUCKING GUNNED down yesterday and it's all Kyle's fucking fault. Kyle couldn't fucking help himself and just had to fucking fuck Jordan's fucking sister, even though we all fucking knew Jordan is the kind of fucking guy who would fucking kill someone if you fucking crossed him. Those bullets were fucking meant for fucking Kyle but no, they fucking found their way into fucking Kenneth when he was fucking innocently coming home from his fucking clarinet lessons at school. We will never get the fucking chance to see Kenneth on a fucking stage, playing us a song we would fucking call him a little bitch for, even if we are so fucking proud of him for fucking making something of himself.

Thankfully I have Collin here. He is being a real fucking champ and letting me cry into his chest. He promises distractions, like movies and comics, but the best fucking distraction of all is having someone who will hold me whenever I'm fucking lost and defeated.

COLLIN AND I WERE pumped to see the new *Avengers* movie together—until our girlfriends invited themselves to join us. But like good boyfriends, we let them tag along. Genevieve fought to sit next to Nicole so they could swoon and stuff over Robert Downey Jr. but Collin argued this was a dude's movie and the dudes should get to sit next to each other. Collin even faked jealousy over them wanting to talk about other guys. Crazy.

An hour into the movie, I reach for a handful of popcorn from the bucket on Collin's lap, slyly brushing his arm. I think pretty little of myself for being such a dick with Genevieve directly to my left, and even when she's far away, but Collin makes me happy and that's that.

"Best. Fucking. Movie. Ever," Collin whispers to me, pressing his lips against my ear for a second. This double date is kind of a turn-on, but there's a big hole here: we won't go home with each other.

"I've seen better," I whisper back.

"The hell you have."

I punch his arm and elbow him. (Tip: your girlfriends won't suspect you're sleeping with your guy friend if you're hitting them.)

"Get a room," Nicole hisses after some popcorn flies on her. (Or maybe they will.)

Genevieve calls my name right as Collin leans in to whisper something else to me and I turn to him. I laugh at his dumb joke about a monkey and a dragon in a bar, pissing off others in the theater. Genevieve included, probably. I want to ask her what's up but I can't expose myself for ignoring her in favor of my undercover boyfriend—or whatever we are—so instead I lean in on her and whisper, "I cannot wait for later tonight, Gen."

☹ ☹ ☹ ☹

GENEVIEVE PULLS MY BELT and drags me to the edge of her bed. Her father is out of town until tomorrow, for a reason I can't remember, and it's obvious what her intentions were after the double date. If I want to keep what I have with Collin, I have to play along so she doesn't get suspicious. She climbs onto her bed and relaxes on her knees, pausing in front of my face.

"You want this, right?"

I should tell her something like "Not really" and just walk away and call up Collin. Instead, I grab her shoulders and pull her to me, kissing her neck, face, and lips. "You're beautiful," I whisper right into her ear.

These seem like all the right things to do.

She takes off my shirt and throws it across the room. "Unbutton my shirt," she says, tracing circles into my chest with her fingers. Every time I rip a button off, she breathes this low moan that seems artificial, but it's crazy to think we're both faking our way through this. I drop her shirt and we study each other's bodies. She's in a green bra she probably bought for tonight while I'm in the same boxers as yesterday.

Genevieve falls to her back and turns off her bedside lamp. "Come here."

Hopefully the moonlight doesn't expose the dread on my face that I'm disguising with suggestive eyebrow bounces and smirks as I crawl toward her. I grip her waist and before I can kiss her, I slap a hand on my bare stomach and groan. "I feel like I might puke . . . I think it was the popcorn. Too much butter."

This sensual Genevieve that confuses me switches off and the real Genevieve is back. "Do you want me to go get you something from the kitchen? I have some ginger ale and bread—"

"I think I should try and sleep it off. That usually does the trick."

"Okay, but . . . Babe, are you sure you don't want to stay awake and see if it passes? Tonight's the only night we can finally do this until who knows when."

"I know. I want to do this but—" Whatever lie that follows doesn't matter because I already told her the truth for once: I don't want to do this.

(AGE SIXTEEN—JANUARY, SIX MONTHS AGO)

THIS WAS A BIT of a shock, but Collin got me something for Christmas: a twenty-dollar gift card to Comic Book Asylum.

I've been begging Mohad, the big boss man at Good Food's, for a job and he said he might need a cashier soon. I did a few chores for Dad, like washing his car and running out to get him sandwiches from Joey's, and he gave me fifteen dollars to buy something nice for Genevieve. But I didn't spend it on her.

Okay, I spent four dollars on a blank pad and created a flip book for her, but I spent the rest of it on two copies of *The Dark Alternates*, Issue #1 for Collin and me. It's the start of a new Marvel series where all the heroes are combating their dark counterparts in a medieval landscape of fiery storms and dead warriors. We read them both in his hallway the day after Christmas.

I go to Comic Book Asylum when they reopen for business on January 2. I head straight to the counter before I'm tempted to spend the gift card on some comics I'll never find in the dollar cart. I catch up with Stan about his holidays and then ask, "Could I get a monthly subscription for *The Dark Alternates*?"

"Have you read the first yet? It's epic, bro. When that tornado destroyed their headquarters I lost my head."

"That was my friend's favorite part too," I say. He rings me up for the New Year's promo and it comes out to twenty-four dollars. I use up the entire gift card and pay the difference. "So there are seven issues, right?"

"The magic number. Once a month."

I have six more comics to read with Collin.

Awesome.

I'VE BEEN THROWING MYSELF into a new project lately to distract myself from several things, like Kenneth's death, Kyle's distance from all of us, and my guilt over playing Genevieve. It's a comic book about a hero I've made up, Sun Warden. I once had this dream where I was so hungry I ate the sun and my bones were really hot, but I didn't blow up or melt or anything like that. Seemed like a decent enough idea. I think once I finish the comic, I'm going to give it to Collin as a gift.

☹ ☹ ☹ ☹

(AGE SIXTEEN—FEBRUARY, FIVE MONTHS AGO)

"AARON, YOU CAN TELL me anything."

I'm sitting across from Mom in her bedroom, and my heart is pounding like crazy.

"Since you were a kid, I've told you this. Remember when you didn't want to tell me that—"

"I like guys, Mom." I spit out the words. I stare at dirty laundry on the floor. "Sorry. I just . . . yeah."

She steps to me and lifts my chin, but I still don't look at her. "Baby, there's nothing to be sorry about."

"I've, you know, lied and been a dick," I say. She holds my hand and I almost start crying what Collin would call little-bitch tears because guys don't cry. "I can go stay somewhere, I don't know where, but somewhere if—"

"Aaron Soto, you are going nowhere. Not until college. Then you get your ass out of here, graduate, get a job, and pay me back all the money I've spent on you since giving birth." She smiles and I force a smile back.

"So, what? You going to tell me you always knew or something like that?"

"I'm better than that, my son."

"Thanks. I owe you one."

"You owe me about a million dollars, but that's beside the point. I'm happy you're ready and you seem okay with it. That's always been my biggest worry, that you wouldn't understand it."

I know what she means. I've been hanging out less with Brendan and my friends, and they've seen me crossing the street to meet with Collin. He does come over and hang sometimes, but I try to keep Collin all to myself for the most part. I just know they won't be so accepting of what we're doing, and everyone's mood has been off since we lost Kenneth.

"Is there a young gentleman in your life?" Mom asks.

"Yeah, but I bet you're playing dumb and already know it's Collin." I talk about him enough. When someone makes you happy, it's pretty impossible to cage the excitement.

She sits down beside me on the bed where we all slept together until I was thirteen, before I moved out into the living room with Eric to sleep in our own beds. "Do you have a photo?"

"I'm sixteen, no shit I have a photo." I scroll through my phone's photo album with Mom looking over my shoulders. We slide past a picture of me with Genevieve.

"So I take it you and Genevieve aren't actually dating then, are you?"

☹ ☹ ☹ ☹

TELLING MOM WAS ONE thing. Telling Dad is another.

He's in the living room smoking and watching what he claims is a very important Yankees game. It's in the ninth inning and the teams are tied. I consider backing out, maybe waiting another week or so, but maybe he won't actually care when I tell him. Maybe all that stuff he said when I was younger, about never acting like a girl or playing with any female action figures, will go away once he realizes I am the way I am without any choice. Maybe he'll accept me.

Mom follows me into the living room and sits down on Eric's bed. "Mark, do you have a minute? Aaron has something he wants to talk about."

He exhales cigarette smoke. "I'm listening." He never looks away from the game.

"Forget it, we can do it another time." I turn around to go back into my parents' room, but Mom catches my hand. She knows I may never feel ready to do this, that I may keep finding excuses to push this off until long after my dad is gone, and then *maybe* I'll go to his grave and come out. But the time has to be now so I can feel as comfortable in my home as I am chilling with Collin.

"Mark," Mom says again.

His eyes are still on the TV. I take a deep breath.

"Dad, I hope you're cool with this, but I sort of, kind of am dating someone and . . ." I can already see him getting confused, like I'm challenging him to solve an algebraic equation with no pen, paper, or calculator. "And that someone is my friend Collin."

Only then does Dad turn toward us. His face immediately goes from confused to furious. You would think the Yankees not only lost the game but also decided to give up and retire the team forever. He points his cigarette at Mom. "This is all your doing. You have to be the one to tell him he's wrong." He's talking about me like I'm not even in the room.

"Mark, we always said we would love our kids no matter what, and—"

"Empty *fucking* promise, Elsie. Make him cut it out or get him out of here."

"If there's something about homosexuality you don't understand, you can talk to your son about it in a kind way," Mom says, maintaining a steady tone that's both fearless for me and respectful toward Dad. We all know what he's capable of. "If you want to ignore it or need time, we can give that to you, but Aaron isn't going anywhere."

Dad places his cigarette in the ashtray and then kicks over

the hamper he was resting his feet on. We back up. I don't often wish this, but I really, really wish Eric were here right now in case this gets as ugly as I think it might. He points his finger at me. "I'll fucking throw him out myself."

My mom guards me.

Dad wraps his big hands around her throat, shaking her. "Huh, you still think he's making the right choice?"

I run over, grab his TV remote, and hit him so hard in the back of his head with it that the batteries pop out. He shoves my mom into the intercom phone and she falls to the floor, desperately trying to catch her breath. Before I can check on her, my dad—the man who fucking played catch with me—punches me in the back of my head, and I crash into a tower of Eric's used games. He drags me by my shirt collar and leaves me outside the apartment door. "I'll be damned if I'm alive the day you bring a boy home, you fucking faggot."

I hear the door lock and I cry harder than I ever have in my entire life because I can't change the way I am, not as fast and as easily as my father just stopped being Dad.

LAST NIGHT I WAS left out in the hallway banging on the door for over an hour. I didn't want my father to strangle or beat me to death, but I was so scared for my mom. With all my freaking out, someone called the cops. When they knocked on the door, my father opened up and simply left with them. He didn't even look at me as they handcuffed him and read him his rights. Mom went to the hospital to make sure she was okay.

It's absolutely the worst nightmare stored in my memory bank.

I needed Collin and our hangout at Pelham Park today. He taught me how to be my own compass around the city since I'm always getting lost despite having grown up here. We didn't talk a lot about what happened last night, but we did admit that it's time to break up with our girlfriends. Sure, they shield us from events like yesterday unfolding, but we can't expect to keep leading them on to keep ourselves safe.

"You better not get clingy like Nicole," Collin says while we're riding the train home. "She stays hitting me up in the middle of the night when I'm trying to sleep."

"Unlikely," I say, even though it's very likely. It's weirdly possessive and obsessive to like someone; you want to learn all of his stories before anyone else and sometimes you want to be the only one who knows at all.

I bump my leg into his, and he bumps mine back. If we were the typical boy-and-girl couple, we could kiss and hold each other and no one would give a flying fuck. But if you're two guys like us, riding the Bronx tracks, you better make sure you hide any sign of affection if you want to fly under the radar. I've known this for the longest—I just hoped it wouldn't matter. Someone whistles at us and I instantly knew I was wrong.

These two guys who were competing in a pull-up contest a few minutes ago walk up to us. The taller one with his jeans leg rolled up asks, "Yo. You two homos faggots?"

We both tell him no.

His friend, who smells like straight-up armpits, presses his middle finger between Collin's eyes. He sucks his teeth. "They lying. I bet their little dicks are getting hard right now."

Collin smacks the dude's hand, which is just as big a mistake as my mom trying to save me from being thrown out the house last night. "Fuck you."

Nightmare after nightmare.

One slams my head into the railing, and the other hammers Collin with punches. I try punching the first guy in his nose, but I'm too dizzy and miss. I have no idea how many times he punches me or at what point I end up on the sticky floor with

Collin trying to shield me before he's kicked to the side. Collin turns to me, crying these involuntary tears from shock and pain. His kind brown eyes roll back when he's kicked in the head. I cry out for help but no one fucking breaks up the fight. No one fucking does the right thing.

The train stops and the doors open but there's no chance for escape. For us, at least. Those two guys laugh while they run out onto the platform. New passengers walk in and some just grab a seat before there are none left. Others act like they don't see us. Only a couple of people come to our aid. But it's too late.

COLLIN REFUSED TO GO to the hospital. He said he couldn't afford it and even though my mom could probably help him for free, he knew she would call his parents and maybe tell them everything, including that thing he never wants to share.

I get home thirty minutes later, still holding my balled-up shirt to my nose to soak up the little blood coming down. I came in through the garage so I wouldn't have to pass any of my friends all fucked up like this. I limp straight to the bathroom and the door is cracked open, lights on inside. Eric's supposed to be working at GameStop, and Mom's visiting one of her patients in prison. I open the door and when I see who's sitting in the bathtub, I drop the shirt and blood just spills down my face and chest.

Holy shit.

Dad.

His eyes are open but he's not looking at me.

He didn't take his clothes off before getting into the tub.

The water is a deep red, stained by the blood spilling from his slit wrists.

He came home to kill himself.

He came home to kill himself before I could bring a boy here.

He came home to kill himself because of me.

All this blood.

All this red makes me black out.

☹ ☹ ☹ ☹

MY LEGS HURT LIKE hell but I don't stop running through the park. I hop onto a bench and soar off of it, landing hard on my bad leg from when I got jumped, but I keep going. I usually slow down when I'm racing Collin so he doesn't feel as bad. But not today. These pigeons eating bread from a knocked-over trash can scatter when I charge through them. I keep running, but the memory of my father dead in a bath of red keeps chasing me and it's impossible to stop until I trip over my shoelaces and tumble into dirt.

Collin catches up to me and falls to his knees, panting heavily. "You . . . okay?"

I'm shaking and ready to pound my fists on the ground like a child throwing a tantrum. He places a hand on my knee and I lunge up and hug him so hard I pop his back.

"Ouch! Shit," he says, breaking free. "Cool it with that."

I look around to see if anyone else is in the park. We're alone. But Collin has his own ghosts too because of the last time I did something as simple as bumping his leg with mine; naturally someone would burn us at the stake if they caught us hugging. "I'm sorry."

It's only been two days, but I miss his face without the bruises and swollen eye.

Collin stands and I think he's about to help me up but he just scratches his head. "I gotta go get cleaned up before I meet up with Nicole. She wants to talk."

"Can you stick around for a little bit longer?" I see a *no* forming so I quickly say, "Forget it. Go do what you gotta do."

And he does.

☹ ☹ ☹ ☹

(AGE SIXTEEN—MARCH, FOUR MONTHS AGO)

NONE OF US WENT to the funeral. There was a closed casket. I'm sure the service was poorly attended. The hated and hateful aren't exactly a popular crowd. Besides, he wouldn't have wanted me there, which made it a missed opportunity to piss on his grave, but I ended up meeting with Collin instead and that's poetic enough for me.

I'm sitting on the ground, and Collin is pacing back and forth. He still hasn't really offered any real condolences or even hugged me, and it's starting to get to me.

"He did this because of me," I tell Collin, even though I've told him this over and over already. "Because of what we do together."

"Maybe we should take a break," Collin says. "Some time apart could be good for you."

"That's the last thing I want right now." I don't add the obvious, that we just got jumped *together* and my father killed himself. "We need to talk to the girls soon. I need you, uh . . . I need us to figure this out. I can't have something else going wrong right now."

"This is shitty timing, I know, but I actually can't break up with Nicole, Aaron. Everything between us has been a slip. Look at everything that's happened to you alone . . . You get why nothing else can go down between us, right?"

This is one of those times where you swear you have to be sleeping and living a nightmare because it's so impossible that your life can only be a string of bad things until you're completely abandoned.

"You can't do this," I say. "I told my mother about you. My father killed himself because of us. We got jumped on the train because of who we are."

Collin keeps pacing and refuses to look me in the eye. "We chose to be the wrong people. It just can't work. Nicole's pregnant and I was trying to talk her into not keeping the kid before I told you, but she is, so I gotta be a man again."

Another bad thing but not unexpected, that was always a risk. "So you knocked her up, whatever. That doesn't make you straight and you're never going to be—"

"It's not happening, Aaron." He walks to the fence. I expect him to come back like he's still pacing, but he just crouches down and leaves without another word.

Something snaps in my head and I'm fighting back tears.

I slipped too.

Whatever, I have a girlfriend too.

I don't need him.

(AGE SIXTEEN—APRIL, THREE MONTHS AGO)

I KNOW DAD KILLED himself because of me.

Mom thinks that his recent jail stint tipped him over the edge, that his many chemical imbalances caught up with him.

Now I keep searching for happiness so I don't end up like he did.

I learn about this town called Happy in Texas and think about how that must be the greatest place to live.

I teach myself how to say and read and write *happy* in Spanish, German, Italian, and even Japanese but I would have to draw that last one out.

I discover the happiest animal in the world, the quokka. He's a cheeky little bastard that's always smiling.

But it's not enough.

The memories are still rattling around my head, twisting

into me like a knife. I don't want to wait around to see what comes next for me in this tragic story I'm living. I open up one of my father's unused razors and cut into my wrist like he did, slit in a curve until it smiles so everyone will know I died for happiness.

I was expecting relief but instead it's the saddest pain I've ever experienced. I never once stop feeling empty or unworthy of anyone's rescue, not even when the thin line on my wrist makes everything go red.

I DON'T WANT TO die and I didn't.

I spent a few days at the hospital where I met with this therapist, Dr. Slattery, who was the worst. I thought it was just me who couldn't stand him, but I read his reviews online and saw I wasn't the only one who thought the man was a joke:

"Dr. Slattery drove me crazier."

"Dr. Slattery wouldn't shut up about his own problems!"

And on and on.

Genevieve is taking much better care of me than that clown did. My mom finally let me out from under her watch, and Eric's watch, too—both of them missing a lot of work as I stayed home from school. They let me out to celebrate my one-year anniversary with Genevieve.

She must've thought we'd run around the city having fun to keep my mind off of things, but instead I'm stretched out on her couch crying with my head on her lap because of all the pain I can't reach. Pain someone else *can* remove.

"I don't see how a Leteo procedure would really help you," Genevieve says. "When my mother died, it was brutal, and—"

She doesn't understand. She didn't have to find whatever was left of her mother's body on the plane's crash site like I had to find my father dead in the bathtub. "I would forget finding him. That's gotta be fucked up enough for Leteo to scrub out."

"Yeah . . ." Genevieve says, crying too. "It's gotta be."

The TV's volume is raised high so Genevieve's dad can't hear me cry. I'm not embarrassed, but I think it makes him uncomfortable. A commercial for this new movie, *The Final Chase,* comes on and it's like a punch in the gut when I think about all the new movies I won't see with Collin, all the comics we won't read together, and how he's basically acting like I never happened.

He's undoing himself and I need to do the same.

(AGE SIXTEEN—MAY, TWO MONTHS AGO)

AFTER AN HOUR WITH Dr. Slattery, where I cried and cried out of frustration, I decide I want to spend some time outside—even if it means my mom has to sit out here with me. There's a moving truck parked in front of Building 135. When I go to check out the new neighbor, I see Kyle wheeling a shopping cart of boxes into the back of the truck. I still half expect to find Kenneth right behind him, minding his own business.

One of the boxes falls out of the shopping cart. I pick it up and hand it over to Kyle, who won't look me in the eyes. "Going somewhere?"

Kyle nods and drops the box into the truck.

"Where?"

"Doesn't matter. Just can't be here anymore."

Brendan, Baby Freddy, Nolan, and Fat-Dave all come over. Brendan nods at me while everyone else looks at my bandaged wrist. He looks into the truck, sits down on the ramp, and asks, "What's up, guys?"

"Kyle's moving," I say, throwing him under the bus because I'd really like an afternoon off from talking about my problems. "He won't tell me where."

"Because where I'm fucking going doesn't fucking matter! I can't go to Good Food's anymore without Mohad calling me Kenneth. I can't play Skelzies with you guys without making tops for Kenneth he'll never use. I can't even look at you, Aaron, because you get to live after trying to throw away your life and meanwhile Kenneth is nothing but bones by this point."

Kyle's parents come out of the lobby, and he snatches a box from his mother and throws it over Brendan's head into the truck; we hear something shatter. "Just forget about me." He heads back into the building and we all go into the third court before he comes back out.

Baby Freddy says, "That was awkward."

Brendan shrugs. He turns to me and says, "You good?"

I nod, though really I feel like shit.

"That Collin kid coming to check on you?"

"No. And I don't want him to," I say, and we all drop it. Brendan even pats me on the back. We hang out for a bit like I never stopped being part of the crew, but then my mom calls me over and I run over ready to argue for more time to stay out.

"Dr. Slattery called," Mom says, still clutching the phone in her hand.

"Is he giving us all the money back you've wasted on him?"

"He knows someone at Leteo." Her eyes are closed, like she can't face me. "He's spoken with this woman, Dr. Castle or someone, and he'd like to refer us to her to discuss possibilities."

Holy shit.

I look back at my friends. I know how to make everything right so they'll never hate me again. I think about how I won't have to think about Collin anymore.

"I want to do it."

☹ ☹ ☹ ☹

(AGE SIXTEEN—JUNE, ONE MONTH AGO)

IT ONLY TOOK ONE session with Dr. Evangeline Castle for me to admit the root of my problems: my liking guys. She still made me sit through some sessions before approving me for the procedure, but the day is finally here. Mom can't come with me because she's missed too much work after everything and her boss's sympathy could only go so far. Someone has to pay for our apartment and this procedure, after all, but at least I'll have Genevieve with me.

"You're going to be okay, my son."

She once promised me that nothing bad would ever happen, and then I grew up and everything went wrong, but I believe her this time because the worst thing that can happen is that nothing will happen at all. "I know."

"Aaron, you understand I'm signing off on this procedure for you, right? It's not because I want to change you or think you need changing. I believe this will be a fresh start for all of us. I really want my son back, the boy who didn't hurt my heart by using Genevieve and didn't try to leave me." She keeps hugging me, and what she says stings. Luckily I won't ever have to remember being a complete disappointment to her and my father.

☹ ☹ ☹ ☹

(AGE SIXTEEN—JUNE 18TH)

I TRACE THE SMILING scar and I feel like mirroring it. I'm insanely happy.

I qualify for the memory-relief procedure. The operation is

scary-sounding and pretty extreme—it is experimental brain work, after all—and the doctors are cautious about administering it to those under the age of twenty-one. But I'm a danger to myself so they're letting me shake the old ways and days out of my head.

The waiting room is crowded like usual, the complete opposite of the hospital where I saw Dr. Slattery. People aren't exactly lining up outside for hours to meet with him. But at least the guy got us a pretty big discount with his referral. Silver lining.

Genevieve won't stop shaking her leg. She can't keep her hands still. It's partly why I wanted to do this solo, but she and my mom wouldn't take no for answer. I consider reading something from the table littered with mental health magazines and booklets and forms, but I know all I need to know already.

They turn away potential clients who only want a procedure to forget spoilers of *Game of Thrones* or someone who broke their heart. But this isn't that movie. Leteo helps people who hurt themselves because of harmful memories—you won't die from heartbreak but you'll die from, well, killing yourself.

Like this elderly Hispanic guy who won't stop reciting the winning lottery numbers he lost to; he'll likely get sent home without a chance to forget.

I recognize some of the patients from the group therapy sessions they forced me to attend, just to see if time was enough to resolve my problems.

Fun fact: sitting through those sessions only made me want to hurt myself even more.

A middle-aged woman banshee-wails from her seat, rocks back and forth, and punches the walls. An orderly rushes to her aid and tries calming her down. I know who she is, not her name or anything, but she's constantly reliving the memory of her five-year-old daughter chasing a bird into a busy street, and yeah, it's pretty fill-in-the-blank from there.

I try to keep my eyes low and ignore her screams, but I can't help but look up when another orderly approaches with a strait-jacket. They carry her away through the same door I'm about to walk through. I wonder how much of her life she'll have to forget to live without a straitjacket—and maybe a muzzle if she doesn't keep it down.

The waiting room is silent now. Any chatter has stopped. Lives depend on this procedure.

This really obese dude—Miguel, I think—told our therapy group that he could stop overeating only after he forgets his childhood traumas. He's here now, the ketchup stain of his last meal on his shirt. I almost want to hug him. I hope he's deemed unfit enough to get the procedure so he can be healthy again, physically and mentally.

Like him, I'm here because I don't want to be who I am any-more. I want to be so happy that bad memories aren't following me around like unwanted shadows.

Dr. Castle encouraged me to give her a list of happy things I should think about whenever I started thinking about things I shouldn't. During sessions, I always faked smiles while unhappily answering because she was so nice. She was trying to help.

I hold Genevieve's hand to calm her down, which seems pretty backward if you ask me. There's blue and orange paint crusting around her fingernails. "What were you working on?" I ask her.

"Nothing good. I was playing around with that idea I was telling you about, the one with the sun drowning in the ocean instead of setting behind it. I didn't know how to finish it though . . ."

I have no idea what she's talking about. Not surprised.

She reaches across me and stops me from tugging at my sleeve, which I didn't even realize I was doing. She knows all my signs and I can't even pay attention to her when she talks. "You're going to be okay, babe. You have to be."

Empty promise. No one ever thinks they'll get cancer. No one expects a gunman to open fire at the bank. "I'm more nervous that nothing will happen instead of something going wrong."

Some of the risks include severe memory loss, anterograde amnesia, and other shit like that. But a small part of me thinks I would be better off brain dead than waking up the way I am.

Genevieve looks around the waiting room with its stark white walls and crazies and patient employees. I bet she would consider painting something Leteo-related if it weren't for the signed nondisclosure agreement that allows her to be with me today provided she never discusses her presence here with another human being unless she wants to pay a zillion-dollar fine.

"I wouldn't worry," she says. "We read through all those brochures a thousand times and watched a marathon's worth of post-op videos and everyone seems fine."

"Yeah, but they probably wouldn't show us the patients who have to be spoon-fed for the rest of their lives." I fake a grin for her. I'm tired of faking, which is ridiculous considering the circumstances about to unfold. But at least I won't know I'm faking, and that's honest enough for me.

Genevieve looks behind me and immediately tears up. I turn. Dr. Castle is standing by the door. Her sunken-in sea-green eyes are always kind of comforting, even now as she stares at me, but her tousled mass of red-orange hair reminds me of living flames. I fight back panic. She probably hasn't announced herself so I could have a few more minutes with Genevieve—maybe even myself.

I pick up Genevieve by her waist and spin her around a couple of times. Getting dizzy before someone plays with my brain is stupid, I know. Before I can ask, Genevieve holds my hand and says, "I'll walk with you."

The closer we get to Dr. Castle, the more it feels like I'm

marching to my death, and I know I sort of am, at least the part of me everyone is better off without. The panic melts away.

"I'm ready," I tell Dr. Castle with zero doubts.

I turn back to Genevieve and while I'm kissing the girl who has been keeping my secret without knowing it, I wonder again if maybe she's known all along. We've never gone as far as saying we love each other in the year we've been together. It's simple, I know, but she's smart enough to never admit loving someone who can't love her back.

I never thought I would say anything like this to her, that I would rather hold this secret in my tight fist until the day I die, but I go ahead.

"I know you know about me, Gen. I won't be like that tomorrow, okay? We're going to be happy together, for real."

She's speechless, so I kiss her one last time and she weakly waves to me, probably saying bye to the person she found a way to love despite that wall I'm about to knock down.

I quickly turn around and head through the door, sick that all my lies and chaos have brought me to this breaking point. I know it's what has to happen. I can't be like Collin who can pretend like nothing ever happened between us and who can fucking forget everything that did. I no longer have to be ruined by another guy. I no longer have to hurt the girl who thinks I love her.

At the threshold, Dr. Castle places a comforting hand on my shoulder.

"Remember that this is for your own good," she reminds in her light English accent.

"I think we both know that remembering doesn't really do anyone good around here," I half joke, and she smiles.

I won't remember that this is for my own good, because I won't remember why I came here in the first place. Leteo will make me forget my relationship with Collin. My insides can stop burning me alive with how much I miss him. I won't ever get jumped on the train again for liking another guy. My friends will stop being suspicious of what I'm doing when I'm not hanging with them. We're going to kill that part of me that's ruined everything. I'm going to be straight, just like how my father would've wanted.

☹ ☹ ☹ ☹

THIS PROCEDURE ISN'T A promise I'll stop being you-know-what, but using science against nature is my best shot.

I'm stretched across a narrow bed with wires sealed to my forehead and heart. I've lost count of how many needles they've stabbed into my veins and how many times someone has asked me if I'm comfortable, and if I'm positive I want to do this. I've said yes and yes and yes a lot.

Some doctors and technicians are running around and setting up monitors; others are typing away on computers and doing analytical stuff with blueprints of my brain. Dr. Castle has stayed by my side the entire time. She fills up a glass of water from a small basin, drops two blue pills in, and hands it to me.

I stare at the pills, but don't drink yet. "Do you think I'll be okay, Doc?"

"Absolutely painless, kiddo," she says.

"And my dreams will be altered too, right?" Some dreams are unwanted flashbacks; others are nightmares, like the one last night where Collin put me on a bike, even though I wasn't ready, and pushed me down the steepest hill, laughing at me as he walked away.

"To avoid our work being unwound, yes," Dr. Castle says. "This wouldn't be an issue if we could simply erase memories without consequence, but memory manipulation is far less of a risk. When we put you under, you won't even have to relive the memories—that would be cruel. It'll feel like a long, long sleep."

"Sounds a lot like dying."

"Think of us less as reapers and more like genies."

"And I won't suspect anything when you come around?"

"We'll manipulate your memories so you believe I'm an old babysitter. The few people who know about your procedure will be clued in to this," she explains. But I know this already; it's been drilled into me and repeated a dozen different ways in the forms I've read and videos I've seen. The Leteo employees disguise themselves with permission all the time so they can check in on post-procedure patients without raising suspicion.

I won't have anything to remember Collin by. No memories, no treasures. I threw away his bad drawings, gag gifts, and an X-Men sweater he gave me. I burned funny notes over the stove as if I could forget what they said once they were ashes piling up in the pot.

Dr. Castle fluffs my pillow. I wonder if she cares for all her patients like this. "May I ask you something, Aaron? Completely off the books?"

"Sure."

She averts her eyes and whatever she's about to ask, it's clear she's reconsidering. "I hope I'm not out of line. From the moment your case was brought to my attention, I understood the struggles you must've been going through. But I can't help but be curious . . . Would you still carry on with this procedure if your sexuality weren't an issue? Would you want to change being gay?"

Lucky for me, I've thought about this even before my father went and killed himself. "It's not a matter of what I want. I need to do this."

A technician approaches. "Ready when you and the patient are, Dr. Castle."

I down the entire glass of water and hand it back to her. "Battle."

One doctor fits a mask around me while a technician turns some dials on the monitor. The sleeping gas hits. It is fresh and crisp and tastes like fiery metal in the back of my throat. It's so hard to stay awake. Evangeline isn't tugging at her sleeve, but I know she's nervous too. My eyes are shutting and I remember something. I pull off the mask, take a deep breath, and say, "Before I forget, thank you."

The mask falls back on my face.

The doctors count down from ten and my eyes shut at eight. Next time I wake up, I'll just be an ordinary straight guy in his bed.

PART THREE: LESS HAPPY THAN BEFORE

1
THIS TIME AROUND

I'm just as surprised as anyone else to be alive.

Pain rocks my bones in a way I didn't think was possible. Looking back to when I cried over falling on my knees on my ninth birthday seems stupid now, completely laughable. That time I was jumped on the train for liking Collin is a pinch in the cheek compared to this last assault, this hate crime. It's not even the heartache from Thomas that's shredding me apart.

Every mistake I've made, every wrong I've repeated, every unhealed heartache: I feel it all and more as the weight of my old world crushes me. If you looked inside me, I bet you'd find two different hearts beating for two different people, like the sun and moon up at the same time, a terrible eclipse I'm the only witness to.

My worlds collided and I can't get up.

☹ ☹ ☺ ☺

UNDERGOING THE PROCEDURE WAS like a blackout. Leteo dealt the cards on how I woke up. Some of my memories were altered, little disguises forced onto them to trick me. Others were beaten over the head with shovels, buried alive and out of my reach. But Leteo fucked up. Somewhere in the uncharted territories of my mind, they failed to scrub something clean and I became the person I forgot.

The goal was for me to forget I'm gay. Easier said than done since there isn't exactly an off switch like my father thought there was. To beat nature, Leteo fostered the shortly lived straight me by targeting and burying memories connected to my sexuality: my relationship with Collin, my dad's cruelty, my childhood crush on Brendan, etc. If I could simply believe I was straight, I would *be* straight. Life would be easy. But Leteo didn't have the power we both hoped they did.

My eyes are too heavy to open.

It's hard to breathe, like whenever Fat-Dave pins me down.

This headache feels like someone's playing a game of jacks inside my skull. Thoughts bounce around like a rubber ball.

My face feels swollen. Maybe that's because my friends beat me up because they hate me.

"Aaron, blink if you can hear me," I hear Dr. Castle call to me.

Evangeline.

I can't face her or anyone right now, so I keep my eyes shut and hide in the darkness where the awful pain drowns her out.

☹ ☹ ☺ ☺

I CAN'T SLEEP ANYMORE, no matter how hard I try.

I can open one eye easily, but the other still feels too heavy and hurts, so I leave it alone. I see half of a midnight-blue room I don't recognize, and it reminds me of a starless night. I turn my neck a little bit to see Evangeline asleep in a chair with a clipboard on her lap. It's hard to believe she sleeps. Maybe this visitor's chair is cozier than the one in her office; that one looks like it's made of concrete to prevent her from getting too comfortable. Next to her is my mother, sitting forward with her face in her hands, praying.

"Mom—" I can barely breathe her name without my throat aching, but she hears me anyway. Evangeline, too; she snaps awake like her boss caught her sleeping at her desk.

"Baby, my son." Mom kisses my forehead and it hurts like hell. She's apologizing to me and thanking God I'm okay until Evangeline pulls her to the side, giving me some much-needed space.

"You're stable, Aaron," Evangeline tells me. "Try not to move too much." She invites my mother to give me water through a straw. She presses an ice pack wrapped in a hand towel against my bad eye and forehead. "I imagine your head hurts, but we're all so impressed with how you're recovering."

"So impressed, my son," Mom adds.

I sip more water and it soothes and stings. "Why am I . . . not in . . . a hospital?"

"You were originally, but your mother contacted me when she heard you screaming things you'd forgotten," Evangeline says, and it hurts my neck to look up at her. "The ambulance drove you here and we've spent the past four days returning your mind to its former state before it could collapse entirely under the weight of the unwound memories. We'll perform some test work when you're feeling up to it to make sure all is well."

Four days. I've been knocked out for four days.

I feel like I know everything I once knew, but I can't be sure. I remember believing Evangeline was my old babysitter, as sure as I know Santeria is stupid or how I'm an asshole and a coward. "Did you . . . change anything?"

"Certainly not, kiddo. Too many complications."

My mind is once again busy with terrible things: my father's body, his hateful words; Collin turning his back on me, Collin's kisses; Eric giving me shit for dumb things; the judging looks of the other guys on the block; and, the most pressing, my mom and one of our last moments together before my procedure.

The memory of coming out to her the first time feels both familiar and unfamiliar, like an old bully you haven't seen in years but still kind of recognize, even all grown up. I know she knows I know she knows, so I just shut up and focus on what needs to happen next.

"When can you change me back?" I ask, my throat aching less and less. "Make me straight again. For real this time."

Evangeline doesn't answer. Mom cracks the silence with fresh tears.

My voice hardens. "Your procedure didn't work . . . and we paid a shitload of money for it to work so you need to make it work."

"The procedure cannot be faulted for the heart remembering what the mind forgot," Evangeline says.

"Bullshit," I say.

"I warned you that this procedure was still very experimental, remember?"

"Yeah, I remember. That's the problem."

I turn to my mom, who shakes her head. "No, I'm not signing off on this. Not again. I have my son back and I'm not giving you up again."

I wish I could've just been exorcised or spent the summer at a conversion camp or something.

"Can you both leave? I want to be alone."

"I can maybe give you five minutes to yourself," Evangeline offers. "But anything longer isn't allowed with all things considered, I'm afraid."

"Fine. Five minutes."

Evangeline hooks my mom's arm in hers, escorting her out.

I have to piss, and I'm not doing it in one of these bag

things, so I rip off the wires from my forehead and chest and try steadying myself on my feet. I'm dizzy. It feels like the awful combination of a head rush and a hangover. I balance myself against the wall and make my way to the bathroom.

I piss myself when I look in the mirror.

I have one black eye. My other eye is swollen and purple, like a bruised plum.

There are stitched-up gashes on my forehead with some dried blood the nurses didn't wipe clean.

My lip is cut open.

There are tears sliding down my face.

Something primal explodes from my aching throat, and the mirror smashes when my fist connects.

☹ ☹ ☺ ☺

GLASS SHARDS WERE PINCHING underneath my skin until the nurses pulled them out and bandaged my hand. Another war wound. Now they all refuse to leave me alone, period, scared I might slice a smile into my throat if I can't get what I want. Mom is keeping me company, telling me that Eric was here this morning, but he's not who I care about.

"Any other visitors?"

"Genevieve and Thomas have stopped by every day," Mom says. "Genevieve was here late last night and Thomas hung around for a few hours this morning. You have great friends."

I stare at the blue wall.

"Genevieve says you broke up with her."

"I guess this means you're not disappointed in me this time around."

She's crying again and hides behind her hands. "You weren't supposed to remember . . ."

But I do. And I need her to help me forget again.

2
TOUGH STUFF

I wake up from the same nightmare I usually had after my father killed himself. It's the one where he is getting completely undressed in the bathroom while calling me a faggot and telling me how I'm not worth living for. He turns on the bathwater and relaxes inside the tub before cutting his wrists. And then I'm drowning in red. I never wake up when the drowning starts like you would expect. I'm always suffocating for what seems like an unfair amount of time, considering I never chose to commit the crime he hated me for. I never chose anything. I just was.

I just am.

"Nightmares again?" Mom asks.

I nod.

I eat breakfast, chat with doctors about how I'm feeling ("like shit"), and read through all of Brendan's apologetic text messages. I don't respond. A couple hours later, Evangeline tells me I have guests. Thomas and Genevieve. Together. More worlds I don't want colliding.

My mom invites them in and leaves us alone.

I should be happy to see them, and they should be happy

to see me alive, but no one's smiling. "You've looked better," Thomas finally says. He has dark circles under his eyes. He isn't looking his best either. If this were my first time meeting him I'd have guessed he was twenty-two-years old, not seventeen. "No homo," he adds while completely avoiding my face. "That's not funny. Sorry."

"It's okay," I say. Then silence, except for Genevieve rapping her knuckles on my bed frame. "Thanks for visiting."

"Thanks for waking up," Thomas says, still not looking at me. At least he's here. I don't know if word got around to Collin, and I'm not sure if he would give a shit if it did. I wish I didn't give a shit about him either, even if the person I really care about is standing right in front of me. I don't know if that's even right. This whole situation is impossible.

"Me-Crazy was arrested," Genevieve says. "Baby Freddy's mother told Elsie he's being moved to a juvenile detention center upstate."

"Good."

Thomas palms his fist. "I wanted to snuff Brendan when he was let out of jail, like you taught me, but I haven't seen him. They must all be grounded."

Doubtful. "Don't worry about it," I say, hoping to clock Brendan in the chin myself.

It's quiet again. I can only assume they've been chatting it up with each other, and I both hope they weren't talking about me, and also that they were. If they weren't talking about me, it wouldn't make sense because they only know each other through me and without me they're nothing to each other. If they *were* talking about me, I hope Genevieve wasn't telling Thomas everything about what led me to Leteo, everything that I couldn't remember to confess to him myself. Those are my stories, not hers. And I hope Thomas wasn't telling her about that time I kissed him and he didn't kiss me back.

"Can I catch up with you in a few, Genevieve?"

She looks at me like I just punched her in the face and kicked her while she was down. "I'll be outside," she tells Thomas—not me—and punches his arm.

I'm dizzy again. The door practically slams behind her and there's a ringing in my ears.

He paces back and forth and it hurts my neck but I keep my eyes on him.

I say, "So what's new?"

"Heart stuff and insanity," Thomas says. I feel something awful rising inside of me. He better not be talking about Genevieve. "I've been giving thought to my life chart and overheard something on the radio about love addiction. It's a real thing. People who are in love with love. I think I'm a love addict. It explains why I always pull away from a girl when I'm not in that honeymoon phase anymore and start searching for someone new. It's a cruel cycle, Stretch."

"That's where your mind has been while I was laid out here?"

It's quiet except for the sound of my heart monitor beeping.

"I don't know what you want me to say," Thomas finally replies. "Okay, I know exactly what you want me to say, but those aren't words I can tell you. I'm not even a hundred percent sure who I'm talking to right now."

"The Stretch you're talking to is a guy who didn't want to like other guys so he tried changing that," I say.

"Let me get this straight," Thomas says. "Leteo made you forget you were gay?"

"Yeah. You thought I told you my story before—hell, *I* even thought I told you everything there is to know—but you have no idea what I've been through."

Thomas sits down, his head hung low. "So who are you?"

"I don't know. I'm sort of two people who want very different things, but even with all this confusion, I'm still pretty sure who you are and it kills me that you're not."

He almost looks at me, but his head drops again. "I don't know what to do. I don't know if I should be apologizing for something or going back to your block to fight those guys or if I should stay here and figure out who you are or if you're better off without me being around. I just don't know. What do you want?"

"You," I say, and I actually say it, because I want him in the same way I wanted Genevieve when I was straight, and the same way I wanted Collin months ago. Except I want—no—need him more than the others. "And if that's something you're not ready for, I think I need a little space to try and forget these feelings."

"Okay." Thomas stands and gives my resting hand a fist bump. He looks at me—finally—and I know I'm punishing him just as much as I'm punishing myself. "I wasn't just self-diagnosing myself while you were laid out. I was distracting myself however I could because thinking of you never waking up and being okay was fucking killing me. I missed you and I hope that's okay to say."

Then he leaves and I feel like the biggest idiot in the universe.

3
DEAD END

When Genevieve comes in, she sits down on the bed and holds my hand like we didn't break up the last time we saw each other. She asks me how I'm feeling. I tell her I'm okay, when I'm really still struggling with Thomas walking out of my life, but it seems like too much to share that with her.

"Do you like the blue walls?" she asks. "I suggested a room this color might relax you when you woke up."

Of course she did. I hold my aching arms up and she hugs me, resting her face against mine. "Remember that time I sort of told you that I liked guys and we were going to live happily ever after? And remember the time before that where I was the worst person ever and used you?"

Genevieve sits up and shushes me. "No, stop. You were confused and had every right to be nervous. This moment here proves that." She lowers her head. "As for me, I should've pulled myself away. Even when I knew you were only mine because Leteo crossed your wires, I stayed with you. Wrong move."

"I'm sorry we broke up."

She cries a little. "You're not for me to love, Aaron. It was a dead end and I kept trying to go forward."

And we crashed because of me. "Can you be real with me about something? You never told Thomas why I got the procedure, right?"

"I thought maybe you told him yourself. I even thought the procedure started unwinding while I was in New Orleans because you two were so close when I got back. But later I realized he knew nothing. I would never tell your secrets, Aaron. Even the ones I know you're hiding from me."

I not only screwed her over; I never deserved her. "So you don't hate me?"

"Of course I don't hate you, but as your friend, I have to be real with you about something else. It's about Thomas." Genevieve pauses, and the heart monitor's beeping elevates for a few seconds. "I'm worried you're going to wait for him the way I was waiting for you. I think the sooner you realize he can't like you, the happier you'll be."

"Wait. Do you think he likes you or something?"

"I already said no! Why are you repeating yourself?" Genevieve tilts her head, looking at me funny. "Are you okay?" She reaches across and grips my shoulder; I'm struck with flashbacks of all the times Thomas steered me somewhere from behind, and all the times Collin and I would bump into each other on purpose. "Aaron, should I get Evangeline or someone?" She's tearing up.

"No, I'm fine. I zoned out," I say, feeling a little short of breath. "Look, trust me, Thomas isn't straight. I know him."

"No one really knows who Thomas is," Genevieve says.

I know she's not being haughty about it, but I don't like how matter-of-fact she is about someone no one knows better than I do. "Gen, you're the one who falls for guys who won't like you back, not me."

"Whoa." Genevieve stands up and I swear she's about to punch me. "Just so you know, you apologized for the wrong thing, Aaron. I understood why you dated me, and I let it happen even though I shouldn't have, but that doesn't make it okay that you were seeing scratch out Collin behind my back. You made me feel like no one. You don't get to keep ignoring the past because you don't like it."

My breaths are quick and uneven. My temper rises. "You're right. I'm sorry I'm not straight. I'm sorry I went after someone I could feel real emotions over. I'm sorry I needed to hide so strangers wouldn't try and beat me to death. I'm sorry my dad killed himself because of me. And I'm sorry my past is so terrible I couldn't live in it anymore. But forget the past, okay? Forget *our* past."

Genevieve doesn't cry or flip me off or punch me. She just turns around and walks to the door. Her arm shakes as she holds the doorknob. She looks at the blue walls she personally requested for me and says, "You forget that I cried with you when all those bad things happened."

And I think she has more she wants to say, but she finds the strength to turn the doorknob and leaves. Once the door closes, I'm hit with this fear that I may never see her again.

4
PSYCH ME OUT

I'm about to have my psych session with Evangeline. It's been a while.

The first time I came into this office I didn't actually think a memory-alteration procedure was possible. Even after I met Evangeline, I was sure she was going to turn me away because I was this kid who didn't even know what to ask of Leteo. I definitely wanted to forget finding my father in the bathtub. But the more she and I chatted, the more I pieced together that my problems ran much deeper. It all came together like connect-the-dots, revealing a boy who understood the impossible things ahead of him.

Months later, I'm back in this office with its white walls, a tablet on a sleek desk, certificates I never bothered to read carefully enough, and my blueprint architect waiting for me to share why I need the procedure again.

Evangeline put on a good show, for sure. I never suspected she was a Leteo specialist. The only people in my life who knew about her were my mom, Eric, and Genevieve. Brendan and the other guys on the block didn't remember me having a babysitter as a kid but never questioned it beyond Family Day—who would think to suspect someone manipulated my memories to get close to me? It's just clicking now, but it was no coincidence when Mom sent me to the post office at the same time Evangeline was there. And when Evangeline accompanied me to Leteo and ran off to speak to that woman from "Hunter College's Department of Philosophy" it was probably some coworker or patient.

I even remember that Hannah chick at the info counter now. Hopefully this show comes with an encore of the forgettable variety.

Evangeline tries to warm me up with small talk, no doubt to gauge what kind of mood I'm in. So I just tell her: "I'm feeling a hundred things right now. Betrayed. Disappointed. Guilty. Desperate. You need me to go on?"

"You only listed four things. Hit me with the other ninety-six."

"Regret. Love. Pissed off. Grief. Just trust me, there's more."

"I believe you, kiddo."

I crack my knuckles, one finger at a time, and tug at my sleeve afterward. "You can make me better."

She shakes her head. "It's not up to me to sign off on the procedure. But let's review what happened the past few months. We gave you a glimpse into what your life would look like if you were straight. Your true nature burst through our seams. I can't elaborate much further than this, but many of our other clients who have undergone similar work remain as we left them. Is being gay really at fault here?"

I know the answer but I stay quiet.

I need the noise in my head to get loud again to drown out all the memories of rejection and heartache. So much has been left behind because of Leteo's screwup, and she wants me to tell her how happy I was, so she feels better? No. No, I won't do that. No, I wasn't happy. I mean, sure, I thought I was, but I found happiness in the wrong person and that doesn't count. It didn't count with Collin, it didn't count with Genevieve, and it doesn't count with Thomas.

"I won't survive this," I say. "You all understood how hard this was for me the first time, but now I'm carrying extra weight. How is that not clicking with anyone?"

"As I said, kiddo, this isn't up to me. I agree that the memories you're carrying around are painful, especially for someone your age with your history . . ." Her eyes fall on my smiling scar. "The day we were here together, Hannah scheduled you for an appointment on the twelfth of August. It was for a consultation, but if your mother signs off on your procedure, we'll take care of you . . ." She goes on about how she couldn't talk me out of it the first time, but I tune her out.

August 12th. Two days before my birthday.

I'll try to make it that long.

5
WINDING BACK THE CLOCK

I have to see him.

All my memories are so warped right now. I'm pushing my father's suicide out of my head as best as possible because it hurts too much with everything else I'm suffering.

I want to turn back the clock, back to the days where being who I am didn't get me thrown through glass doors; back to the days where he and I ran around laughing; back to the days where there was a chance of happiness despite our circumstances.

It's against my better instinct, but I reach for my phone and dial his number like I never forgot it. I press CALL and don't expect him to pick up.

"You're okay," he says.

"I've been cooler, Collin."

WINDING BACK THE CLOCK

6
ONCE MORE

I'm forgetting about Thomas and Genevieve without any help from Leteo.

Talking with Collin has made recovery pretty easy these past three days. There's been zero reminiscing or any shit like that over the phone. We're trying to keep everything cool and not gay between us, I guess. We talk about meaningless things like movies we've seen—he also hated *The Final Chase*—and how I need to catch up on *The Dark Alternates* because the last issue comes out this month and the story line has gotten crazy. The biggest taboo of all is his pregnant girlfriend; he never even hints at her.

I'm finally being released from Leteo today. Evangeline thinks I should stay for another couple of days as they run more tests, but I will hang myself with an IV if I have to spend another hour in this room. (Not really.) I promised to let her know if I have any dizzy spells, cases of vomiting, or the attention span of a goldfish.

The only time I speak to Mom on the way home is to ask if Mohad is firing me for missing work on account of getting my ass beat. But she's already been in contact with him and he's not. I have that going for me.

I'm a little on edge when we arrive on our block. Brendan, Skinny-Dave, and Nolan better not come at me again. Mom holds on to my arm, squeezing, and I bet she's nervous too. I see Baby Freddy and Fat-Dave playing catch by the trash cans, and Baby Freddy drops the ball when he sees me and runs over.

"No!" Mom screams, guarding me with her body. "Stay away from my son, or I swear I will have you all thrown in jail."

Baby Freddy backs up a little. He looks straight up embarrassed. "I just wanted to see if he's okay. I'm sorry they did that, Aaron. It was messed up." He leaves before my mom can threaten him again.

I swallow a deep and sharp breath when we get to our lobby entrance. I used to run through those doors as a kid when we played tag, and manhunt later as a teenager. I would race to hold the doors open for our neighbors, and they would tell my mom she raised such a well-mannered little boy. Now there's nothing but a door frame and a little girl jumping back and forth over it, like someone wasn't almost killed here.

Next thing I know, I'm riding up the elevator with Mom.

Once she crashes onto her own bed for the first time in a week, I change into different clothes and sneak out to meet Collin.

☹ ☹ ☺ ☺

I GET TO JAVA Jack's, this run-down diner on 142nd Street, in no time. Without thinking, I settle into the booth by the window Collin and I always opted for whenever we came here together; it's a prime spot for people watching/mocking. Collin used to hate coffee, but I'm betting now he thinks drinking coffee proves you're a man or something. It's pretty dumb, but I know he struggles with this side of himself way more than I ever have in both of my lives, so I won't call him out on it. I'll also keep everything about our history airtight so we don't tip anyone off.

I stop the waiter. "Can I bother you for another coffee?"

"Be back in a moment," he says.

The door opens and I shoot up. It's not Collin. It's just some guy in baggy clothes and long surfer hair. If I had the power to snap my fingers and change him, I'm not convinced I would've dressed him in a basketball jersey or made him taller with Collin's golden curls. Maybe I would've transformed him into Thomas, watching his skin turn a shade darker than the weak coffee this place serves, and his regular, boring eyebrows would've grown into the thicker eyebrows I had no business touching before I kissed him.

I just don't know.

Snap, snap.

There's a hand snapping a few inches from my nose.

"You cool?" Collin sits down across from me like we've spent no time apart. "You certainly don't look it."

My swollen eye is less swollen, but it's still pretty much an eyesore everyone can't help but stare at when I'm just walking down the street. "Yeah. I ran into a lot of wrong fists. How'd you find out?"

"Genevieve told a friend who told a friend who told Nicole," Collin says. "What else is new?" He picks up the menu as if he doesn't always order the same thing—omelet with a side of hash browns—and it's a good tactic; I'll give him that. Focus on what's new and what's next instead of what brought him here. "Hey! Can I get some coffee over here?"

"Make that two!"

"Why do you need two?" Collin asks.

"I downed mine already."

Collin points at the steaming mug in front of me. I could've sworn I drank mine already, especially because of how badly I have to pee now. Maybe the waiter refilled it while I was lost in my head.

The waiter looks confused too. And a little annoyed as he brings two steaming mugs. "What the . . . ? You still haven't finished the second cup."

"Uh, no. Sorry about that."

"Great. I'll just make another batch for the next time you want to waste some more."

Collin pours sugar into his coffee and tells the waiter, "Don't be a dick, dick." The waiter curses under his breath and leaves. Collin always used to tell off the asshole waiters who never hang around Java Jack's longer than a month. It started a game where I would draw something crude on the bill to make him laugh. Becoming that person again would be cold and distant, but safe.

"So you were about to tell me what's new with you," he says.

"Nothing besides getting thrown through doors."

He stares at his coffee. "Where was Genevieve when all this went down?"

"I kind of quit her." I lock eyes with him when he looks up. "What's going on with you and Nicole? How's her pregnancy coming along?"

Collin covers his mouth, coffee dribbling down his chin. "Uh, she's about to enter her third trimester."

"Boy or girl?"

He takes a second to answer. "Boy."

Now would be a good time to have a fully functioning crystal ball so I could divine whether or not Collin is going to be a good father to his little boy. I don't just mean whether or not he'll take his son out to play and feed him spoonfuls of medicine when he's sick, but if Collin will let his son listen to songs sung by women and let him date a dude if it made him happy.

"Congratulations," I say.

"I know you don't mean it."

"No, I think it's cool," I lie.

"That sucks about you and Genevieve."

"I know you don't mean it," I parrot with a grin.

Then we just look at each other, the same way we did during school when we passed each other in the halls. "Want to get out of here?"

"Let's get the check," I say.

"And the waiter's pen," he adds.

WE'RE GOING TO COMIC Book Asylum, laughing as we throw the waiter's pen at each other, overdramatic, like gladiators hurling spears. After we started hanging out last year, we would go to the comic shop when it was too cold out to do anything else. It didn't matter to me as long as we were chilling. We'd spend hours sitting in the aisles, as close to each other as possible, checking out what we wanted to read but were positive we didn't want to buy. Man, I spent so much time at Comic Book Asylum that Genevieve brought me there for Trade Dates. Then again, she also created Trade Dates because there was a strain in our relationship, also because of Collin.

He always surprised me whenever he brought up things that weren't related to comics and fantasy books. One afternoon I thought we were about to leave the shop, but he pulled me back down to the floor beside him. I was both nervous and hopeful he was going to kiss me, but instead he said he was done caring about what others thought of how he lived. That sentiment didn't survive any longer than a shadow-basilisk did against a black sun phoenix, but in the moment it made me happy to believe it. And then I lost him and his conversations and touches, and I couldn't fill that hole. So forgetting the hole was even there turned out to be the next best, saddest thing.

But I have him back now, I think.

Stan is by the door, doing a poor job installing a Captain America gumball machine. He smiles at us. "You two done fighting?"

Collin is looking at me funny, sort of like that time I echoed the ending to his bad haircut story because he'd forgotten he told me already. I paid attention, made him feel worth it, and I promised I always would.

"We're good," he answers for us. He leads me to the graphic novel section.

"What was that about?"

"I came in here a few times without you, and Stan kept asking me where the Robin to my Batman was."

"That's bullshit," I say. "I'm totally Batman."

Collin snickers. "For a while I made excuses, said you were sick or working, but eventually I accepted we probably wouldn't ever talk again. It sucked, but it made sense with how I ditched you." He trails a finger across the spines of graphic novels and says, "I gotta ask you something."

"Shoot."

"When you saw me here and were being extra nice and fake, were you doing it to impress that guy you were with? Was he your boyfriend?"

I completely forget that happened on account of having forgotten my relationship with Collin. Two worlds, ten feet from each other—and Collin was the only one who knew, the only one who was affected by it. "He was never my boyfriend and you were barely anyone to me. I went through the Leteo procedure and forgot my time with you."

"Sure you did," Collin says.

He doesn't believe me. Why would he? But I told him.

We sit against a bookcase, our elbows touching. We're both

reading the same graphic novel about zombies invading a heavily guarded garbage dump, where they find their master's decapitated head. Not really sure what the zombies plan on doing with the head if they manage to retrieve it, but we lose interest anyway.

"Remember our spot behind the fence?" he says out of nowhere.

It's not a game of Remember That Time.

"It's been a while," I say.

"Want to go?"

I close the graphic novel. We tell Stan we'll see him later and I wonder if he knows about Collin and me. As long as he's not outing us, it doesn't matter.

We head to our spot between the meat market and flower shop. I steer Collin toward the fence from behind, but he shrugs me off and I don't give him any shit for it, even though there's not a single gay-hating soul in sight. The smell of dead cow is way more pungent than the flowers this evening. There's a sign that reads: COMMUNITY SERVICE GATHERING ON FRIDAY, AUGUST 16TH. Who the hell knows what that entails? But it's pretty awesome to find our graffiti still on the wall.

We crawl through the open spot in the fence into the side where history is pulsating with memories of our first time, second time, third time . . . you get it. Collin scans the area for any wanderers or birds with cameras on their heads before coming back to undo my belt buckle. It's so dark someone could murder us and get away with it, which we prefer—the darkness, not the murder part. I pull him into a rough kiss and I don't doubt that whenever he's kissing Nicole he's pretending she's some other guy—maybe even me—and as I kiss him now I pretend he's someone else, and it's just so fucking sad.

He hands me a condom and I rip open the wrapper with my teeth.

7

HEART-TO-HEARTS AND HEARTBREAKS

It's only been a day and I desperately need to see Collin to stay sane. I know he's working two jobs—one as a busboy at an Italian restaurant, the other as a stock boy at a bodega—and doesn't get a lot of sleep. But I need him as badly as I should be pushing him away. It's too weird a mix of ugly and hopeful.

Collin has a few hours free before work, so at 2:00 he meets me at the track field where I watched trains speed by with Thomas. I look around for him lying on the grass or sitting on the bleachers, thinking about how he can be the architect of his life, but Thomas is not here. It's okay, it's okay: I have Collin, my first gateway to honest happiness. I tell Collin I chose this spot so we could run around and get him in shape for basketball try-outs, but when we race he's so far behind, and it reminds me of Thomas losing too. But unlike Thomas, Collin doesn't just quit, be it a job or a dream or a race. He charges on to the end and then throws himself onto the grass beside me.

"Can we talk about it?"

His question throws me off. "About . . . ?"

He looks around before tapping my scar. "Was it really that bad?"

"Yes." I lie back and stare at the sun until it hurts. "Life felt like it was going to be too long. I wanted out."

"It wasn't because of me, right?" he asks quickly.

I shake my head in the grass. "Not completely. I'm not some kid who was pissed someone didn't want him back." Except I was. Even having forgotten all the things that led to Aaron 2.0. I was still aching for a Leteo procedure because of fear and disappointment in someone who couldn't love me back. And I was despicable enough to try and play my suicide card to forget heartbreak. "There were a lot of reasons. But trying to live when my father refused to stay alive—because of who I am—broke me in a way I don't think will ever be fixed."

"I was so pissed at you, Aaron," Collin says. "Nicole told me what you tried to do. I was stuck on this level of Vigilante Village and I was *this* close to throwing my controller at the TV. But I kept it together because I didn't want to ruin her the same way I wrecked us. I always thought we would be the endgame, even when I knew I couldn't afford to be that person."

"You walked away from me."

"It's taken me a few months to realize how badly I miss you. I know I'm living a lie, but I'm thinking about this kid, Aaron. My son. What is having a gay dad going to do to him? I sometimes think I'd be better off not being in the picture at all, but I can't get myself to be a deadbeat dick either."

I sit up. "What do you want from me? Are you going to bounce again?"

"I can't promise anything," Collin says, which is basically promise-speak for *Don't count on me.* He sits up with me and—for a second—holds my hand. "I just want you to be alive when I figure it out."

So, I have another *maybe* to wait around for. Maybe Collin will stick around or find me again later in life. Maybe Thomas will come out for me. Maybe I'll get another do over from Leteo. Of all the maybes, Collin's making me happy is the safest bet.

☹ ☹ ☺ ☺

WE RETURN TO THE track field the next day, but this time we sit on the bleachers to reread *The Dark Alternates* before the last issue drops this week.

Collin flips through Issue #5, the happiest I've seen him since I told him my mom was cool with me being gay. All his money goes to Nicole and the kid so he's only been able to read each issue at the store and always in a rush because of customer demand. His smile fades when he reaches page twenty-four, where Thor is beaten bloody by his Dark Alternate and left for dead in a pub.

"The day we got jumped," Collin says. "I was so fucking scared for our lives. I really thought that was it."

"That's how I felt when my friends ganged up on me," I say.

"Why did they do it?"

I ask myself this every fucking hour. Hate, ignorance, feeling betrayed—I don't know, but they turned against me and there's no taking it back or forgetting. But I answer honestly: "They didn't like my friendship with Thomas, that guy you saw me with at Comic Book Asylum. They had the wrong idea about us."

"Did anything ever happen between you two?"

I won't tell him we kissed. "He's straight," I say. That's what Thomas claims, and I roll with it to protect him. If my instincts are right and he does come out to me, I don't want to have betrayed his trust. He never betrayed mine.

"That sucks," Collin says. "Everything happens for a reason, right?"

Collin is the reason. Full circle.

☹ ☹ ☺ ☺

AFTER MISSING HIM YESTERDAY—Collin had a doctor's appointment with Nicole before work—we didn't get to hang. Now we're back at the track field for the third time. We get ready to run a lap when I see Thomas on the bleachers eating Chinese food. With Genevieve. It's like a sucker punch. I can't breathe. I have never been so hurt seeing someone else so happy.

She cracks open a fortune cookie. I hope it reads: YOU'RE JUST ASKING FOR HEARTBREAK AGAIN.

Thomas brought Genevieve here, one of the more public places where he thinks, and I hate the idea that he is sharing his thoughts with her. Maybe he's even taken her up to his roof to watch movies, shirtless. If it has gone that far, I don't have it in my soul to be happy for them, especially when he's bullshitting her and she's bullshitting herself again.

I take off, hoping to get the fuck out of here before I can be seen, but then Collin calls my name and both Thomas and Genevieve look around and find me. Thomas doesn't take his eyes off me, but Genevieve's eyes dart back and forth. Her face falls when she sees Collin.

I jet out of there even faster and don't stop until the corner of the next block.

Collin catches up to me. I'm heaving and spitting over a trash can, pressing a hand against my aching rib cage.

"You okay? Your face is mad red."

I cover my mouth so he doesn't have to watch me try and throw up.

"I saw Genevieve back there with your boy Thomas. She's not going to tell Nicole she saw me, right?"

"I don't think they even talk anymore," I manage. He'll be lucky if Genevieve doesn't take on a Dark Alternate herself and rat him out. "I think I should go home and rest. See you later this week?"

"You still like Thomas, don't you?"

I don't want to lie to him, but the truth might cost me him.

Collin shrugs. "It sucks, but it's for the best. I'll see you later this week, Aaron."

He walks away. I watch him. I really wish people would just start punching me in the face again. At least a punch in the face would make me feel worthy of being hit. All this—Thomas and Genevieve laughing without me, Collin not giving enough of a fuck about me—makes it clear that no one would have any problem forgetting that I existed.

Maybe that's the only way Leteo can work. For the forgettable. No one wants to be forgettable. But I'll take that risk.

8
IMPOSSIBLY FORGETTABLE

I try not to be home when Eric is around. Out of all my relationships since being unwound, ours is the only one that hasn't changed. Even remembering all the times he teased me doesn't shift anything; we've always given each other shit, after all. But I'm kind of, sort of, definitely awkward around him because even though he knows, I never actually came out to him. Still, the apartment is small, and the arguments with Mom to approve me for another procedure are loud and daily.

I get to Good Food's early to dodge Eric before he wakes up.

Mohad has been really cool about me missing work. But on Tuesday I asked him to give me some extra shifts because I needed to get out of the house. My mom only agreed to it because Mohad banned Brendan, Skinny-Dave, and Nolan from the store. He even told me I could call the cops if they showed up while he stepped out.

More than anything else, I thank Mohad for not firing me yesterday when I completely zoned out during a customer transaction. I gave this guy change for a fifty twice. That asshole naturally took the cash and bounced, but Mohad could see on the cameras that I didn't pocket it—just got really distracted, I guess.

I spend the afternoon doing the same bullshit: cashiering, taking inventory, cutting conversations short about why my friends jumped me, sweeping, more cashiering, cutting more conversations short. It's nearing the end of my shift when Mohad asks me to mop the beverage aisle. I prop up the CAUTION: WET FLOOR sign, dip the mop in the bucket, and almost freak out when Thomas and Genevieve appear. They slowly approach me.

His head is low, like when he couldn't face me at Leteo.

Her head is high, like she's won a prize I could never have.

My head is spinning, like I'm drunk on worthlessness.

"Hi, Aaron," Genevieve says. "Do you have a chance to talk to us after work?"

"You can talk to me here." I start mopping, but then Thomas's cologne hits me and I retreat back to my corner.

Genevieve peeks into the next aisle and says, "Your mother told us about Leteo. Why would you do this again to yourself and everyone who loves you?"

"You'll never get it."

It's impossible to explain the emotions cycling through me to someone who never forgot her life, later remembered it, and now has all these memories bleeding into each other. Every day feels more like chaos, like I'm never going to get my life straight—no pun intended—like starting over again is better than game over. Surely there's some Leteo support group for those whose buried memories have been unwound. On the other hand, I don't need any more sadness in my life listening to other people's tragedies.

"Aaron, it's *you* who's not getting it," she says. "Leteo fixes some things, yes, but it ruins everything else. I've been with you every step of the way, as much as I could, and pieced together everything else myself. This is not the happiness you want."

I throw the mop onto the floor. The clattering makes Gen flinch.

"I can't have the happiness that I want. On top of everything else, why should I have to carry around that weight too?" What I feel for Thomas is the loudest thing I've ever had ringing through me. I can be me again—or some form of me—when that ringing shuts up.

Thomas steps toward me. "I'm trying to make sense of this, Stretch. This guy, Collin . . . The one we saw at Comic Book Asylum and at the track field. You forgot him, but still knew him?"

"I forgot my time with him," I say.

Thomas looks me in the eyes and I turn away. "What does that mean for me? Do we have enough history that you would still recognize me? Would you forget me?"

"Maybe," I say, wishing I were somewhere else, even back home with Eric. "I don't know exactly how Leteo puts together their blueprints."

Thomas sniffs. I look up. His eyes are red and watery. I haven't seen him cry since Brendan laid into him. "Remember back in June when we left that Leteo rally? You agreed with me that everyone serves a purpose. Is our friendship really so worthless now?" he asks.

When I don't answer, he turns to Genevieve. "I'm going."

It doesn't sound like an invitation, but she looks at me one more time before following him anyway.

Genevieve is right: I don't want this happiness, but blind happiness is better than inhabitable unhappiness.

AFTER MY SHIFT, I go straight to my building, ignoring Baby Freddy's shouts to hang out. I enter the lobby just as my mom exits the downstairs Laundromat, pushing the heavy load of clothes in a shopping cart. I come up beside her and take over, heading to the elevator.

"Genevieve and Thomas stopped by," I say, keeping my cool.

She doesn't even try and play it off or explain herself. "Thomas too?"

I press the elevator button. "Yeah. Did you only recruit Gen for the mission?"

"Outside your family, she loves you the most," Mom says. "I thought that was my best shot." Maybe so, but I guess Gen thought bringing along the guy I want to be my happiness might be a better bet. That girl is really something else. "I'm tired of this fight, Aaron. I know it's my responsibility as a parent to give you the life you want, especially since I failed at getting you your own room and finding you a father who didn't get so lost in his own head, but I don't want to lose my son."

The elevator arrives but we don't get on. "I just don't think I'm that different from him."

"You are, my son, you are. You are kind and too good for the bad you've lived through. If you're sure, if you promise me that in this moment, you'll forgive me for signing off on your procedure, I'll do it."

I hug her, promising over and over that this is what I want, what I *need*, that there would never be any reason to forgive her.

"Hold on," she says. Here we go. "I'll sign off on one condition. I want you to visit Kyle and his family on Saturday."

I get to see Kyle. That's more than enough.

9

KYLE LAKE, THE ONLY CHILD

When Kyle and Kenneth were younger—twins still so identical even I couldn't tell them apart—they made up this game called Happy Hour. They didn't know what "happy hour" meant in the real world, but they heard it enough from grown-ups. They would come home from school and shout, "Happy Hour!" whenever their parents asked them to settle down and do their homework. They'd be granted one hour of playtime, relax time, whatever, before having to do work and chores. Happy Hour changed as they got older, transforming into a therapeutic judgment-free hour of bitching.

I don't even know who Kyle bitches to now.

It required a lot of back and forth, but my mom teamed up with Evangeline to make this meeting happen. Mom had to sign a permissions request and a confidentiality form, and some other papers promising never to disclose the location of the Lakes to anyone except me.

I'm not sure what the penalties are, but I guess it would just be really shitty of her to send the block flooding to 174th Street, right off the Simpson Avenue train stop. I guess their housing budget post-procedure wasn't very high; otherwise, they would've escaped to the deep end of Queens, not thirty blocks and several avenues over from where they started.

When I get to their apartment building, right beside a video rental store with a CLOSING sign, I feel shaky. I press the intercom.

"Who is it?" Mrs. Lake asks.

"Aaron," I say.

They buzz me in without a word. I walk straight to apartment 1E and knock twice. Both Mrs. and Mr. Lake—their first names lost on me—look taken aback when they open the door; it's the wounds on my face, no doubt. I'm surprised at how happy I am to see them considering how little time I've wondered about them. But now I remember the sleepovers where Mrs. Lake would play video games with us, and I remember the times Mr. Lake would accompany us on school trips to the Bronx Zoo, always sneaking us candy. I hug them both at once.

They welcome me inside. It hurts to see an apartment so different from the one I saw my friends grow up in: the walls are beige, not rust orange; the windows have bars, like a prison cell; the TV in the living room is gigantic, not the flat screen Mr. Lake won from a sweepstakes last year. The game consoles are all still here, but all of Kenneth's trivia and soccer games aren't. The cat-shaped clock Kyle gave Kenneth for their tenth birthday isn't hanging in the living room like it was in the last apartment. It really is like Kenneth never existed.

"You want some iced tea?" Mr. Lake offers.

"Just water, please." Iced tea brings back another memory: of Saturday mornings over at the old Lake apartment. We had cereal in bowls of iced tea because we all don't like milk.

She brings me the water and they sit across from me.

"How are you both doing?" I ask.

"Do you want the truth?" Mr. Lake replies.

I nod, knowing I'm about to regret it.

"Hurts every day," Mrs. Lake chimes in. "There's no forgetting. You see Kyle, and you expect big brother Kenneth to be tailing after him. There are still mornings where I almost ask Kyle to wake his brother up. It doesn't matter that it's been ten months or that we're in a new home. I can never believe I lost one of my boys."

Mr. Lake stays quiet. He used to make jokes about how Kyle isn't actually his own person, just an alternate-universe version of Kenneth-gone-wrong.

"I miss when Kenneth would get rage-y whenever someone called him Kenny," I say. As soon as the words come out, I wish I could take it back. It's not like I was invited to share a story, but I can't stop. All at once, I'm spilling out more and more things about Kenneth, like when he faked his eye exam in order to get glasses so people could tell him and Kyle apart. And when they dressed up as storm troopers for Halloween. And that time we were with Brendan in the band room while he rolled up a blunt, and Kenneth discovered he could play clarinet—which I hope to God still exists somewhere in this fake home and isn't in the hands of some stranger. The Lakes are crying by the time I have to take a breath.

"I'm sorry," I say.

"Don't be . . . Aaron, thank you," Mr. Lake says, staring into my glass of water he's still holding. "We never get to talk about our son anymore. It's . . . energizing to hear someone remember him so fondly. Makes me feel less crazy, like I didn't just make up this second son."

"How do you do it? How do you not find yourself banging down Leteo's doors to give you the same procedure Kyle got?"

"We couldn't dishonor his existence like that," Mrs. Lake says. "Parents have done it and it breaks my heart tenfold. You move on, you have to—but you don't write someone out."

Mr. Lake looks at the timer on the microwave. "Kyle should be getting home soon, Clara. We should fill Aaron in on everything."

They tell me the story of why Kyle thinks they moved. He had a history of fights with Me-Crazy—no love lost for that psycho when the Lakes moved away—starting from slaps to the back of the head on the school bus to being pushed into lockers and eventually straight-up fistfights. Whoever served as the architect for Kyle's blueprint—not Evangeline, I learned—tapped into very real emotions to create a very believable narrative that would never send Kyle back to our block. He just accepts his new life as a barber's apprentice, and boyfriend to some girl Mrs. Lake hopes is around forever.

The intercom buzzes.

"Always forgetting his keys," Mrs. Lake says. "Why don't you go wait in his room? We'll send him in to you."

I head to his room and Mr. Lake issues out one more obvious and painful reminder: "Aaron? No Kenneth . . ."

I nod, even though he can't see me. If there's one thing that hasn't changed, it's the smell of week-old socks and underwear. Kenneth wasn't exactly a laundry fan either, the two of them putting it off until Mrs. Lake gave in and did it herself. But everything else is different, like the queen-sized bed Kyle now has—bunk beds gone—and the memorabilia from times I wasn't around for.

The door opens. Kyle, an oblivious "only child," walks into his room and laughs at me. "Your face is busted, Aaron."

There's no hug or fist-bump or how-have-you-been moment. We just are, like we were never separated at all.

"Me-Crazy got me, too," I say, careful with my words. I'm crossing a field of mines. I want to tell Kyle that Me-Crazy is in jail, but maybe he'll think the block is safe for visits. God knows what would happen if someone, just to be a dick, straight up told him he went through Leteo and unstitched his shielded memories. "I see why you bounced."

Kyle leans against his wall, a map thumbtacked to the space above him. "I couldn't keep risking it. Good thing our lease was up anyway so we could get a fresh start. Shittier neighborhood, but some good people here."

"I hear you got a girlfriend," I say, picking up a handball from his bedside drawer. I toss it to him. "Who locked you down?"

We play catch as he tells me all about Tina, a Chinese American girl he met when she brought her little brother into the barbershop. Kyle was giving a Caesar cut and almost messed up. His mentor thought he was distracted because of the work, but it was all because of Tina. I try to pretend I'm interested, but find myself almost tuning out until he asks: "How's Genevieve?"

"We broke up." I remember what Thomas told me when he broke up with Sara. "We just weren't really right for each other anymore."

"Damn, man. Any new prospects yet?"

"Nope," I lie.

I want to come out to Kyle, but he'll have no idea what I'm talking about if I ask him to set the clock for a judgment-free Happy Hour. He's changed—not matured, but he's *been* changed, obviously. Maybe this new Kyle will be cool with Side A. Maybe it'll make him uncomfortable. I used to know the person in front of me and I'm tempted to bring him back, to unwind him, since Kenneth's death is his fault and he should have to live with that. He should know about how Kenneth could walk on his hands, how Kenneth always ate junk food and never had a single cavity, how Kenneth casually played ding-dong-ditch on his neighbors to get a rise out of us.

He should know Kenneth, his twin brother, existed. But it's not my decision to make.

I hang around for a little while longer until it's time for him to shower and meet up with Tina. He puts his girl first now, which I like. I promise to visit him again sometime soon, and he tells me to tell everyone on the block he says what's up. I hug Mrs. and Mr. Lake again, whose faces silently plead: *Don't forget.*

10
LETEO: TAKE TWO

It's the day of my procedure and I'm standing on the corner, outside the Leteo Institute.

Memories: some can be sucker punching, others carry you forward; some stay with you forever, others you forget on your own. You can't really know which ones you'll survive if you don't stay on the battlefield, bad times shooting at you like bullets. But if you're lucky, you'll have plenty of good times to shield you.

Being gay wasn't, and isn't, the problem. It only seemed that way because of everything that branched out from it—my father taking his life, Collin abandoning me, getting jumped on the train, and all the uncertainties ahead. The problem was that I didn't know any better because I forgot my life. And now I know I can't forget.

It won't be an easy life, but I'll soldier through. Thomas didn't even know he was helping me with this—hell, I didn't even know I would become myself again in need of this guidance. The boy with no direction taught me something unforgettable: happiness comes again if you let it.

I close my eyes and count to sixty, zoning everything out like Thomas taught me to do. I reopen my eyes, turn my back on Leteo, and walk home. I owe my mom and brother an apology.

11
MY UNHAPPY BIRTHDAY

Ever since my first birthday, my mom has written me a letter recording my greatest hits of each year. She leaves the letters in my baby album. She even attaches newspaper clippings so I know what was current.

I caught up on all of them on my twelfth birthday. I wasn't surprised that the first letter was pretty uneventful, aside from me spitting up on my mother's graduation gown as she accepted her diploma. Before my second birthday, I walked for the first time when my father came home after being gone for a week—which I learned later was because he got kicked out after assaulting my mom in the street. In the fifth letter, I learned I was once obsessed with collecting key chains. A drawing paper clipped to the eighth letter showed me holding my mom's hand.

These letters are a map of my life. They bring into focus years that are hazy to me. It hurts to admit it, but there were things in those letters that feel like Mom was taking a shot at me. Why did she write down that I was obsessed with singing songs from girl pop stars? Or how when she took Eric and me shopping for toys at CVS, I didn't let him bully me into buying a blue Power

Ranger because I wanted to play with a Jean Grey action figure? I feel like it was her coded way of saying, "This is when I knew about you."

I think liking Brendan was the first time I knew. Sure, singing girl songs was a tip-off too, I guess, but that's when it all clicked that maybe I wasn't who everyone would like me to be. It's funny the way that ran full circle. A couple years ago, I threw away old magazines my mother left sitting in the bathroom, but not before I ripped out pages of hot cologne models and stashed all of them inside an old binder for whenever I had urges. But I got rid of all that before the procedure.

I haven't gotten around to apologizing to Eric or my mom yet, but I will. They were relieved enough the other night when I said I didn't want the procedure anymore. A cloud over our tiny home had lifted. I went straight to bed.

So now I'm acting like this Leteo episode never happened. Eric has agreed to play Avengers vs. Street Fighters with me. When Mom gave me the game this morning, I didn't comment on the scratches on the disc. I don't deserve a mom who works too many hours a week so she can afford our outrageous rent, keep food on the table, and even make sure she has something to give her boys on their birthdays. I lose to Eric because I chose Captain America instead of Black Widow, not trying to draw attention to my growing desire to tell him Side A and be done with it.

Before I leave, I go into Mom's room to thank her again. There are some bills fanned out next to her and on her lap is my baby album. We have a birthday ritual where we look through it together, but maybe she realized the last thing I want to do is reflect on the old days. I see a photo of myself as a five-year-old holding a figurine of Belle from *Beauty and the Beast*.

"First love, right?"

Mom strokes the picture as if she can twirl my old curls. "You carried her everywhere."

"I remember telling everyone she was my girlfriend." I remember believing it too.

"Until you broke up with her for the pink Power Ranger." Mom half smiles. "Tale as old as time."

She flips through the album and this reel of my life is lost to me. There are pictures of me on my father's shoulders when he was still Dad; one of me taking a bath with Eric when we were kids; another one where I'm wrapped in a towel, lying across his lap. Another, another, another, another, and in all these photos is something hard to find now: smiles. "I'm going to go run out for a bit." She looks up at my face and I know she's studying my bruises, yellowed but almost healed. Sometimes I look out the window to try and catch Brendan chilling, thinking maybe I can run downstairs and snuff him. "I'll be fine."

"How's Genevieve?"

"Happy," I lie, and it's a lie because you can't be happy with someone who can't love you back.

"Are you meeting up with her today?"

"Nope," I say. She hasn't even called or texted me.

"Going to go see Thomas?"

That one stabs me hard. I haven't heard from him either. "I'm linking up with Collin."

She holds my hand and nods. "Okay, my son. Go have fun. Be safe." She dismisses me but doesn't release her grip on me, not for a while, and when she does, she holds on to the baby book the way someone would hold on to the edge of a cliff, feet dangling.

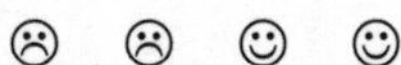

I THINK COLLIN HAS legit forgotten it's my birthday. But maybe it's because he's been really stressed lately. Nicole is demanding more attention from him since he's been spending his free time with me behind her back. His other complaints are small, like how she's craving ice cubes. The crunching bothers him.

Screw all his bitching because it's his fault she's pregnant—okay, our fault for being cowards—but he's 100 percent to blame for letting her fall in love with him. I never really understood why he "liked" Nicole, and you can argue that I'm looking at her with the wrong lenses, but I know she's the type of thoughtful girl who will wish you happy birthday every hour of the day and get you presents you never realized you wanted. I can't pretend Collin is the only guilty one—I'm not an asshole, too. I let Genevieve fall in love with me. But that means Thomas is also an asshole because he let me fall . . . Yeah, he definitely let me fall and couldn't bother to pick me up.

But I have Collin. I never admitted loving him to his face, not even to fill these holes of loneliness. When he tells me to follow him, I'm expecting a surprise, but instead we end up at our spot behind the fence. We have sex quickly, and he heads off to work without wishing me a happy birthday, just a pat on the back after he pulled up his pants from around his ankles.

I go the long route so I can walk past Thomas's building in the hopes of seeing him outside or staring out of his window. Yeah, there's the risk of seeing him holding hands with Genevieve as they go upstairs and probably have sex so he can feel straight. But I've been through that pain before with Collin, and I just want to see him for at least a moment.

I spot Skinny-Dave across the street and when he sees me, he stays underneath the traffic light even though it's signaling for him to cross. He knows better now that Me-Crazy isn't around.

Maintenance has finally boarded the lobby door with plywood. I check the mail. There are two birthday cards from my eighty-year-old aunt with dementia; I'm not as surprised that she sent two cards as I am that she remembered my birthday at all. I walk down to the elevator and—just like he surprised me the day Me-Crazy almost killed me—Thomas is there.

He's leaning against the wall and I want to smile, but I don't because he isn't.

"I didn't get the procedure," I tell him.

He looks at me for a second. The circles under his eyes are darker than when I last saw him at Good Food's. He opens the staircase door and rolls out a dark blue mountain bike. It's either a new bike or something he waxed and fixed up until it looked new. I'm not sure which it is because he's capable of both. He presses down on the kickstand and walks over to me. I'm scared he's going to walk past without saying anything but instead he hugs me hard, and I hug him back—also hard because there's something that feels very final about this hug.

When he lets go, I do too, which feels insanely stupid. Then he starts walking toward the door.

"Thomas, I fell . . ."

Not once does he stop or even hesitate. He walks straight out and leaves me. And now I'm alone with the bike he once promised to teach me how to ride since no one else ever did, both of us unaware at that time that it was a lie: Collin tried and I sucked.

I eventually find the strength to go upstairs, gripping the handles of my shiny new blue bike tightly. I collapse onto my bed with the bike at my feet. Seeing him was what I wanted, no, *needed* for this day to even feel somewhat right. But now I'm just staring at the clock as the hours run by, wondering if I'll hear from Genevieve before it hits midnight.

And then the weirdest shit happens: it's already 1:16 A.M.

Eric is sleeping. There's a dinner plate at the foot of my bed where I always leave it, except I don't remember eating whatever it was or even being hungry. On my phone there's a message from Genevieve wishing me a happy birthday at 11:59

P.M. I should respond to her and say thank you, but she's probably asleep, too.

The last thing I remember is throwing myself on my bed. Nothing after that. Total blackout. I'm so scared I'm crying, except I don't really know if I can pinpoint the moment when I started crying. I turn to the clock that's jumped from 1:16 to 1:27, and I cry harder because something impossible is happening to me.

I shake Eric awake, and he curses at me before his face registers something is off. I don't even know what to tell him at first, still not even convinced that this isn't a nightmare, but finally I say, "What the fuck? What the fuck is going on?"

He asks me what I'm talking about, but the words sound far away.

I'm suddenly disoriented again. I find myself in the middle of my mom's bed, crying so hard my throat aches. As a kid, I would pray at the edge of the bed for new action figures or my own bedroom. Then I would crawl into the space left open for me between my brother and mom because I couldn't sleep without holding her hair. But as my mind continues steering itself, going this way and that, I find myself praying only to wake up.

12
NO MORE TOMORROWS

"Anterograde amnesia," Evangeline tells my mother and me.

We're in her office. It's 4:09 A.M. I've been keeping my eyes pinned to the clock for my own sanity, though I can't really tell if there has been any other crazy skip in time like a few hours ago.

"It's an inability to form new memories," she adds.

The clock reads 4:13 A.M.

"What's anterograde amnesia?" I ask. It sounds familiar. I think she mentioned it before my procedure, but I can't remember what it is.

"It's an inability to form new memories," Evangeline replies, exchanging looks with my mother, who's crying. She's pretty much been crying since I ran into her bed. When she called Evangeline, she was crying. On the cab ride over, she was crying. I can't remember her not crying.

"Are you following, Aaron?" Evangeline asks.

"Yeah," I say. "You think that's what's happening to me? That I'm not remembering stuff that's going on now?"

"Can you recall any other issues with your memories recently?" she presses.

"You're asking me to remember something I probably forgot?"

"Yes. Something that may have confused you since your attack, but stuck out to you like earlier tonight?"

Thinking is hard. No, remembering is hard. I'm proud of myself when I remember how odd it felt when I couldn't remember drinking my first cup of coffee at the diner with Collin, and how Genevieve told me I was repeating myself at Leteo. I only told her Thomas didn't like her once—or I thought I only said it once. And when I blanked out at Good Food's. Who knows what else?

"Yes," I answer, my heart pounding. "I can remember forgetting stuff." I just can't remember what I'm forgetting. "I feel like I should be crying or having a panic attack."

My mother buries her face in her hands, racked with silent sobs. Evangeline takes a deep breath before telling me, "You already did."

"What does this mean? How do you fix me? Another procedure?"

She sounds like a robot when she speaks. There are a bunch of options, though nothing sounds promising. The condition is still a mystery even to top neurologists because no one's locked down the exact science of storing memories. She says something about neurons and synapses and medial temporal lobes and the hippocampus, and even though it's all doctor-speak, I do my best committing it to memory because I can already feel the words slipping away. The treatments used for those suffering from anterograde amnesia aren't all that different from the ones used for Alzheimer's patients. Medication can enhance the cholinergic brain functions. Psychotherapy is not necessary; this is about brain function. Probably for the best, because I would punch someone if they tried using hypnosis on me; the last thing I need is someone else playing with my mind.

What I want to forget is when she says, "Unfortunately, in some cases it's irreversible."

I can't help but notice she sounds tired, and not because it's in the middle of the night or because she's bored, but possibly because she's exhausted of repeating herself in the event she's told me this several times already.

"Has this happened to any of your patients before?"

Evangeline nods. "Yes."

"So? What happened?"

She meets my gaze. "The amnesia takes hold quickly, sometimes within a few days."

"So I have less than a fucking week?" No one scolds me for my language.

"Maybe more," Evangeline says in that clinical and robotic tone.

My heart pounds harder and I'm scared I'm forgetting how to breathe, a basic instinct. I feel like I'll faint, and then I'll probably forget how to wake up. "What the hell will my life look like?"

"Challenging, but not impossible. This was all in the literature, Aaron. For the most part, you might be limited to the knowledge you had before the procedure. I know of a musician who writes his own songs and forgets them soon after, but he still plays guitar beautifully because it's a skill he learned before the trauma he wished to erase."

I understand what she's saying. Before. Before is all I will have left, and Before destroyed me before.

"Why bother living?"

I'm thinking out loud and my mom cries harder. Shitty of me because the smiling scar on my wrist speaks for itself, but right now, like Before: dying seems easiest.

Evangeline leans toward me. "You have so much to live for," she whispers.

"Like what?" I ask, and either she told me and I already forgot or she has nothing convincing to say. This is going to be a long night. Well, a long night for them anyway. It'll fly by for me.

"What's anterograde amnesia?" I ask Evangeline at 4:21 A.M.

13

ONLY YESTERDAYS

I sort of, kind of, definitely always took yesterdays for granted—and now yesterdays are all I have left. Some of them, at least.

Yesterday.

A lot of people will remember a hug with a friend, but will have forgotten what time they woke up and ate for lunch. Others will share the crazy dreams they had last night, but the clothes they wore or books they read on the subway will slip away. And some will keep their stories to themselves, a secret left in the past only they can revisit.

I will do none of those things.

Tomorrow I might not remember hugging anyone, if there's anyone even left to hug. I won't know what I ate for lunch and will only know if I ate at all depending on whether or not my stomach is growling. What time I wake up won't matter because I'll always be waking up. And I'll probably wear the same shirt and pants over and over while endlessly recommending *Scorpius Hawthorne* because new words will have zero weight in my head.

The only way I can see myself getting through this is by saying goodbye. Even if I never change, everything and everyone around me will. No one's going to hang with the guy who doesn't know what day it is or can't keep up with their lives. I'll always be lost and lonely or surrounded by strangers constantly repeating themselves.

Lose-lose.

WHEN I TRY THE door; the chain is on. We never used to use it. We weren't even using it in case any of my friends tried breaking in to finish the job Me-Crazy started. This can only mean that they're locking me in so I don't get lost outside.

I feel sick but they're right; I could forget where I am in the middle of a street or even in the middle of the air after a car sends me flying. On the other hand, I can't just wait here while my mind withers away. I quickly unchain the door, but Eric is fast and catches me before I can run out.

"What the hell are you doing?" he demands, holding my arm tight.

"I have shit to do."

Mom appears from her room, but stays silent.

"What's that?" Eric asks.

"Something I need to do for myself."

"That's not a surprise—" He stops himself and takes a deep breath. "I'm going to shut up and be a good brother and not talk to you until I'm sure you won't remember."

Low blow. "Fuck you. Say it now and don't hide behind my amnesia. You owe me that."

"Okay. I'm game," Eric says, his grip on my arm tightening, his eyes ablaze. "You're selfish, Aaron. You used a cheat code to make life easier without thinking about how it would affect us. We've had to watch you walk around like a zombie. You did this to yourself, okay?"

I stare back at him. "Maybe I wouldn't have raced to forget myself if you made me feel more comfortable with who I am instead of giving me shit for choosing girl characters in video games."

"I never gave a flying fuck about any of that. They were just jokes. I thought you were tough enough to handle them. I'm sorry!" His words, his *apology*, take us all back, himself included. The last time I saw him this red was when we told him what happened to our father. So it's no surprise he adds: "You stopped being your own man to please someone who abandoned us."

"He committed suicide because of *me*. Not you."

"Baby, he didn't kill himself because of you," Mom finally jumps in. "Your father had it rough and—"

"Stop it! When he was arrested, I thought we were finally safe from him. And then he came home and . . ." I'm crying, but I'm happy that I can remember when the tears started falling: it was when I admitted his absence was a good thing.

That shuts them up.

Shuts me up too because I now understand why they threw away all his stuff. They always knew better.

"You messed up," Eric says. But his voice softens, and there's something different in his eyes. It's sympathy. He turns to Mom, rapping his knuckles against the wall with his free hand, his other hand still gripping me. Our father rapped his knuckles against the wall like that once when he was pissed we wouldn't go downstairs to get him a slice of pizza from Yolanda's. Then he punched a hole in it. I feel something like hope, just because of the fact I remembered. "You should've never signed off on that procedure," he says to Mom.

Mom looks back and forth between us, like she's just been outed for a crime. "I was trying to save your brother—"

"No," Eric snaps. "This is about you and losing control of

your family. You treated Aaron like he would've been helpless without this procedure and look where that's landed him!"

I wrench myself free of Eric's grasp. Maybe he has cracked. Maybe he had some things he wanted to forget too. Maybe he wasn't quite right in the head either after our father committed suicide in the same bathtub where he bathed us.

In this moment, I know Eric is not going to grow up to be like our father. He loves us. He should've been paid the same attention from not only our mom, but from me, too. I never asked him how he was doing.

Mom catches herself in the grimy hallway mirror. Maybe she's really seeing herself now. She's lost so much weight these past few months, maybe twenty or thirty pounds. Eric leans back against the wall and slides down, "This isn't about me being jealous of you, Aaron. Maybe I am a little bit. But I agree that we're better off without him."

I'm tempted to reach down and take his hand, but I don't.

He looks up at me.

"Remember when we had trouble beating the last few levels of Zelda? We pooled our allowances and bought the walk-through guide to help us out." He softly adds, "You should've asked for help before cheating."

Sometimes pain is so unmanageable that the idea of spending another day with it seems impossible. Other times pain acts as a compass to help you get through the messier tunnels of growing up. But the pain can only help you find happiness if you can remember it.

"Do we still have anything that belonged to Dad?" I ask. And then the box is in my hand. It's not even half full, just a couple of old sweaters and track sneakers. Eric opens the door for me without a fight, and he and Mom both follow me to the garbage chute down the hall. I cling to every detail. This will make for a memory. And despite everything, I can't help but hesitate when

I think back to the days where my father wasn't a monster. Then I turn the box over and everything thumps down the chute until it's quiet.

☹ ☹ ☺ ☺

IN SCHOOL I ONCE read about gypsies and how they grieved for loved ones by covering all the mirrors in their caravan for as long as they needed. Sometimes days, sometimes weeks, sometimes months, and in rare cases, years. As of now, we're done covering the mirrors. Together we've searched the apartment for any last scrap of him we don't want.

Eric puts on his sneakers after we get back inside the apartment. Without looking at me, he says, "If it's worth anything to you, I'm sorry for everything I ever said." I want to thank him for swallowing his pride, but he quickly adds, "So where are we going?"

"What?"

"You said you have shit to do, right? Mom's not going to let you go alone."

I don't remember saying that, but I do have shit to do. I have four people to see, four goodbyes to make. I keep my head low and let my brother follow me out so I can strike names off this bucket list of mine.

14

THE SORT OF BEST FRIEND

It's a dead giveaway where we can find Brendan; we spot his client go into the staircase. I want to see Brendan first, not because he lives closest to me, not because I've known him the longest, but because he needs to see the damage he's done. I'm about to go into the staircase when Eric stops me.

"I shouldn't have let you have sex with Genevieve," he whispers.

I'm so confused that I almost laugh. "That had nothing to do with you."

"I knew the truth. That's enough to put me at fault if you got her pregnant. I didn't stop you because I thought your life was going to be easier when you weren't gay. It didn't matter to me if you unknowingly led someone on."

And then Eric is pacing from wall to wall in the lobby.

"That had nothing to do with you," I say, and immediately after I say it, I can't get aboard the train of thought that brought me to those words. "I don't know what's going on."

"It's okay," Eric says. He recaps the conversation. "It's crazy how you still turned out to be gay. You must really like that dude you kept hanging out with."

Now this is so awkward I actually *do* want to forget it. "I have to go take care of this," I mumble. "Wait here for me."

I hand him the comics I want to give Collin and run into the staircase before he can protest. I don't hear Brendan or that girl Nate running off so I keep jogging down. Brendan looks like he's seeing a pissed-off ghost when I turn the corner. I swing at him and he ducks, which is fine because I was really hoping to kick him in the balls, which I do.

He crumples to the floor. Nate picks up the weed and runs away. No doubt she lost a dealer after stealing, but she won't give a shit while she's high today.

Brendan holds his crotch, his manhood, and groans. "I had that coming."

I almost have sympathy pains for him because getting hit in the balls sucks hard. Almost. "You fuckers fucked up my fucking brain!" I shout, ready to pounce on him all over again. "Major fucking memory loss and there's a chance I'm going to fucking forget this fucking conversation but I'll never fucking forget how my fucking friend almost fucking killed me because he fucking hated me."

No matter how many times I say it out loud or to myself, I can never wrap my head around the fact that Brendan could've gone to jail forever for killing me.

Maybe it's okay to forget. I'll never play cards in his hallway again whenever it's snowing outside or too chaotic to hang out in his house. I'll never throw popcorn at his grandfather while he's snoring in front of the TV again. I'll never sleep over again and kick at the top bunk where he almost got this girl Simone pregnant before he learned the magic of condoms. I'll never sit at his computer with him and write crude customer reviews on insane products, like a banana slicer and dog-shaped dog whistles. I'll never leave his sneakers outside the window so his room won't smell like feet.

"I don't hate you," Brendan says. "I just don't understand why you're being gay."

"I can't change that," I say. Except for that time I could, and even then, I still kind of couldn't.

He sits up and rests his elbow on his knee. "You chose that Thomas kid over us. We're your blood, not him or anyone else."

"Maybe that's true. But I never knew. And I'm basically a toy without batteries because of you guys."

"Your boys will take care of you, A."

"Even if I'm gay?" I say the word out loud, about myself, because even though I never chose this, I can choose to accept it before it's too late.

Brendan says nothing. I have my answer. I head back up the stairs and hope one day Brendan will find his happy ending. I really do want this for my very confused, former sort of best friend.

15
THE BOY WHO WON'T MAN UP

I'm about to sit in the alleyway between the meat market and flower shop and maybe flip through one of the comics I brought for Collin—Issue #7 of *The Dark Alternates*, the big finale—but community service do-gooders are painting over the spray-painted black-and-blue world Collin and I made.

And then he's here.

"'Sup," Collin says, nodding at me. He looks around, probably for spies with cameras, and finds the community service team in our spot. "Hey, what the hell are they doing?"

"Community service," I say.

"Where can we go instead? You need to go buy a condom too because Nicole was finally in the mood last night and I used mine."

Of course he uses a condom *after* she's pregnant.

"Don't need them."

"You want to do it without . . . ?"

"Look, our graffiti is gone."

"Yeah. That sucks. Oh shit, you got the last issue! Let's go read it." I hand the comic over to him. In another life, this could've been cool. He speculates on what might happen: "Who do you think the redhead in the scarlet robe is? Do you think the Faceless Overlords will go through with the siege? Shit, they have to, don't they? Man, this is going to be insane."

I sit down on the curb and ask him to join me. "I can't keep wrecking things, Collin. The way I feel about you has changed, and I don't think it's because there are still some memories of our good times hidden in my head or something."

"Wait, you for real did that Leteo thing?"

"Yeah. I forgot everything that went down with you."

"Are you fucking with me again?"

"I'm not."

"Seriously, you no joke had your mind wiped?"

"Don't you feel bad that Nicole has no idea you're with me?"

He doesn't say no or admit to how little he gives a shit.

"Well, I feel bad," I tell him. "This makes us different. I don't think you suck as a person. I legit believe you'll be better than this one day, but if you want to continue faking out your family, that's your unhappiness, not mine."

Collin shrugs, hiding his pain poorly. "So, what, forget we ever happened, right? I don't want you coming at me tomorrow or the day after." He gets up, pacing back and forth to give me enough time to take back my words.

I don't.

"Okay then. I'm going." He's holding on to the comic, in no way about to give it back, and crosses the street to retreat back to his safe life built on lies. But then he freezes. He turns and rushes back over to me. "Are you sure about this?'

I can almost forgive him now. "I can't screw anyone over anymore, Collin," I say. "Look, I loved you, but now isn't the time for us."

Collin flips me off and walks away.

I lean forward on the curb to flip through the comic when I realize it's not in my hands. I look around to see if I dropped it before realizing what's happened.

16
THE GIRL WITH THE UNFINISHED PAINTINGS

I forgot what happened with Collin. And I hope to God he'll change and that it'll be something worth missing. I just hope I remember everything with Genevieve because she's the one I would've been lucky enough to share a happy ending with.

She loves me in a way that's not fair to her. And it's shitty times two because I know the feeling.

Before I knock on her door, I ask Eric to wait downstairs for me. I extend an arm to pat his shoulder. He must think I'm trying to hug him because he leans in and it's awkward and I recover by hugging him for the first time since we were kids.

"Uh, thanks again. I feel like you've been my seeing-eye dog or something."

"Forget it. You owe me one now. But don't forget—" He slaps his hand over his mouth. "Forget I said 'forget.' Um. I'll be downstairs."

"Okay."

I knock on the door, trying to remember everything I have to say while I still have the chance. Her father calls from inside the apartment, asking who it is, and I tell him it's me. He opens the door, studying me up and down. I can smell his beer breath.

"How you doin', Aaron?"

"I'm okay. Is Gen home?"

"Still in her room, I think."

Other fathers wouldn't let a boy into their home the way he does.

Her door is cracked open and I peek in and see her on her bed surrounded by wet paintbrushes and open paint bottles and sketchbooks. She tears a page out of one book, crumples it up, and throws it onto the floor, the graveyard of failed drawings. Then she grabs a new brush.

I knock and let myself in, tensing up when she looks at me.

She drops her paintbrush and bursts into tears.

I rush to comfort her, but there's no room for me to sit with all these open sketchbooks and unfinished paintings on her bed. There's one of a girl talking to a boy made of leaves; another of an ocean monster destroying a girl's sand castle; a third of a girl falling out of a tree while a boy sits idly by eating an apple. I shove them aside. I'm not just wrapping my arms around her to make her happy or to lie to myself; I have to stop her hurting, and for once it's so real I forget my own forgetting problems.

"I know better than to ask if you're okay," I whisper.

Genevieve pulls her hands away from her face. Now probably isn't the best time to point out the fingerprints of paint across her forehead and cheeks. "Seeing you with Collin really messed me up, Aaron. I have no idea if you were at the track field to see Thomas or if it was a coincidence, but it brought back everything I had to pretend never happened."

I turn away. "I'm sorry about that. And about him. I'm really, really sorry I led you on before the procedure. And even sometime after it. I wasn't fully ready to be this guy who liked guys, and needed a girlfriend to protect me."

She strokes my face, probably getting paint on me. "I know. Even after our first kiss, I knew."

"Only a guy who likes guys wouldn't want to kiss you," I say. "I'm sorry for being such an asshole."

Genevieve traces my scar, left to right and right to left, like I have countless times, like she might have too, if I could remember. "I could never hate you for being gay, but when you came back to me, I loved forgetting you were."

"We made a pretty cool faux-couple when I thought it was real," I joke.

She rests her head on my shoulder. "If I could do it over, I wouldn't have lied to myself that it was real. I wouldn't have dated you and I definitely wouldn't have had sex with you." There's a moment where I think she's going to say something more. She sighs and adds, "So you didn't go through with the procedure. What made you change your mind?"

I can't comfortably tell her how Thomas made me okay with myself. I can't tell her how I want to spend my days taking on the world with him and watching movies and drinking Blue Moons late into the night while we draw on each other.

"The procedure promised happiness but it wasn't real. About Leteo, actually . . . my mind is kind of messed up, which is why I really had to see you today. I'm going through this thing called anterograde amnesia which means—"

Genevieve pulls away. "I knew it." Her bloodshot eyes are wide, searching. "It was in the video we watched before, the one about side effects. You also . . . when I spoke to you the day after you woke up, you forgot something I said to you. I thought you zoned out or were trying to hurt me."

I can't be selfish anymore. "Are you and Thomas happy together?"

"We're nothing right now. Honestly. Just hanging out, but I like it. I think I need something real after everything . . ." It stings and burns and kind of kills me too, but I don't take it personally. "I'm sorry this is happening. I'm sure it's not something you're particularly excited to remember."

"Two of my favorite people being happy? Sure it is." While it isn't 100 percent genuine, it's not a lie either. Not by any stretch. As long as Thomas is telling the truth about who he is. She would be lucky to have him and he would be damn lucky to have her.

I glance at her crumpled drawings on the floor. "Maybe you're drawing the wrong things. You should try painting what you want your life to look like. It could be a map of your future. I'm sure Thomas would love to help you with that as long as you don't let him get too carried away with it."

"Or maybe *you* can help me," Genevieve says, scooting over.

"I can't." I swallow and choke out the last two words, suddenly remembering my brother is downstairs waiting for me. "You're beautiful."

"Beautiful enough to turn you straight?" She wipes a tear away and laughs a little. "A girl's gotta try. I love you, Aaron. I don't mean it in a weird way."

This is probably the last time we'll stare at each other like this. I lean in and kiss her, and it's genuine and happy and all final kisses should be like this.

"Genevieve, no matter what . . ."

She rests her forehead on mine.

Without having forgotten I said it before, I keep repeating, "I love you in a non-weird way too. I love you in a non-weird way too. I love you in a non-weird way too . . ."

17
THE BOY ON THE ROOFTOP

My senior citizen illness keeps getting the best of me.

I'm going to lose my job at Good Food's. If I become a bus driver, I'll forget my route. If I become a teacher, I'll forget my students' names and lesson plans. If I'm a banker, I'll have no money in my safe after I keep handing over cash. If I'm in the army, I'll forget how to use the gun and get all the wrong people killed.

The only thing I'll be good for is being a failed lab rat.

I doubt I'll be able to concentrate enough to finish my comic, but I've made peace with that. It's okay how some stories leave off without an ending. Life doesn't always deliver the one you would expect.

I'll never be in a relationship again. If I met someone new only to forget him later, it's not fair.

So now there's only one apology left to make.

It takes some convincing, but I do it. I get Eric to back off and let me head over to Thomas's house by myself.

Once Thomas knows about my condition there's no way he'll let me wander the streets alone. I just don't want to rush my time with him.

Now I'm slowly climbing up the fire escape. I'm getting used to these jump-cuts in my life. I don't scramble up the steps with the thrill I had all summer, but with the fear of someone marching to his death. When I reach his window, the curtains are drawn. But I can still see a sliver of Thomas leaning over his table and writing. I bet he's journaling.

I knock on the pane and he jumps.

And then, like Genevieve, he blinks a few times, fast. His eyes fill with tears. I shake my head.

"Meet me on the roof," I tell him.

He nods.

I head on up and just wait, reminding myself again and again what I'm doing and why I'm here. I check out the streetlamps turning on below, glowing orange as evening kicks in, and then up at the few stars hanging out in the sky. I see him step off the fire escape, and all of a sudden he's sitting on the ledge.

I'm trembling a little bit. This is another forever moment. "So something crazy is happening," I tell him. I lie down on the ground. The stars don't shift, and I'm very appreciative. "There's been a trauma in the part of my brain where you store your memories. It's only partial right now, but my doctor thinks there's a chance it'll take full effect at some point or another. If I don't remember something you say, I'm sorry."

Thomas is now down beside me. For a while we don't say anything else. Or maybe we have an entire conversation I don't remember.

What I have is this:

He asks, "Do you think there's a chance you were someone really awful in a past life? Like a long time ago in a galaxy far, far away you were Darth Vader? I feel like you can't catch a break."

I laugh and quickly repeat it in my head several times.

"Sure feels that way," I say. "I honestly don't want to live anymore, Thomas. I think it could be freeing to just get up and fly off this rooftop . . ."

"If you love me, Stretch, you won't leave me with the memory of you jumping off this roof now, or ever. Okay? If there's one thing I'm begging you to remember from this conversation, it's that promise."

"Okay, but in exchange you have to promise to never die. I can't stand the pain of someone telling me every day that you're dead. You need to always be alive and happy, okay?"

He laughs through his tears. "You got it, Stretch. Immortality. No problem."

"And happy too," I say.

He props his knees up and cracks his knuckles. "Okay. I need to come clean about something. I suspected you liked me after you came out with Side A. You understand me in a way a lot of other people don't. If I'm being one hundred percent honest, I think our friendship even confused me a little, but I'm also one hundred percent sure that I'm still straight because I would've been chasing after you if I wasn't."

I try to say something, but I can't.

"We can't ever be together," he finished. "But I always want to know you, even if we're in the same room and you're just saying hi to me over and over again, I'll be perfectly happy. I'll always want to be sitting across from you."

So now in this moment I have this fantasy: Thomas is straight—which I now believe is either very real or who he needs to be right now—but he goes to Leteo and convinces them to give him a procedure so he can forget he's straight. Once he's gay, he finds me just like he said he would and we build a life of happy memories together.

But like with everyone else, I know better. I can picture Thomas and Genevieve making each other happy. Genevieve will glow whenever he leans in to her to whisper a joke that isn't my business. He'll sweep her off her feet, as if they're newlyweds, and carry her into a world I can never share with either of them.

"What would Thomas Reyes do if he were in my situation?" I ask.

Thomas sits up. "I would do my damn best to be more happy than not. You've already experienced so much bullshit so you can always look back on how things could be worse. That's my two cents."

I may never get to see the person Thomas grows up to be. If he becomes a director or wrestler or deejay or set designer or gay or straight, I may be too lost in the past for it ever to click.

"I don't want to forget, Thomas."

"I don't want you to either. Just remember that I love the hell out of you, okay?"

I repeat it over and over because there are so many memories crowding my head that don't need to be there. "I don't want to forget, Thomas."

It shocks me when he starts straight-up sobbing, but it's even more shocking when he holds my hand. But there is the happiness he promised, too. He loves me without being in love with me and that's all I can ask of him. I don't even need to hear him say it to believe it.

"No homo, Stretch."

"I know." I smile, and squeeze his hand back. "Hell of a happy ending, right?"

PART FOUR: MORE HAPPY THAN NOT

THE DAY WE START OVER

The Leteo Institute, or more specifically, Evangeline, is able to get me short-listed for a reparative procedure they've been developing in Sweden.

In exchange, I'm going to help them out with some of the safer experimental science. The hope is to find a cure for amnesia one day. It may never happen in my lifetime, but maybe someone will figure it out eventually and I'll have played a part in that. Funny how I once turned to Leteo to forget and now I'm counting on them to help me—and maybe millions of others—remember.

My mom considered moving us all upstate to get away from the sucker-punching memories, but we're done running. Instead, we're painting the walls white and starting over. I'm helping Mom with the bedroom. I know it's hard. My father was the one who chose gray.

I ask her what color she'll paint her new room.

"I think I'll leave it white. It's pure and reminds me of a rabbit I used to have. It's nice to reflect, sometimes."

☺ ☺ ☺ ☹

THE DAY I LOOK AHEAD

Eric and I take a break from painting our living room green with a round of Avengers vs. Street Fighters. He chooses Wolverine, of course. I choose Black Widow because I'm tired of going easy on him.

He sucks his teeth when I win.

There is no judging. There are no jokes made.

He challenges me to another round.

I remember enough to remember that this is the first time we've really had fun in a long time, like we did when my father wasn't around.

☺ ☺ ☺ ☹

THE DAY I MOVE ON

During the cleaning, I find a bunch of my old composition notebooks. I leaf through the childhood drawings, not caring about how I didn't have a good eye for color or how careless I was with my shading. I just laugh over and over at the memories there. I haven't thought about that funny villain I invented, Mr. Overlord King, in years. He and Sun Warden will likely live in harmony in my character's afterlife world. Either that or they'll fight to the death over and over again.

But the whole thing sparks me to chronicle my life—all the good stuff, at least—in pictures. And I'll start off every illustration with a header that reads, "Remember That Time . . ."

☺ ☺ ☺ ☹

THE DAY I FORGET

I'm wheeling my new bike outside as a building super works on final repairs of the lobby door I was thrown through.

I'm only allowed into the second court, where my mom and brother can check in on me from our window. It's a compromise so I can have some alone time. The orange-and-green playground, the black mat where we all used to wrestle, the picnic benches where we drank quarter juices, the monkey bars we used for pull-ups, the old friends who watch me from the other side of the courtyard . . . this will forever be the place where I grew up.

Today I'm teaching myself to ride a bike so it doesn't feel like *the* end.

I don't need my father or Collin or Thomas to do this.

I adjust the seat before relaxing into it. I grip the handlebars. I rest one foot on the pedal and keep kicking off with the other, sort of like I'm a stallion about to race, until both feet are on the pedals.

And then I'm sailing forward with an amateur's balance and some wind in my ears. I get the rhythm down until I'm faced with a wall and sharply turn.

I try steadying myself but I drop and the bike slams into my knee.

It hurts, but not any more than that one time Baby Freddy threw a doorstopper block at my shoulder for losing his softball, or when I was skating downhill and crashed into a garbage can.

Brendan, Skinny-Dave, Nolan, and Fat-Dave are still staring at me from the same spot where we used to play card games and drank our first beers in brown paper bags. Brendan is the only one who gets up and steps forward like he's going to come and help me, but I hold up my hand and he stops.

Our friendship is over.

I stand, get back on the bike, ride for a bit, and fall again.

Stand. Ride. Fall.

Stand.

Ride.

I'm riding, riding, riding. I ride past Good Food's where I can never work again. I ride in circles, really having a handle on this thing that my father should've taught me if only he were more of a dad, until the worst thing happens:

How am I on a bike?

REMEMBER THAT TIME

I play Remember That Time a lot.

I've become this happiness scavenger who picks away at the ugliness of the world, because if there's happiness tucked away in my tragedies, I'll find it no matter what. If the blind can find joy in music, and the deaf can discover it with colors, I will do my best to always find the sun in the darkness because my life isn't one sad ending—it's a series of endless happy beginnings.

I've lost count of how many sketchbooks I have. Sometimes my drawings are unfinished because I'll forget what memory I'm recalling, but I don't get discouraged and stop, not always at least. I wear the pencils thin, the markers dry, and I keep drawing. I keep trying to remember the next thing in case it's the last chance I have.

Remember that time Brendan taught me how to make a fist?

Remember that time we were all wrestling, and me and Brendan went up against Kenneth and Kyle in a tag-team match where we pinned the twins down in less than five minutes?

Remember that time my mom did what I begged of her, even

though it broke her? And how she saved me from repeating my first mistake?

Remember that time Eric had my back in a way I would've never bet on?

Remember that time Collin chose me and I chose him?

Remember that time I met Thomas, a guy who desperately wants to walk into a Discovery Factory to figure out who he's going to be?

And remember how before Thomas and Collin unlocked something in me, there was Genevieve, the artist who started up this game with me and loved me in a way that wasn't fair to her?

I definitely do and always will.

It's storming outside right now. I stare out the window. I can't tell you if it rained yesterday or even what day it is. It always feels like I'm waking up, minute after minute, like I'm in my own little time zone. But as I trace my smiling scar—unable to do so without remembering the time Thomas poked two eyes onto my wrist with dirt—I still have hope in what Evangeline and Leteo hope for, too.

And while I wait, happiness exists where I can get it. In these notebooks, where worlds of memories greet me, almost like a childhood friend who moved away for years and finally came back home.

I'm more happy than not.

Don't forget me.

CONTINUE READING FOR AARON'S MORE HAPPY ENDING

MORE HAPPY ENDING

Does anyone remember me?

I know time is moving forward because that's how time works, but I feel stuck in the same day and it's maddening. I can't prove that there are more drawings on my tiny-ass desk here today than there were yesterday because I can't remember a damn thing about yesterday.

I sketch random memories as they come and go: standing shirtless in the sprinklers with Thomas as he rested his hands on my shoulders; Genevieve sitting in my lap as she hugged me and cried and told me she loved me; sitting on the rooftop with Thomas when I gave him the news about this anterograde amnesia; Evangeline telling me the truth about who she was; Mom flipping through my baby book on my birthday; playing video games with Eric; chilling in an aisle at Comic Book Asylum with Collin; playing Skelzies with Brendan, Baby Freddy, and the rest of the crew. There's a balled-up piece of paper that I unfold, and it's a drawing of Me-Crazy throwing me through the lobby door downstairs and it strikes my heart so fucking hard.

He could've killed me.

I'm alive, but he ruined my life.

I put down my pen, breathing in the smell of pasta. Mom is making lunch. I turn to the window and it's dark out. Dinner. She's making dinner. I can't remember what I had for lunch. Maybe there's a drawing of what I ate somewhere in this pile.

I look down again at the drawing of Me-Crazy. The line work around our bodies is chaotic.

How many times have I drawn this? How much time has passed since then? Days? Weeks? Months? I still feel young, but I don't know if that's normal since it's not like I can remember those stretches of time where I would've matured. Am I still seventeen? Am I now eighteen? Nineteen? Twenty?

I get up to check myself out in the mirror to see how old I look.

I slide my chair underneath my desk, which is close to the TV where Eric plays his games. Then I turn around and freeze.

What did I get up for?

I don't have to pee. I'm not hungry. I don't know, but I'm pissed off at myself. What if it was important? What if I figured out how to save myself from this amnesia with a stroke of genius that Evangeline and the rest of her team would never consider because it's so out of the box? What if I was going to leave myself a note on how to keep finding happiness even though my life is a mess? I know I was optimistic about making the best of my situation. I ran my mouth about finding the sun in the darkness, but I don't want the darkness at all—I want sunburn, I want blinding lights, I want happiness.

Why am I standing?

"What am I doing?!"

Mom is by my side and guiding to me my bed. "It's okay, my son, everything is okay."

"No it isn't!"

I don't know the day, the month, the season. I get this pull to check myself out in the mirror to see if I will recognize myself the way I recognize my hands. This hand that held Thomas's hand on the rooftop. This hand that held Genevieve's hand around the city. This hand that turned into a fist when I had to fight off my friends.

Eric appears out of nowhere, almost like he's a glitch in a game. I didn't even know he was home. He has shaving cream on his face, and I have no idea how old my brother is.

"Aaron, chill out."

"Get him his books," Mom says, crying and exhausted. "Please, God, let this next surgery work."

Surgery?

Eric hands me a stack of notebooks.

What the hell is this, homework? There's no way I'm still in school, right? Evangeline told me people with short-term memory continue advancing through lessons, but I was struggling with school when I had it all together.

"The blue journal is all your private thoughts," Mom says through her tears. "The green one has messages from all your loved ones that they write when they visit you."

Story of my life, but I don't recognize these journals, let alone remember writing in them, but when I open up the blue one, it's definitely my handwriting. I flip to an entry about having fun playing Othello with Mom; a page later I'm writing about how suicidal I am.

I shut the journal and look at the smiling scar that's still on my wrist. It's too scary to think of that being a possibility, to feel so hopeless that I would call it quits. I open the green journal. The entries are all signed so I don't have to fight to remember who wrote them. Mom tells me how much she loved hearing me laugh when she told me a joke. There's a sketch from Genevieve of the two of us drawing side-by-side—she's meta that way. Then there's a paragraph in Thomas's beautiful penmanship

(I remember that) about how he saved up and bought me a polaroid camera, so I can capture moments with all of my favorite people. I turn the page and there's a stapled polaroid of Thomas with his arm wrapped around my shoulders, and we're both smiling. I blush, remembering what it feels like to be touched by him—but I don't remember this fucking moment at all.

I burst into tears because my people never forgot me.

I'm the one who forgets.

☺ ☺ ☺ ☺ ☺ ☺

"OPEN YOUR EYES, AARON."

I know that voice. Who knows how many new people in my life aren't really new? But I know this English accent. Evangeline Castle, my Leteo architect who gave me my memory-alteration procedure, posed as my former babysitter to discreetly check in on me, and the doctor who has promised to take care of me during my amnesia.

I don't recognize the room. The walls are gray, the orange sky outside the large window suggests that it's dawn or sunset, and there's a bathroom in the corner. It's not the same room, but it does remind me of the blue room I was in when my procedure first unwound. This has got to be Leteo.

"Aaron, do you know who I am?" Evangeline asks, staring at me with her green eyes. Her red-orange hair is pulled back into a bun and she's in her gray jacket.

A simple nod makes me dizzy. "Evangeline."

"Good. Very good."

She asks me a series of questions: What's my address? What's my mother's full name? What school do I go to? What brought me into Leteo? I answer everything correctly.

"What's going on?" I ask.

"You're waking up from surgery," Evangeline says, putting

down her tablet. "We're hoping our reparative procedure worked this time."

Surgery? This time? How many times have we done this?

"How old am I?" I ask.

Evangeline looks away and takes a deep breath. "You're eighteen."

I'm supposed to be seventeen.

"I'm sorry I couldn't mend your brain sooner," Evangeline adds quickly. "But I'm hoping all the hard work of the architects proves to be successful and holds—"

"Thank you," I interrupt. My tone is harsher than I'd like, because the gratitude is genuine in case the reparative procedure doesn't hold, in case I don't remember to thank her for everything she's done for me.

"You're welcome," Evangeline says.

☺ ☺ ☺ ☺ ☺ ☺

WHEN SHE'S GONE, I crawl out of bed to look in the bathroom mirror.

I'm expecting to find the bruises leftover from my friends, but those would've been long gone by now, even if for me it all feels like it happened days ago. The bags under my eyes are darker than I can ever remember them. How many days and nights were spent being awake, confused and pissed and hopeless? My brown hair is longer than usual and it's spilling over a white bandage that's wrapped around my forehead. I can't pinpoint everything about my face that's different, but my reflection feels like a really good self-portrait—definitely me, but a little off.

I don't know where to even begin with trying to catch up with myself.

THE NEXT COUPLE DAYS at Leteo are busy with memory examinations. I spend one morning staring at different images of animals on a computer, and whenever there's a repeat, I have to hit the space bar. Then another where I have to remember different numbers in sequential order, which is really tricky. The one tonight was the most fun. I was given a grid of squares and a few light up for three seconds and I have to memorize which ones were lit, and the rounds get harder, but it feels like a video game. No one was expecting perfect scores, but Evangeline needed to see that I was performing in the average range.

Who would've guessed that average would've been enough to send me home?

Outside I try to hug Evangeline, but she steps away.

"Get out of here, kiddo," she says. Her voice is thick. There are tears in her eyes. "I'll see you soon for checkups and counseling."

Mom gives her balloons and gift cards like it's her birthday or something. It's embarrassing, but how else is she supposed to thank the woman who was my brain's MVP?

WHEN WE GET TO the block, I'm already struck by how much has changed. There are new awnings for the ice cream and sandwich shops. Then when we get past the gate, I see the sandbox has been replaced with a garden that has the kind of plants that make me want to travel to a rainforest. I stop and stare at the playground, which is not the same one where we used to play Don't Touch Green. This new one is blue and white and built on an orange mat that's not fun on the eyes. How is it possible so much has changed? Mom tells me all about the new management team, who she's got to reintroduce me to—for the last time—and they've been very understanding on late payments because they were in the know with what was going down with me.

I stop outside the lobby, remembering the attack from Me-Crazy, Brendan, Skinny-Dave, and Nolan. There's been construction that makes it a little easier to forget what happened here. The mailboxes, laundromat, hallways, and elevators have all gotten makeovers for the better. It's not familiar, but I'm not against it. If I were an outsider, I would've bet money that you have to be rich to live here. Outside our apartment, I remember all of the wrong things; banging on the door after my father threw me out because I'm gay; coming home after Collin wanted a break from me, and I found my father dead in the bathtub. I want to get lost in the good times, like when I invited Thomas inside and we read my Sun Warden comic.

I open the door and step in. It's familiar, but there are so many drawings, and I don't recognize a single one. Some are taped to the wall. Others are spilling over my desk. There are marker caps on the floor.

For the past year I've been drawing my life, over and over.

"There are so many," I say.

"That surprised you every day," Eric says.

This is the last time I'll be surprised by my own creations. But I still don't know how I'll feel about them when I wake up tomorrow.

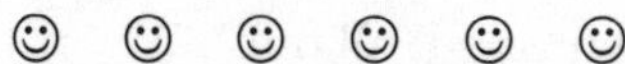

I'VE BEEN SLEEPING ALL day, trying to make sense of my dreams. Was kissing Thomas a lost memory or some fantasy? Who I am kidding? I know the truth.

Eric is still asleep since we spent all night catching up. Mom wanted to stay home, but she has to keep an appointment with her client and earn bank too. I don't have a phone right now because Mom had it disconnected. She kept paying the bills for three months, hoping that I would recover, but she snapped out of it because she needed the money. I could read up on everything I've been up to in the journals, but I'm not ready, so I grab the cash she left behind to go downstairs and get lunch and candy. My teeth are pretty good, I gotta to say. I don't know if it's because Mom and Eric kept me away from sweets or if I've been brushing ten times a day because I kept forgetting I already did it.

I lock up behind me and go downstairs, avoiding the staircase where Brendan could usually be found selling weed. I don't know what he's up to these days or where he is, but I know he hasn't moved away. Mom and Eric have been busy catching me up on everything else to get into what's good with Brendan.

I walk into Good Food's and it's seen some changes. There are cleaning supplies where the candy rack used to be, hardware where the chips were, and Baby Freddy behind the counter where I used to work.

"Aaron!" He runs around the counter and he's shaking a little. "Is it true? You're okay?"

"All good, Baby Freddy."

"It's Freddy now, I told you that—I'm stupid."

"It's okay."

"So what's up, man?"

"I don't know. Figuring it all out."

"Wow. You're really back."

I wonder how often he's seen me in the past year. Enough that he apparently got sick of me calling him Baby Freddy. He looks good. Kind of cute. He's got his ear pierced, a Yankees fitted that I'm surprised Mohad is letting him wear while working, a baggy shirt that goes down to his knees, and fresh kicks.

"Just Freddy, huh?" I ask with a smile.

"I'm grown now," he says.

Grown? We're the same age.

"What's your plan, man?" he asks, forcing a little laugh. "Don't take my job."

I shrug. "Playing catch up, I guess. What's been going on here?"

Freddy fills me in on all the block news: Fat-Dave has taken up wrestling, and he loves it so much and his girlfriend cheers him on ringside; Skinny-Dave was dating someone too, but she dumped him after he cheated; Nolan got into a fight with Eric apparently and got his ass beat, and he moved shortly after; Me-Crazy is still locked up somewhere as far as anyone knows, which is damn good news.

"Oh, Collin had his kid," Freddy finishes. "Wild."

He's watching me closely, almost like he's studying how the news might affect me. I don't know what anyone on the block officially knows about us, but you're not going to catch me outing Collin.

"Wild," I repeat.

"Brendan is cleaning his act up," Freddy adds, avoiding my eyes. "He's mad sorry, Aaron—"

"I lost a year of my fucking life. I need more than mad sorry."

I should've stayed home.

Freddy nods, sheepish, like he just got in trouble and was scolded. He's Baby Freddy all over again. "You're right, you're right. That's everything here. Seen your girl and your boy a lot. Starting to think Thomas isn't gay after all."

"What do you mean?"

"They were always visiting you. Saw them holding hands once."

I feel hot and sick.

☺ ☺ ☺ ☺ ☺ ☺

BACK HOME I OPEN the green journal and frantically flip through it, eyes seeking only entries from Genevieve and Thomas . . . Here's Genevieve reading me my favorite chapters from Scorpius Hawthorne over and over; making Skelzie tops with Thomas and playing outside with Eric; Thomas and I apparently had a conversation about how he wants to track down his father and confront him; being the subject of Genevieve's painting; Thomas giving me a haircut, which apparently didn't go well because I would forget what was happening and flinch; getting away from the block during Family Day and having a picnic at Fort Wille Park with Mom, Eric, Genevieve, and Thomas; Genevieve holding me as I cried myself to sleep, and even passing out with me; spending my eighteenth birthday at home, reading and rereading everyone's cards; journaling side by side with Thomas and him saying that I was always so happily surprised to find him right next to me. Thinking about that moment is gutting—it's everything I wanted for our future and it's fucking lost in the past.

Then an entry from Thomas hits harder: *I made you cry the hardest I've seen you cry, Stretch, and I hate myself.*

He doesn't say what happened.

He must've told me about falling for Genevieve.

I close the journal and stare at all the drawings on the wall.

For the first time since being back, I wish I could forget.

☺ ☺ ☺ ☺ ☺ ☺

I'M WATCHING THE LAST Scorpius Hawthorne movie when there's a knock on the door.

"Who is it?"

"Me!"

Genevieve.

I open the door, my heart wild inside my chest. She's stunning.

Is this the Genevieve I dated? Her dark hair is shorter and curlier, kind of styled like her mom's hair used to be, and she's in a white button-down shirt with black pants. The only thing that's familiar is the green tote bag I got her, the one with all the song lyrics on it; I can't believe she's still using it.

"Remember that time Aaron Soto was back?" Genevieve says with a smile. "Ugh, that sounded better in my head. But I've been dying to say that to you for over a year."

"I'm glad you did," I say. I'm being honest but I can't smile back.

She hugs me so hard and—

It triggers a memory: the last hug we had in her bedroom when I first told her about the amnesia. We had cried and kept repeating that we love each other in a non-weird way. There's a part of me that loves Genevieve. It's the part that makes me hug her back just as hard.

"I can't believe I'm seeing you. I've seen you a lot obviously. But I can't believe you're actually going to remember this." She lets herself in and even though she's been here who knows how many times, it's still a new sight for me. "I missed you so much. Is it weird to miss someone who has been here all along?"

"I don't feel like I've been here all along," I say.

"You were here," Genevieve says. "We were all with you too."

"Thanks for not forgetting me."

"Impossible, dumb-idiot."

We're sitting on my bed. Everything she's telling me is good, like her plans to return to New Orleans for college if she can get a scholarship and how her dad is in AA and met his new girlfriend there who keeps him accountable, but my chest is still tight as I wait for her to bring up Thomas.

"You can tell me," I say even though it feels like asking her to punch me in the face.

"Tell you what?"

"About you and Thomas. You two were getting close before I . . . before all of that."

"We got closer because we missed you."

It feels like she's saying it's my fault, that I brought this heartbreak on myself.

"We took it really hard, Aaron. We were crying and missed you and hated what you were going through."

I wonder if she held Thomas as he cried to sleep too.

I feel sick thinking about Thomas and Genevieve in bed holding each other.

"You get that it's hard that two of my favorite people got to live on without me? When you wouldn't have known each other without me?"

"I promise we kept you moving with us." Genevieve is talking more quickly now. "There were so many times Thomas and I were together where we would make note of something to tell you because we knew it would make you happy. He's at work right now, but he really wants to come over after his shift and see you too and—"

"I need some time," I say. "I gotta wrap my head around all of this."

She's quiet. "Oh. of course. I'll tell him you'll reach out when you're ready. I'm always around for you, Aaron." She kisses the top of my head, lovingly punches me in the arm, and leaves.

MY FIRST SESSION OF Unwind Therapy has been okay.

Evangeline is leading the group because she's not busy enough with all her regular day-to-day work or with promoting the recent success of my reparative procedure to counter Leteo's declining reputation. I've been thinking about how she truly is one of the good ones. She could've sent anyone to go undercover as my babysitter or some other character after my memory-alteration procedure, but she chose to do the work herself. Like now.

The group is small, only four people, and as we all talk, I pick up pieces here and there about their stories. There's Claribel Castro, who is struggling with her faith as a Christian after she felt pressured to go through a procedure to forget her abortion. She's understanding now that it was always her body, her choice, but she had given in to the procedure to feel better about her strict upbringing. Then there's Liam Chaser, whose leg won't stop bouncing as he talks about whether or not he wants to visit his uncle in prison after all the ways his uncle harmed him. I don't know the specifics, obviously, but it was serious enough that he got the greenlight from Leteo to go ahead and forget it, and serious enough that it broke past Leteo's walls. And lastly there's Jordan Gonzales Jr., whose brown, muscular arms are folded over his chest. He has a streak of silver in his gelled black hair like some comic book superhero. Jordan hasn't shared a single word about his own history.

Evangeline turns to me. "Would you like to talk about what brings you here, Aaron?"

Jordan flinches like my name is some curse.

"I don't know where to start," I say.

"Wherever you want," Evangeline says.

"Um, okay. I, uh, forgot I was gay."

Jordan perks up. "You're the one?"

"The one in the news?" Claribel adds.

I never thought people would know-know me like this. "Yeah."

"Aaron, this is a safe space," Evangeline reminds.

"She'll make us forget anything you don't want us to remember," Jordan jokes.

"Shut up," Claribel says.

"What, I'm kidding. Besides, he's different. I mean, we

unwound, but he had amnesia after that. He forgot, he remembered, he forgot."

I forgot, I remembered, I forgot.

"What's been hard for you?" Liam asks.

"I know life isn't supposed to stand still, but I'm scared to catch up on everything I missed. The first guy I was ever in love with had his first kid. The first girl I thought I was in love with is now seeing the second guy I was in love with, and neither of them would've known each other without me. I don't know how to be happy for them."

"You don't have to be happy for them," Evangeline says. "You're allowed to take time for yourself."

"But Genevieve and Thomas were there for me the entire time I was out of it."

Evangeline is about to say something, but Liam beats her to it. "You don't want to find yourself pursuing another procedure, right? You have to protect yourself."

"What works for everyone else in the circle may not work for you," Evangeline says.

I get that, but as I look around at everyone in the support group, I think about how we all thought Leteo was the answer, and how we're all lost souls trying to find our way back into our own lives.

☺ ☺ ☺ ☺ ☺ ☺

I'M BACK ON THE block, setting up my new phone, when I look up and see Brendan, Fat-Dave, and Skinny-Dave sitting on the playground mat and eating sandwiches. I haven't seen any of them since my surgery, and now they're all there together. Fat-Dave wasn't part of the attack, but I can't mess with someone who's still down with Brendan and Skinny-Dave after what they did to me.

Brendan looks like he's seen a ghost. I see my former sort of best friend.

He stands. It reminds me of the day I fell off my bike and he looked like he wanted to help me. I had held up my hand to stop him then, but as he tries coming toward me now, I just go straight into my building and don't look back.

I don't know if I'll ever forgive him, but I damn well know that I won't ever forget.

FROM BED, I STARE at the dark blue mountain bike Thomas got me for my seventeenth birthday. He thought I didn't know how to ride a bike, and I didn't. Not then. Leteo took the memory that Collin had taught me. Thomas wanted to teach me, too.

When I would get too lost in my head, Thomas taught me how to be free. When I thought coming out would mean everyone hating me, Thomas loved me harder. When I couldn't remember a single thing, Thomas didn't stop creating memories with me.

I get Thomas's number off Eric's phone and I call him before I change my mind.

"Hello?"

"Hey, Thomas."

"Stretch!" Thomas says, like nothing has changed.

I love the familiarity even though I know so much has changed.

"Hey. What's up?"

It's such a simple question, but asking someone how they're doing when the answer might hurt you is really intense. My heart is really going for it, hoping he doesn't say that he's with Genevieve right now.

"Nothing, I was just journaling a little before work."

"Where's work?"

"Remember when you came with me to go look for jobs?"

"Big Job-Hunt Saturday," I say, legit surprised I remember what he called it.

"Yeah! I work at that barbershop now."

"Is that why you tried giving me a haircut?" I ask.

Thomas laughs, and I wish I could see him laughing.

"No, you just really needed one. So you read the journals?"

"Some of the one you wrote in," I say. "None of mine."

"Why not?"

"Not sure I can handle that," I say. Those words are going to be too raw. "I'm calling you because I wanted to see you, but you're going to work."

"I want to see you too. We can catch up after? Or during my lunch break at two?"

I want to spend as much time as possible with him, but I gotta to be smart about this. If I see him after work there's more of a chance we'll end up at his place, watching the world from his rooftop, getting comfortable in his bedroom, and I'll remember a relationship that doesn't really exist. But I don't want to spiral over every new thing I don't recognize in his bedroom, wondering if it came from Genevieve as some girlfriend gift or if it's just a random little item Thomas came by innocently.

I tell him I'll meet him at the barbershop at two.

"Awesome. I'll see you then, Stretch. I'm so excited to see you."

MY HEART IS POUNDING as I turn the corner and see the sign for Stooj's Scissors, and through the window I see the back of Thomas's head as he's sweeping up a mass of black hair. I go in.

There is only one barber working, someone I don't know cutting someone's hair. He asks me if I have an appointment.

"Sort of," I say.

Thomas turns. "STRETCH!"

He's got the biggest smile as he drops the broom and runs at me and hugs me. I wonder if he notices that my heart is hitting his chest. I'm not familiar with the cologne that's coming off his neck, and I have to stop myself from wondering if he sprayed it on for me. We just stand there hugging for a couple of minutes, none of that No Homo nonsense either. Then when I really see his face up close, he's rounded out a little, the stubble is definitely new, but the thick eyebrows are Classic Thomas. I fight back a cringe as I remember tracing those eyebrows before kissing him.

"It's kind of, sort of, absolutely, definitely great to see you, Stretch."

"It's kind of, sort of, absolutely, definitely great to see you, Thomas."

Thomas pats me on the shoulder, unbuttons his black button-down, tells the barber he's going on his break, and we head back out. "How's it going?"

Everyone keeps asking me that. Naturally.

"Still catching up on my life. How are you liking the job?"

"I'm not quitting on the spot like I did at that ice cream place last summer," he says.

"Progress."

"I like it. It's a new team here, so no one's telling stories about the women they're sleeping with. All I really do is sweep hair and shelve new supplies and go on random errands, but I get a lot of good thinking here. I'm writing a script for a short film."

"Oh, cool. What about?"

I'm scared it's going to be some love story about Genevieve.

"It's about you." Thomas is quiet for a sec and scratches his head. "Stretch, I can't imagine what you're going through right now, but watching you live through it is the most difficult thing I've ever done. There were times you were so happy and times where you were miserable and times where you were scared. This one time you got upset and you swore you were never going to speak again until you could remember it, and then a few minutes later you forgot and you were rambling about a plot hole in Scorpius Hawthorne."

"I'm sorry," I say.

"What are you sorry for?"

"You put yourself through a lot for me."

"Stretch, you couldn't stop me from hanging out with you, even though you were going off for the hundredth time that it makes no sense why it took so long for Scorpius to figure out that his father's traitorous best friend was still alive when he had the Hunter's Map."

I laugh. I'm sure it was more than a hundred times I bitched about that. Then I look at him. "I need to ask you about one of your journal entries. You said that you made me cry and you hated yourself. What happened?"

Thomas stops at the corner of a bodega, leaning against a lamppost. "There's a bright side to your best friend not being able to remember anything," he says, and even though it should sound like a joke, it doesn't. "I told you a lot of dumb secrets that I never trust with anyone. But there was one day where I was questioning myself—my sexuality. You wanted to kiss me and then I stopped you. You were pissed off and crying, and I couldn't wait until you forgot everything. Every good time we were having seemed to slip away too suddenly, but this went on for so long." He can't even look me in the eye. "When you finally forgot, I made up some lie about why you were crying. I'm so sorry that I can't be who you want me to be, Stretch. I really wish I could."

I think about Genevieve. I don't know if he loves her yet, but if he doesn't, he's going to because she's the best and he would have to be an idiot to let her go.

"I hope you don't hate me," he says trying to look me in the eye again.

"I don't hate you, okay? But I need to figure some stuff out."

Thomas nods. "I'm here for you."

He holds out his fist, hopeful. We bump fists.

It's hard to walk away, but I do. I don't know how to stay as long as I love him.

☺ ☺ ☺ ☺ ☺ ☺

UNWIND THERAPY TODAY IS a jumble of bits and pieces; I am unable to fully tune in as I get lost in obsessive thoughts about Thomas and Genevieve. Every thought makes my stomach hurt—the two of them laughing together, kissing, having sex, going on dates, being happy without me. I don't know how to make sense of the fact that they were there for me and also managed to make me feel booted.

When I leave Leteo, Jordan follows me out.

"Hey, Soto," he says. "You're not okay."

Not even a question. "Not really."

"I'd ask if you want to talk about it, but if you're not talking about it in therapy then you probably don't," Jordan says.

"That's really cool of you, but I'm feeling kind of drained. You know how when you're going through something and people check in on you and you have to go through the story again? I'm kind of tired of reliving my pain over and over."

"I've been there. I left behind all my drama in Texas three months ago when I moved here with my older sister. No one outside this group knows about my Leteo links. Fresh start."

"That sounds kind of nice."

"Except for me it feels like running away all over again. That's what it all is, right? The procedure, the cross-country move. Even though I'm building a sweet life out here, I do miss my people back home. Even the ones who wronged me."

"All of them?"

"Fuck no," Jordan says with a smile. I like his fanged canine teeth—he's got a cute vampire thing going on. "But some. I wonder where we would be if I had stayed. If we had tried. You hear me, Soto?"

"When did this Soto business start?"

"When you walked in with my ex's name." Jordan's gaze falls to his sneakers. "Anything else people call you?"

I almost tell him Stretch, but shrug. "Soto works."

We cross the street.

"Have you shared your story at Leteo?" I ask.

"Not with the other Unwinders. Only Evangeline when I transferred over."

"Okay. You don't have to tell me obviously, but if you want to I'm here for—"

"I forgot someone," Jordan interrupts. "The Aaron guy. I had to—I was hurting myself because of him. It was toxic and terrible and I don't want to fully get into it, but I'm telling you because we're alike."

I don't know how Jordan harmed himself, but I'm happy he survived.

"Alike how?" I ask.

"Love was trying to kill us, Soto."

Collin was toxic for me, but looking back, I wouldn't say Thomas was. He told me who he is, and I wanted to believe he was lying.

"I don't want love to hurt," I say, "but I don't know how to love Thomas right now without being hurt by that love. And I don't know how to accept that he got to live all the good stuff with me and I don't remember it. I mean, Thomas and everyone had my eighteenth birthday party with me, but also not really with me. I missed out on all of that."

"Who says you have to miss it? Who cares if your birthday passed. Throw yourself another party, one you'll remember."

"I never thought of that."

"Soto, if you want to take back your life, you have to actually take it back. Your memories are yours again. You don't have to obsess over the ones you lost. You can create new ones. Better ones." Jordan checks the time on his phone. "I have to get home to help out my sister, but what are you up to tomorrow?"

"Nothing."

"Great. Show me around."

"What do you want to see?"

"Your favorite spots in the city. You can tell me about why they're sentimental to you."

"I don't know if I'm ready to step into my past like that just yet."

"We don't have to, I'm sorry," Jordan says. "I only suggested it because I know what it's like for my favorite arcade to feel haunted because of everything I experienced with Aaron."

"I don't want to feel haunted," I say, and I agree to meet Jordan tomorrow to prove that.

Where do I start?

FIRST STOP ON THE Aaron Soto Tour: Comic Book Asylum.

The front counter is still manned by Stanley, and his familiar face is comforting as I walk Jordan through the aisles and my complicated history with Collin. I tell him about the moment I bumped into Collin when I was here with Thomas, having forgotten everything romantic with Collin because of Leteo. Jordan didn't have any weird bump-ins with his Aaron, which, good for him because looking back, Collin was so hurt and I never want to do that to someone.

We then go to the spot between the flower shop and the meat market where Collin and I had sex for the first time. Jordan tells me about losing his virginity with his friend John from homeroom when he was sixteen and bored and horny. He doesn't look back on it as fondly as I do with Collin, even with all the heartbreak that followed.

I hope Collin and Nicole and their kid are good. Beyond that, I don't think I need to know what's up with him or see him ever again.

I take Jordan to Fort Wille Park, where I asked out Genevieve, and tell him about how much I love her and how I wish I could've loved her more. Jordan's former best friend, Dane, was in love with Jordan too, and years ago Jordan tried—he really, really tried—to give that a shot, but then Aaron came along, and Jordan had to answer that call and he lost Dane for good. Jordan still thinks about Dane, especially since things didn't continue blossoming with Aaron, but Dane is in college and happy with his new boyfriend and Jordan knows he missed out.

Timing is everything. Who knows what—and who—I missed out on because of the year I couldn't remember.

I've been avoiding it, but I finally get around to Thomas. We walk through Thomas's high school track field, and I tell Jordan about how we ran around there until our rib cages were aching. And then I'm honest about how much it hurts remembering when I rolled through here with Collin and found Thomas and Genevieve sitting together, especially knowing that they're coupled up now—maybe even together right this second—and I'm alone. Jordan knows the feeling too. His relationship with Aaron ended after Aaron thought it was okay to hook up with a guy Jordan always suspected had a thing for Aaron.

On the way back home, I point out the movie theater Thomas

snuck us into, and then his building. I tell Jordan all about the times we spent on that rooftop—Genevieve's birthday, Thomas's, the time Thomas and I chilled under the sun with our shirts off, and when I cried telling him about my amnesia. It's a lot to take in, and even Jordan doesn't try to fill the silence with a story of his own.

We were back on my block, standing outside the little alleyway.

"This is where I met Thomas," I say.

"Ending the tour at the beginning," Jordan says. "You a poet, Soto?"

"It's more convenience," I say.

"How do you feel?"

This is the spot where Thomas broke up with his girlfriend. Where I first focused on his eyebrows. Where he nicknamed me Stretch before knowing my name. This is where Thomas and I began, and now I have to figure out if we're going to have another beginning or if it ends now because his happiness with Genevieve is too much for me.

"I think I want to try," I say.

"Try what?" Jordan asks.

"Try trying? I love Thomas and Genevieve and they love me and maybe it won't work out, but at least I'll know, right?" I take a deep breath and look at Jordan, happy that I brought him here and that he walked through memory lane with me. "What are you doing this weekend?"

"No plans."

"Get ready. You're coming to my eighteenth birthday."

I get a vibe that Jordan is a keeper. Maybe we'll be good for each other. I hope my name doesn't haunt him so much and he'll stop calling me Soto. But if I'm being honest, it's growing on me.

I'M TURNING EIGHTEEN AGAIN. (Well, we're all acting like that's true today.)

I originally wanted to have the party outside so we can celebrate with the community that's looked after us this past year, but it's been raining all afternoon, and I didn't want to cancel because all my friends already shifted things around to be here today. So I invited everyone to come over to the apartment. I've spent so much time being ashamed of my home, this place where I have lived my entire life. I'm done hiding my home from my people just like I'm done hiding myself from the world.

It's already my favorite party.

Freddy is talking mad shit to Eric as he beats his ass in Mario Kart, and I haven't had Freddy over in years because I was embarrassed that I didn't have my own bedroom like he does. But he doesn't care. Mom is having so much fun playing host to her friends and making sure we're all stocked up on chips and soda while we wait for the pizza from Yolanda's. Genevieve arrived first, but Thomas wasn't too far behind, and I bet they were ready to arrive at the same time but wanted to play it cool for me. It's funny, I'm struggling with them being together, but I also don't want them apart because of me.

I wonder if my feelings will ever feel crystal clear to me, like how I feel a little guilty for not inviting Brendan even though I'm pissed at him, or remembering how fun my father was on birthdays but still hating him for everything I did to myself because of him.

I don't want to throw away everyone in my life, not while I still can see there's more good than bad with keeping them.

But when Thomas and Genevieve are laughing over something I can't hear, my stomach twists until Eric lets Jordan in. Then I feel a little better.

"Happy birthday, Soto," Jordan says, handing me a present.

"What the hell is this?"

"You'll find out when you open it," Jordan says.

"Can I open it now?"

"You're old enough to vote now, you make your own rules."

That last part is far from true, but I smile.

Before I can rip into the present or introduce Jordan to anyone, Mom and Evangeline come out of the kitchen and begin singing "Happy Birthday." Jordan steers me toward everyone, and they're all singing off-key. I'm red in the face even though I damn well knew this was going to happen. I blow out the eighteen candles with a big-ass smile.

Then, everything is quiet for a few moments, like we all know what a miracle it is that we're able to do this today. I look around at how happy everyone is: Mom and Evangeline are crying; Eric toasts me with his Pepsi can; Freddy is ready to dig into the cake; Genevieve blows me a kiss; Thomas reaches over the cake and we fist-bump; and Jordan is smiling with his beautiful canine teeth, a little smug, like this idea wouldn't have happened without him—and he's right.

Look, it's not a perfect eighteenth birthday party, but it's one I'm always going to remember and that alone is the best gift.

I'M BEGINNING AGAIN.

I get on the bike and kick off. The wind is in my ears, my fingers are tight around the handlebars, my legs are powering me through a fast trip around the courtyards and away from the bad memory of me crashing last year. This is how I'm going to win—not from running away from the memories, but from confronting them dead-on.

I park the bike in the lobby, take my journals outside my backpack, and sit down. I have to understand the power of these journals. I'm going to read some stuff that makes me feel left out, stuff that pisses me off, that makes me sad. But it's okay to hurt. And I see what I've been missing. Evangeline was right. Now that I can remember the past, bit by bit, I am reconnected with time. I don't have to read all these journals right now. I can take it a page a year if I have to. But I'm excited to find the sun in the darkness in these stories, and if I can't, I will work to create my own light.

I'm more happy than not.

Remember that.

AFTERWORD

I sort of, kind of, definitely can't believe we're all reuniting with Aaron Soto after so many years.

Since this book was first published, readers have asked me for more words in this More Happy universe. Sequels, companion novels, official Scorpius Hawthorne stories. I always wanted to write more Aaron, and I tried many, many times over the years, but I couldn't find his voice. *More Happy Than Not* was the first novel I ever wrote, and I got to live with Aaron intimately before it became a book that was going to be published, before critics could enter my head. But since my debut, I've written four books with eight new narrators and I felt like I was never going to access Aaron's head again.

Then I reread *More Happy Than Not* for the first time in five years, and it was like opening a time capsule. I remembered all the devastation in this book, but I'd forgotten how young and light and hopeful Aaron is. I was charmed by so many moments between Aaron and Thomas. I flinched at lines I would never write today. I admired the story's pacing. I fell in love with Part Zero all over again. But rereading the book confirmed what I knew needed to happen since publication.

A new ending.

Back when I wrote the book, I wanted an ending that felt true and surprising, and I believe I did that. But Aaron is too much a part of my heart, too real to leave him where I left him. I was genuinely haunted by this ending, and I wanted to give Aaron a long overdue win.

I'm not going to lie, I wrote *More Happy Than Not* for myself. I could've never imagined that this book was going to mean so much to people. Over the years I've had readers come out to me, tell me Aaron saved their lives, show me tattoos based on the book, fan art, and so many more memorable experiences that keep me publishing queer stories for all of you.

I may have written this book for myself, but I wrote "More Happy Ending" for all of us.

—Adam Silvera, 2020

AUTHOR'S NOTE

I GREW UP THINKING being gay was a choice, which was so much more comforting than thinking I was born wrong. If I had subconsciously chosen to like boys, I could switch back to "normal" before any of my friends noticed that I was different, before they would take it into their own hands to straighten me out.

Being gay, of course, was never a choice. Many make this assumption, which never made much sense to me as I got older: Why would I subject myself to judgment? Why would I design such a complicated life for myself? Why would anyone when being normal is straight-up easier?

These are questions that threw me into writing *More Happy Than Not,* latching onto a speculative element to help me explore a character, sixteen-year-old Aaron Soto, who no longer wanted to be gay and could rewrite his history—and his life—with the help of a memory manipulation service.

I hope you will relate to Aaron's journey even if you're not gay yourself because his journey is ultimately about the pursuit of happiness, which is universal. If you've ever suffered through a tragedy you wished you could forget, you may empathize with Aaron's story. While we can't always engineer our own happy endings, we can learn how to be more happy than not with the cards we've been dealt.

(More) Happy reading,

ACKNOWLEDGMENTS

MAD LOVE TO THOSE who knew becoming an author would make me More Happy Than Anything:

First shout-out goes to the guy who makes it all happen, Brooks Sherman, the coolest and weirdest agent in all of Agent Land. It takes a lot for an obsessive-compulsive person—writer, no less—to give up the reigns and I absolutely trust this guy to keep steering me in the right direction. He's ensured my debut experience is unforgettable in all arenas, and I'll help him carry a couch down the crowded streets of New York any day.

The top-notch team at Soho Teen: Daniel Ehrenhaft, my editor, who not only pushed me to great distances under his guidance, but trusted me to find my way out of the battlefield, too; Meredith Barnes, my publicist, who was the first at Soho HQ to believe in this book, cranked the volume on what I always thought was a quiet book, answered my many emails within minutes, and partnered with the talented Liz Casal to create my dream cover; Bronwen Hruska, my publisher, whose pride radiates; Janine Agro, who is an interior design wizard; Amara Hoshijo, editorial assistant/salad date extraordinaire; Rachel Kowal, finder of things I've missed; and the other hardworking champions in-house, including Rudy Martinez, Juliet Grames, Paul Oliver, Mark Doten, and Abby Koski.

Luis Rivera, for everything I learned from our nothing, and for everything he could give me. He sort of, kind of, maybe, definitely knew how to make a guy more happy than not during the Code Adam era, and he continues to keep the good times and fist-bumps coming every day.

Corey Whaley, who must never stop existing. I'm super grateful he gave me a summer home so I could write my story, and for the crazy amount of happiness he energized within me so I could survive reliving it.

Cecilia Renn, my best friend and wilder half. Fingers crossed the world doesn't end on June 6th or I'll never hear the end of it from her. Our Gemini handshakes will echo across infinity—or at least across her kitchen where she's surely left another cabinet open.

Hannah Colbert Kalampoukas, for being the perfect first person to come out to, and for the strawberry frosted birthday cake she baked me and shaped like an A. The cake was a small gesture that meant as much to me as The Great Coming Out of 2009.

Christopher Mapp, for being such a great Life Coach that I couldn't possibly model a character after him in this book or Aaron Soto's journey would've been too easy.

Amanda Diaz, who not only passed along her love of literature and fan fiction, but also read this story more times than was necessary. Michael Diaz, for countless nights of gaming and playing "Draft" with our candy. Ana Beltran, for dinners (which she always cooked) and debates (which I always won).

College didn't appear to be in the cards for me, but growing up in bookstores after high school was way more rewarding anyway, especially thanks to the following: Irene Bradish and Peter Glassman, my former bosses who doubled as mentors; Sharon Pelletier, for hitting me hard with tough love edits; Jennifer Golding, for cheering me on since the beginning; Donna Rauch, for ongoing duck jokes; Allison Love, who changed my life with a bookstore application; Maggie Heinze, for being the first eyes on work I didn't want anyone seeing; Jonathan Drucker, for keeping it really real, bro-style; Gaby Salpeter, for being an ego-boosting cheerleader all day, every day; Joel Grayson, for unwavering kindness and encouragement whenever he passed me in the aisles; and my many other booksellers-turned-friends whom I met at Barnes & Noble and Books of Wonder.

Lauren Oliver and Lexa Hillyer, for not only revealing their plot guru ways to me, but for saving my life when I was literally drowning. This book wouldn't be a thing without them—seriously, I wouldn't be a thing without them.

Joanna Volpe, for her genius book-changing pointers and keeping me sane on my first flight ever; Suzie Townsend, for loving and believing in this book before it was sellable, and loving it again when it was done-zo; Sandra Gonzalez, my Hubby, who puts my all-nighters to shame and all my human feelings to good use; Margot Wood, my partner-in-crime and wife in another life, for taking photos of my face and wanting to go gay for me and my narrator; Julie Murphy, my Texas slide, for our Dallas writing dates; Holly Goldberg Sloan, for being the greatest LA mom a kid from NYC can ask for; Tai Farnsworth, for an invaluable insight that reshaped things; Hannah Fergesen, who came into my life late in the publishing game, but has proven herself irreplaceable time and time again.

I've lucked into many writer friends, and I've been especially fortunate to go on this journey with my Beckminavidera squad: Becky Albertalli, my literary twin, whose love for these characters and their story outshines her great distaste for Golden Oreos, which is silly since it's clearly the superior Oreo, but whatever, more cookies for me; Jasmine Warga, my Swedish Fish–loving, Art Bar–going sis who can always be counted on for fun road trips and great song recommendations (except that one time); David Arnold, my bro who I want to hug to death every time we have solid chats about Life, capital L intended. I can't wait until we finally get that house in Beckminavideraville, my friends.

Jennifer M. Brown, a fellow night owl, for opening so many doors for me when she took me under her wing.

My family and friends, for the pride they find in me, and the happiness I find in them.

My mom, Persi Rosa, for raising me with summer reading challenges, spelling bees with swear words, subtitles whenever I watched TV, and for editing my book reports. She inspired a love for words that's proven pretty important in this field I'm writing myself into. And, most importantly, she's always loved me as I am—I know she wouldn't change a thing about me, and likewise.

Finally—we got here!—thank you to the incredible community of booksellers, librarians, readers, writers, bloggers, and imaginary characters who keep our industry and literature alive. Let's make sure books and bookstores remain a thing, please and thank you.